HER SISTER'S
BONES

HER SISTER'S BONES

GERALDINE HOGAN

Bookouture

Published by Bookouture in 2019

An imprint of Storyfire Ltd.
Carmelite House
50 Victoria Embankment
London EC4Y 0DZ

www.bookouture.com

ISBN: 978-1-83888-263-1
eBook ISBN: 978-1-78681-909-3

Previously published as *Silent Night* (978-1-78681-910-9)

To my wonderful family,
I count my blessings every day.

'There's no thrashing the ties in the land or the blood...'
Old Irish saying

COUNTY LIMERICK, 1990

'Out you go, the pair of you.'

It was the coldest summer in fourteen years. A forbidding storm loomed across the Atlantic, already ripping apart the eastern coast of the United States and hardly wearing herself out before she made her crossing. The baby had arrived two days earlier and, although her mother had not yet registered a name for her, to Anna's mind she was and always would be baby Janey, just like her perfect baby doll. She'd even drawn a small pink heart on the doll's right thumb, and one to match on her own. They were triplets now. Her mother had spent almost ten minutes the previous evening scrubbing the pink away, complaining and irritated. She wasn't usually so brusque. Anna knew it was a mixture of the new baby and the storm warnings. Soon, everything would settle down. Once more, they'd sit and read stories and Anna would stroke her mother's mane of soft red hair that smelled of Shalimar and glided across her face like a protective armour of silk.

'Make the most of it now; when that storm comes, ye won't get out for days,' her mother called as she made her way back into the cottage.

She'd wrapped them both up, extra blankets for the baby, but it wasn't cold, not really. The old tabby wound itself around Anna's legs a few times, its fur warm against her cool ankles. She would usually bend down and stroke her, pick her up and snuggle deep into the soft fur. Today, the cat was ignored; and in the way that most cats seem to know everything worth knowing, she cocked her tail high and strode away with dignity. Anna hardly noticed her slip deep beneath the thick summer hedging that hid most of the garden from the small track beyond. Anna stood gingerly beside the large pram, afraid to move in case she missed anything. She peered down at the tiny peach face below. Jane's eyes were wide open, blue and grey and green. Anna had never seen anything like them; soft buttons that transfixed her so she could hardly breathe. Even now, with her hands stuck stubbornly in her pockets, she wanted to thrust them inside the pram and touch the baby's cheek.

'Give her a little space,' her mother had said a hundred times already since the baby arrived. But Anna couldn't help it; she loved her more than she'd ever thought she could love anything in the world.

She marvelled at her mother who seemed to take the baby's utter perfection in her stride. From what Anna could see, her mother spent all her time washing, cleaning, feeding or crying. 'Baby blues,' she said as she blew her nose and got up to fold more clothes. 'I'll be fine once your father gets back.' Her father was due in four days' time; he'd be here then for a few weeks before heading back to the lighthouse on Tarbert Island once more. 'And before we know it, we'll be headed for Christmas, all here together,' her mother said between sniffles. 'That's something to look forward to.' Anna didn't see anything wrong with right here and now. They had the baby; her father was coming home soon. Of course, it would be somewhat improved by the arrival of her Barbie Fairy Castle with matching Ken and fairy clothes, but really, sunshine or not, this was the best summer of her life.

'Come on, Anna.' Ollie Kerr, a small square-shaped boy with an expression belying his sensitivity, eyes so icy blue they looked cruel in one so young, was standing at the end of the house. 'Come on, we have time for a quick kick-about.' Ollie lived in the next house up. He seemed to lurk constantly somewhere between the two properties. When Anna thought about it, she wondered if he ever spent any time anywhere but outside her house, waiting for her to play some stupid boy's game.

'Can't today,' she said pointing at the pram, 'I'm minding my new sister,' and she thought once more how much she liked the sound of the words. *My sister, my little sister, Janey.*

'Oh.' She could see he was disappointed; he would never have any sisters or brothers. His parents had adopted him. *Married too late,* her father had said ominously and she figured, years later, that he was thinking, *There but for the grace of God.* Her dad was fifty-six when Janey was born; strong and handsome in his uniform. Anna thought he was the greatest man ever.

'Maybe later?' Ollie murmured, head low, walking away from the cottage. Anna knew that often he went no further than the copse and watched from there.

'Yeah, maybe.' She had no intention of wasting one second on him, not now she had Janey.

She stood for a while, just watching the baby, listening for the very low sounds that Janey was trying to make. She wasn't gurgling yet, but every so often a small sigh would rise from her and Anna would feel her breath catch in her chest, as though she was waiting for the pronouncement of a great prophet – words of wisdom, words never uttered before, words to treasure for evermore. For evermore.

When the door opened behind her, Anna was hardly aware of it. Her mother's voice made her jump. 'Have you been here all this time, have you not had a run around?' She looked about the garden, as though she'd lost something. 'Is Ollie not here with you?'

'No, he's gone home; I told him I was minding the baby.' Her mother had already told her off for calling her Janey. *We can't call the baby after a rag doll, now can we?*

'You know fine and well, the baby no more needs minding than I do. Come on, you can help me hang the clothes on the line, an hour or so in this wind and we'll have them dry.' She took a cursory glance inside the pram hood, a small stretch upwards of her thin lips confirming that all was well with Janey. 'You need to run around a bit, Anna; you've been stuck beside the baby all day long.' She was talking over her shoulder, having handed the bag of clothes pegs to Anna.

She didn't count them, but it felt as though there were hundreds of nappies and tea towels and hand towels. She passed each one, hot and steaming as it was violently shaken out before her mother pegged it to the line. All sparkling white – almost a blue white – an obscene testament of cleanliness and purity against the overcast backdrop of grey skies and dark-green summer foliage. Her mother had boiled the nappies in a pot, that looked to Anna more like a cauldron, on the range, filled to the top with Omo bubbles, the smell steaming the small kitchen with the aroma of a muggy launderette. By the time they reached the bottom of the basket, it sounded as though the first of the washing hung out was already well on its way to being dry. The energetic flapping on the clothesline was an eternal reminder of wasted time. At the end her mother stood back to inspect the work, then she made her way into the house.

'Don't let me see you bothering the baby now; go and find Ollie and play with him for a while.'

Anna willed herself not to take one more peek and walked towards the gate. She walked the path that bordered the small garden her mother had given up trying to cultivate into something more sophisticated than a square, even green patch. She looked at the copse beyond, her eyes searching the greenery for a hint of Ollie. Surely he was there watching her; she should call out to him, she knew. But usually, unless he was really cross with her, he came to her once she was standing at the gate.

The wind was coming up stronger behind her back. She almost felt it whispering something in her ear. *Janey, Janey, Janey.* Something made her turn, and even from where she was, she knew that something was not right. The neatly tucked-in pram cover had been loosened on one side. Her mother always fastened down the navy cover so it sat in a rigid rectangle, like a stretched canvas guarding the treasure beneath. She ran towards Janey, her voice a strangled squeal now. She just knew the baby hadn't pulled open the covers, and whatever had opened those covers, it had not been her or her mother. She looked towards the cottage door; her mother's face a white oval, her eyes embedded in deep black circles, her hair a wiry bright halo about her thin and frightened frame.

'What is it?' Her mother spoke in a whisper and later, when she remembered parts of those few minutes, Anna would wonder if she could have heard the words above the rising winds, above the scream that hung low in her own chest. She couldn't answer, hadn't looked yet, but she knew. They reached the pram together, running, stumbling through panic and over nervous unsure footfalls. Her mother pushed before her, pulled back the already opened covers. She inched away from the pram and looked about the garden, a woman already possessed. Anna moved closer to where Janey had lain. She placed her hands on the brushed cotton under-blanket. It was still warm, still holding onto the last memory of her, and Anna put her face in, drinking in the final sense of the sister stolen from her.

CHAPTER 1

Iris Locke had three minutes left on the timer. After that, she was giving up and going home. She wasn't sure at this stage how many laps of the track she'd run, but she knew it was enough, feeling it stretch down the back of her legs and drawing the breath from her lungs as though her insides were beginning to burn up. Truth was, Iris hadn't taken a decent walk in twelve months, never mind a run. This was payback for the sedentary lifestyle undercover had forced her into. Her days had fallen into a pattern and it didn't leave much time for little more than work and more work.

She'd spent almost a year in undercover, living the life of a seemingly carefree twenty-something, PA to one of Ireland's most high-profile businessmen. The McCracken case was meant to be the making of her career; for a while it was the sting of the decade. The fact the case had fallen apart had not been her fault, and yet, because of it she'd been thrown to limbo land. In the final analysis, a year of her life had been sucked into something that amounted to a sideways deployment and now she was further away than ever from what seemed like an easy hop into the team she'd always dreamed she'd be part of. It looked like they'd managed to pull McCracken down on several charges of corruption; there was still hope that he might be implicated in the unlawful death of a tax official who'd taken too keen an interest in his affairs. It hardly mattered to Iris's career now, the pronouncements on her future had already been rubber-stamped in Dublin. She'd been shunted back to Limerick, her reputation tainted by association rather than by her own ineptitude. When they'd released her from undercover her face was too well-known by then, a minor celebrity in some ways. It didn't make it easy with her already bitchy colleagues. So, at twenty-nine, she was back in the floaters' pool, a detective sergeant, with nowhere to go. She was filling her time visiting schools and women's groups, not what she'd signed up for.

When her watch bleated out that it was time to stop for now, she slowed to a brisk walk and headed for her car. She recognised immediately the numbers of the two missed calls on her mobile; drank back as much water as she could and decided she'd ring her father later. Even when she'd been working undercover, she managed to talk to him every day. Her job was unfair on everyone, especially her father, who'd spent forty years on the force. He'd have preferred if she'd done something 'safer', perhaps teaching. It was never going to happen. At this stage she figured she was genetically engineered to be a detective; you don't just turn your back on generations of guards – it had to come out somewhere.

'Hi, Diane – you called.' Iris tried to keep her breath even. She doubted that Diane, a perfectly made-up fifty-something, ever broke a sweat – more flight-attendant material than civil servant.

'Yes, Detective Sergeant Locke.' She seemed to sniffle at the title. 'Superintendent Penrose has had a request in for you…' The line seemed to go dead for a moment, as if Diane had forgotten she was there. 'Inspector Grady, Murder Squad. They have three bodies in a fire and they need hands on board.'

Iris racked her brains. She thought she knew everyone in Murder, and certainly, she knew all the senior officers. God knows, she'd approached them all at some point to include her on their teams. Murder in Dublin Castle had always been the end goal – but until now, it was a no-go, it seemed. 'Grady? That doesn't ring a bell for me at all,' she said, catching sight of a single strand of hair. It fell tenaciously from the band currently working hard to hold back her long growing-out fringe. She pulled the stray distractedly, still tossing over the various names in Dublin Castle.

'No.' Diane's voice was sand dry. 'You might not have. He's based in Corbally station.' She seemed to pause for a minute while Iris digested what she was saying. 'Limerick, Sergeant Locke, you're staying in Limerick.'

'Limerick. But I never said I wanted to transfer to Murder in Limerick…' The Murder team in Limerick was too close to her father's back door, so she'd never approached them.

'You said you wanted Murder. There are no vacancies in the Murder teams at Dublin Castle. Superintendent Penrose says there may be one coming up in Limerick.' The voice on the other end of the line lowered. 'This could be your last opportunity to get into Murder, Sergeant.'

Iris knew she could be in the floaters' pool until she reached her fifties if she didn't grab this chance to get onto a team. 'How do you mean, there might be a vacancy?'

'I'm not sure exactly, but I think there's a senior post to be filled and they're hoping the current DI will fill it. You could even be looking at applying for an inspector's job.'

'Hmm, but…' Iris was going to say, people didn't just swan into inspectors' posts, but then she remembered who she was talking to. 'So, when do they want me there?'

'Get there as soon as…' Diane seemed to mull over something for a moment, then she said, as though it had just dawned on her, 'Corbally, isn't that where your father worked?'

When she dropped the phone, Iris wasn't sure if she was happy or not. Sure, this was her shot at Murder, but Limerick? No one wanted to go to Corbally and Iris especially didn't want to work Murder there. But then, maybe anything would be better than staying in the floaters' pool? Another community-watch meeting or bunch of third-year students and she'd crack up. And, it was Murder, after all – even if it was Limerick. Damn, damn, damn it.

*

Ben Slattery wasn't quite sure how Grady had managed it, but he'd pulled in nearly twenty bodies, apart from himself, the DI and June Quinn. They even had a new DS on the way, of course, though what they needed was a superintendent as well to keep Byrne out of the incident room.

'Iris Locke,' Grady said as they drove out of the station; perhaps it was convenient that he couldn't meet Slattery's eyes. 'She comes well recommended. She's spent the last while in undercover.'

'Any relation of old Nessie?' Chief Superintendent Locke had run a tight ship. He was a bear of a man with a monster's appetite, but he'd been a good guard and decent enough to any detectives who found themselves in his division.

'The daughter. Not that it matters but she's the one that was…' Grady's voice drifted.

'A celebrity? That'll go down like a lead balloon. She's hardly out of nappies.'

'She'll get the same chance as anyone else, Ben.' There was a note of warning in Grady's voice; they needed as many good detectives on board for this one as they could get. 'It's headline news, our burnt-out family. It will be front-page news and you know what that means.'

'It means that like every other case, if it's murder we'll work our backsides off to find out who did it.' Slattery and Grady went way back. For the next few miles they drove in silence, each chewing down on the scant details they already knew and the difficult scene that lay ahead.

Slattery narrowed his eyes as the car drew up close to the smouldering ruins. He exhaled, more than muttered a grunt to the DI beside him.

'Give me a drowning any day, or even an RTA, but fires,' Slattery moaned as he opened the door of the Ford. Nine times out of ten, fires were down to faulty wiring, but they still had to come for a look-see to rule out anything more.

'Well, we don't get to choose,' Grady said, but they both knew, fires were the worst.

'Neither did they.' Slattery was thinking about the poor sods that had perished inside. The place was a wreck; hard to imagine what it was like before the blaze, though it hadn't been exactly plush, he could tell that much. Slattery stood for a moment, taking in his surroundings. The cottage snuggled at the end of a narrow track, everything about it was overgrown, from tall evergreen trees to the grass that licked greedily from all sides. The cottage was old and crumbling, with little beyond wind chimes and a few scattered toys around the door to stake a claim on the present decade. It gasped with a neglected mournful air that had as much to do with the desolate temperament seeping from its very fibre, as it had with the peeling paint and dirty windows. The smell of smoke and death didn't help the place either, but Slattery had a feeling that the rot had set in long before the cottage caught fire. They made their way up a narrow road, already a couple of locals had gathered. The fire boys confirmed the worst for them and they stood around taking in the debris that remained of three wasted lives.

'You can have a chat with them in a while,' Grady said to Slattery, and he nodded towards a small band of onlookers drawn to the cottage despite the melancholic circumstances, or maybe because of them. They stood in a shallow semi-circle, their expressions a mixture of grief and morbid curiosity. Perhaps he knew Slattery would prefer to stand and take statements from them than go anywhere near the charred cottage.

'Inspector.' They both turned to see a tall copper-haired detective making her way along the track behind them. She was attractive, no doubt, but there was an air of independence to her that sat at odds with her soft curves and pink cheeks. This was no shrinking wallflower. Here was a girl, Slattery suspected, who

could take care of herself long before she ever had to. 'Inspector.'
She was out of breath, like a woman who'd just run a marathon.
'I'm Sergeant Locke.' She stuck her hand out between Slattery and
Grady, perhaps unsure which of them was which.

'Good to have you here,' Grady said, shaking her hand, and
turned towards Slattery. 'Slattery, you can bring her up to speed.'

'Lovely.' Slattery managed to curb the irony when he caught a
sideward glance from Grady that warned him he was not to create
any trouble. 'Right, we're going in, you might as well tag along.'

It was the smell more than anything. It filled up your senses, so
you were surrounded by death. There was no getting away from
it with a fire. Slattery knew even the most-hardened cops dreaded
this kind of case. You never really saw the victim. Of course there
would be photographs; smiling, sun-filled days where the person
was vibrant and vigorous. But, in Slattery's mind, most fire victims
remained that – just images – with the burnt remains a half-cooked
gruesome reminder of the vulnerability of beauty, youth and grace.
We are all flesh and bone, he thought, *and eventually we rot and
when we do, it's not pretty.*

As they neared the cottage, Slattery spotted two uniforms,
staking out crime-scene markers. The forensic boys had begun
their work and Slattery heard them cursing the damage done by
the fire first, and then the water.

'Inspector, you didn't take long.' The fire chief nodded towards
the two detectives. He was young, probably his second time
overseeing an incident of this nature. He was shorter than most
of the fire fighters, but his eyes were keen and Slattery had a
feeling that he would work day and night to figure out what had
happened here.

Coleman Grady held out a hand. 'It's Grady and,' he nodded
towards his colleagues, 'Slattery and Locke. Well, what have we got?'

'It's not good, I'm afraid. Three bodies, two kids and the mother,
still in their beds. We have names, Anna Crowe, her son Martin

and daughter Sylvie – that's the baby, but no official ID yet. She was an artist. The place is full of burnt canvases.'

'Shit…' Slattery said, his hand partly covering his nose and mouth. The gritty air cut into his lungs, this was far worse than he'd imagined, and he cast an eye in Grady's direction. They needed more manpower; they'd need experienced officers to work this with them alongside the uniforms who could take on the grunt work. Slattery groaned, he hated new people foisted on him, almost as much as he hated fires.

'Shall we…?' Bennett asked, and led the way towards the front door. Inside, it was as black as Slattery had expected, lit only by the raw white of two bulbs running from the fire engine outside. There was still the sound of hissing from the dying fire, still the odd creak of wood, settling into its new form. The cottage was the traditional layout, with the addition of a lean-to kitchen and bathroom at the rear. They walked into what would have been the living room first. Off this room, at either end, were two bedrooms. They would leave those until last. In what Slattery supposed was the children's bedroom, he could hear Professor Rafiq Ahmed gently advising the photographer which particular angles to take of the victims. The place was filled with the disintegrated vestiges of large canvases and littered throughout the sitting room were the remains of various jars of flowers, all charred now, their water dirty, only ash petals left behind. The kitchen was probably the least damaged, which was unusual in domestic fires. Still, Slattery could make out some of the book spines heaped in a sooty corner, mainly art and travel, not a cookbook in sight. Amazing what could survive.

'We've checked the electrics; all seems fine there. Nothing to suggest the fire was electrical,' Bennett said.

'That's unusual.' Locke bent to examine the remains of a mobile phone from beneath the kitchen table.

'Better not to touch anything,' Slattery barked – his voice so loud it startled Locke.

'This is not my first time out, sergeant.' Iris's voice cut across the room icily.

'Anyway, there were no open fires in this grate recently, no chip pans, no signs of cigarette smoking – really, if there was a question…' Bennett looked around the room, as if it might give up its secrets if he stared long enough at its blackened walls.

'So… what can you tell us?' Slattery asked.

'From the damage left, I'd say there were two fires. The bedrooms are badly burnt. Here, well, it's mainly smoke damage. Apart from the lighter stuff, it looks like it was just about to take off, when we arrived.' He exhaled deeply. 'My feeling is, someone set those two rooms alight… and that makes it…' He couldn't finish the sentence.

'Murder,' Rafiq Ahmed said softly from the doorway. 'Our victims were shot, one after the other – a clean, probably silenced shot in their sleep. From what I can see, they may not even have known there was an intruder.'

'Fuck,' Slattery said before he stormed out the door.

CHAPTER 2

The incident room was buzzing by four o'clock. Already the hum of expectation zipped through the place, the odd nervous ripple of laughter, the light banter. It all halted as soon as Grady stood before the group. They were here for one thing only – to get whoever had killed the Crowe family while they slept. Grady nodded across at June Quinn. She was putting up the last of a series of ten by eights taken out at the site. They'd managed to get a decent snap of the family too, all smiling faces. The image made Iris gasp. She knew this woman, Anna, well, she'd met her at least, somewhere, sometime. The intrusion of a ringtone edged past her memories. It was gone – but there was a sliver of familiarity about Anna Crowe, she was sure of it. Iris stepped closer to the case board. Anna had been an attractive blonde woman and her two young kids, a boy Iris would put at about seven, all gap-toothed and freckled, and a small baby, wrapped against the cold Irish summer of last year.

'Settle down now…' Grady's voice boomed across the room. 'Okay, you all know why we're here. Earlier this morning, the local fire brigade got a call out when a neighbour raised the alarm. This small cottage,' he put his hand beneath a photograph of the smouldering ruin, 'was…'

'Lit up like a bloody Christmas tree,' Slattery cut in.

'Yes.' Grady nodded across to June Quinn.

'Three bodies were found in the cottage, each with a gunshot wound. The bodies have been identified as Anna Crowe and her two children, Martin and Sylvie Crowe. Mary Higgins is acting as family liaison officer. She's with Anna's husband – Adrian Crowe – now.'

'They were… estranged?' Iris had nabbed a desk, front and centre.

'Yes. Fairly recently from what Higgins has been able to get from the husband, he's in a pretty bad way at the moment,' Slattery answered. The reality was they'd got nothing out of him yet. The FLO, Higgins, had gleaned as much from the family photographs around the walls and the contact numbers in a neat book by the kitchen phone as she had from Adrian Crowe.

'We'll be going out there a little later to have a chat with Mr Crowe.' Grady looked down at his notes. He nodded to Slattery.

'The house itself, as you can see from the photographs, wasn't in great condition to start with. Forensics are going through the place still, but with the fire damage and what have you, we're not expecting a whole lot.' Slattery took up the chipped mug before him, examined its contents, seemed to think better of actually drinking from it and set it down again.

Next up, Grady went through the site. It was so far off the beaten track, it hardly seemed worthwhile to check out Traffic, but this was a murder investigation, so they couldn't leave any stone unturned. Grady put a big burly guard called Westmont onto all of the approach roads to Kilgee. 'Sergeant Locke, you and Slattery will go and see Mr Crowe this afternoon.' He didn't wait for an answer. 'June, I want you to check up on who's around the area with form. The rest of you, I want you out there, split between Kilgee and Anna Crowe's former neighbourhood. Mary Higgins found Anna Crowe's old diary. It has a few contact numbers – June, maybe you can take that on as well. Put addresses to the numbers and Slattery, you can dole them out. If anyone needs anything, I'll be in my office, putting together notes for our new superintendent.'

*

Iris couldn't be sure, but she had a feeling that she'd never met anyone who got on her nerves as much as Ben Slattery. She drummed her fingers against the steering wheel, willing herself not to make a comment about the fumes of alcohol that settled into any space he filled. Everything about him set her on edge, from his lazy gait to his bitter retorts. Too long on the job. He was a man eaten up by simmering cynicism and it didn't take a genius to see that he was trouble on a road to nowhere. They were going in opposite directions and she hoped with equal speed. She decided she would not let him see he had rattled her. She put her mind, as forcefully as she could, to considering everything she'd heard about the victim's husband. There wasn't much, but surely they would learn more when they met him.

On their way into the estate, they'd passed by a couple of uniforms doing the rounds. So far, they were picking up very little. The victim had kept herself to herself. Adrian Crowe lived in the semi-detached house he'd bought with his wife some ten years earlier. The house faced onto a fair-sized green where kids could play football or mess about on their bikes. *It was all nice kids here*, Iris thought.

'Amazing what a couple of thousand can buy. An entire childhood, when you think about the kids who live in the Cloisters,' she said to Slattery as they pulled up outside the Crowe family home.

'Yeah, well, people do what they can,' he said flatly. 'We can't all be born with a silver spoon in our mouths and have doors opened for us because of who our father is,' he grumbled.

'That's not…' Iris had felt the tension in Slattery from the moment they met. There was no point arguing with him, the only way to deal with relics like Slattery was to show them she was here on merit. It bristled all the same, this old certainty.

'Let's just get this done,' she settled on instead and banged her door a little too loudly, cursing when she saw the satisfied look in his eyes.

The house inside was understated, in various shades of cream and off white. The walls here weren't big enough to carry canvases as large as the ones found in the cottage. It felt somehow sanitised, as if Adrian Crowe had cleaned out every scrap of his wife and children as soon as they'd left the house. There was a tidiness about the place that bordered on compulsive and which was completely at odds with the ramshackle little cottage captured in grey photographs and included in their case packs. The only thing out of place was a small cream business card that sat propped on the hall table, as though left for the specific attention of someone who might call. Iris picked it up as she passed and slipped it into her pocket.

Mary Higgins led them into a small sitting room. She explained that they'd just had tea and Mr Crowe had received medication from his local GP to try to calm him down. The tablets remained sealed on the low coffee table in front of him. Iris knew, when Crowe held out his hand that he did so mechanically; he was weirdly composed, his eyes dead as a taxidermy salmon, glassy and empty.

'Can you tell me, Mr Crowe, how did you find out about the fire this morning?' Slattery asked, taking out a battered notebook that looked as worn out as its owner. Iris watched Crowe – she couldn't help but feel he was a bit of a weasel of a man. He was in shock. Still, she couldn't help but feel as if somewhere between how he looked and who he was there was a disconnect and the man would never be fully at peace with himself.

'One of the men in the village, John Kiernan, I think, he was the first to spot it and he rang the fire brigade, then he rang me.'

Iris knew that this man would feel many different emotions over the next few months, but today's emotions and Crowe's reactions were vital to the investigation. In far too many murders, the victim is killed by the person closest to them, that's murder 101 – every green officer knows that much. Even if he wasn't the killer, being the person closest, Adrian Crowe could reveal more from his reactions today than he'd ever realise he was giving away.

'So you drove immediately out to Kilgee?' Iris leaned forward in her seat. Her hands were spread out across her lap, her body language completely open and relaxed, inviting Adrian Crowe to share his worries, share his thoughts. Slattery had hardly spoken to her on the journey out. He reeked of booze and fags and she wondered how on earth a dinosaur like him still took up valuable space on a murder squad. All the same, she had a feeling that he knew his stuff; and he seemed a little too chummy with the DI to make an enemy of him yet.

'As soon as I got the message.' Adrian's voice was flat. He had no use for words now.

'We'll need to talk to your work colleagues,' Iris kept her voice soft, 'just to get a timeline up and running. It's standard procedure. Can you give us someone we can contact, a number, anything?'

'Sure.' Crowe took his phone from the pocket of his jeans. The clothes he'd been wearing earlier had already been taken for forensic analysis. His wardrobes had been searched. They all knew the score. Wouldn't make it any easier for Adrian Crowe, especially if he was innocent. Crowe passed the mobile across to Iris. 'It's a work phone, I won't be needing it for the next while. Maybe you could drop it in to them when you're there?'

'Of course,' Iris said. It'd give them not only a list of calls, but also a location for Crowe's movements over the time frame they were interested in. 'When did Anna move out to Kilgee?' Iris asked gently. In the coldness of the room the words almost sounded like a lament.

'She's been gone a couple of weeks now. Started out as a creative thing. She wanted to be surrounded by nature, said she couldn't work here any more, the traffic, the airport, too many kids playing outside, what have you.' He waved his hand about, as though the sounds were rushing through the quiet room. 'We converted the attic into a studio; you can see it if you want. But she said it wasn't what she needed.'

'Was it what you wanted?' Iris asked, gentle again.

'Is it what any man wants? I love my wife very much, detective. I wanted her and my family here with me. The last place I wanted them was back there in the middle of nowhere, with God knows who or what lurking about the place.'

'How do you mean?' Slattery cut in.

'Look at what happened to them. I told her this could happen.' Crowe's body began to shake once more, sobs overtaking his torso so his head and neck seemed to wobble maniacally out of sync with the rest of him. 'Some weirdo has been sending her flowers since she moved out there, been watching the place too, I think, but I couldn't get through to her.'

They had seen the jars and jars of flowers, still left intact in the sitting room of the cottage. 'Wildflowers?' Slattery checked, to be sure they were not just a haul from days trawling through the woods and fields that surrounded the little house.

'Yes, wildflowers, bunches and bunches of them,' Crowe said wearily.

'Do you know who this guy was?'

'Of course I knew who he was; she was convinced he was watching over her, protecting her somehow, like her guardian angel.' He sighed, a hollow empty sound that said far more than any words could. 'She'd give him food and cups of tea, encouraging him. I warned her. Too late now. Too late for all of us.'

*

It seemed colder tonight than any night before this week. The ground was damp here, the leaves heavy and black, winter wet; there'd be no drying them back to the crisp autumn carpet of only days ago. Soon darkness would be upon them and he looked forward to this – it was where he belonged, in the half-light; maybe she'd known that too. He crouched down low, waited while they did what they needed to do. They'd taken her away earlier in the day, on a stretcher, her face covered now, the only sound a protesting wheel, which screeched even as it tried to negotiate the rough ground about the cottage. He tried hard not to think of what was beneath that cover. The kids came after, but he hardly noticed, kept his eyes fixed on the ambulance that stood waiting. This was goodbye to Anna, he knew that now. He should have left then. Gone home, for a time at least. He hadn't eaten since early morning – now his stomach rumbled, but that was nothing to the ache that had overtaken his whole body. Was it loneliness or guilt? He wasn't sure. He'd have plenty of time to figure that out now. A lifetime, a lifetime more than Anna and her kids were left with.

He turned, thought he heard something in the woods behind him, probably nothing. He always knew Anna would never love him back, and maybe that just made him love her more. For years she'd been dismissive of him, and now when she'd come back, well… What kind of twisted toxic adoration culminates in this? He shivered, and it wasn't that cold. He pulled close his heavy army coat. Within its pockets he carried an armoury of weapons; knives mainly, but he had more at home, a shot gun and several smaller guns that he'd managed to pick up over the years. A man had to protect himself after all, and he liked the feeling of power carrying a gun gave him. He liked to be in control; liked to have the upper hand. He thought of Anna now, how she'd begged him to make things right. How finally she'd stopped, left him alone, accepted what fate had handed her; and then her joy – she'd been released, ultimately, she'd been freed. The guilt still made him tremble; that and the feeling that he'd never been so desolate in all his life.

The crack of a branch beneath his foot brought him back to the present. He knew he had to do something – but what? He looked down at his weather-beaten hands. It was almost dark, an occasional sliver of moonlight spilling out between fast moving bulbous clouds – it had all been in his hands. He'd been within sniffing distance and then just when she trusted him… *There had to be some way to make things right.* He sat back against the damp earth, pulled out a small tin box where he kept his tobacco and rolled himself a slim joint. They'd all left now. It was just him and the occasional night creature, sitting here, waiting. He would think long and hard, and somehow, he'd make it all up to Anna Crowe and her kids.

*

'Fucking typical,' Slattery said to no one specific and Locke in particular.

'What's that?' Locke said, smiling at the business card in her hand. It was for a local solicitor, but not one who would be of any help in a murder case. There was an air of expectant triumph from her, as if she'd pulled one over on Slattery and he didn't like it one bit, it was almost enough to make him retch.

'Well, there's Grady expecting me to cut corners and I'm doing my best to keep on the straight and narrow and here I am stuck with you, a bloody magpie, stealing from a suspect's house.' He put his cigarettes on the dash and eyed the card that sat between Locke's fingers on the wheel.

'Ah, don't worry, we can tell him it was you anyway,' Locke said, her voice light, joking. 'You look dodgy enough to have done a lot worse than move around a bit of paper and anyway, I'll drop it back exactly where we found it.'

The words could have cut a more sensitive man, but Slattery knew that how he looked was a direct reflection of how he lived. He had always followed any lead before him. He worked off his gut. He patted his stomach now, feeling every one of his years. His beer gut, his grey pallor, his shortness of breath – the accumulation of a lifetime of bad food and too much smoke and booze. He wasn't thirty any more – he was in his fifties, heading for retirement if he was unlucky. If Slattery prayed, it was that he'd die with his boots on. He wasn't looking for any glory; a quick, painless heart attack, an aneurysm, dead before he hit the ground. That would do nicely, thank you. Better than waiting it out, somewhere, just him and his memories. And his regrets.

'Thanks for that, mate.' He closed his eyes, blocking out Limerick, blocking out life.

At least it was something to get started on, before the post mortem. Slattery opened his eyes to see Locke turning down Nicholas Street instead of Athlunkard Street.

'Where are you going?' he grunted.

'Street closures, it's pedestrians only,' Locke said evenly.

'Fuck that, I'm not walking half a mile. Stick on the flasher and away we go, we're on official business.' Slattery grunted again, and began to undo his seat belt, so much for Locke being a rule-breaker.

They pulled up outside Forbes, Stapleton & Gains, and made their way in, despite the dirty looks from council workers nearby. Slattery almost swaggered, as if he was an extra on *CSI*. Alan Gains was waiting for them when they arrived. Quiet times. The man was visibly upset and Slattery wondered if he hadn't been carrying a bit of a torch for Anna Crowe. He brought them into a well-appointed office, offered them tea or coffee and sat opposite them, waiting for them to tell him what had happened.

'She was a good friend, you know,' he said after he had heard as much as they could tell. 'Not that we met up regularly; you don't after a few years, do you? Partners, kids, jobs, they all take up your time. But we kept in touch, the odd phone call. I bought a couple of oils for here, sponsored her exhibition a few years ago, that kind of thing – when it was worth our while getting a tax break.' He smiled ruefully.

'How did you meet her?' Locke asked the obvious question.

'We were in school together; I grew up in Kilgee too. We were all buddies, me, Anna and Adrian.' He smiled at some memory that seemed to cross his mind. 'Back then, it was me and Anna – Adrian was a year ahead, so…'

'Have you kept in contact with Adrian too?' Slattery asked.

'Ah, no. You know the way it is…'

'No.' Locke looked across at Slattery, took the lead from the old man's nod. 'Mr Crowe – Adrian – her husband, he's just not able to help us much at the moment.' She smiled apologetically and Slattery thought, *Well done on the sympathy vote*. Slattery for one always pegged the husband as the most likely suspect. He'd become cynical so long ago, it was his natural default setting now.

'He's a man of few words at the best of times,' Gains said.

'They were separated, were they?' Iris edged into the silence of Gains's thoughts.

'I wouldn't know about that, I hadn't talked to her in about six months. Last time… well, I'd say she was under pressure, but aren't we all now? An artist, sure it's either a feast or a famine when it comes to commissions. She was selling very little these last few years. Even if she was having problems with Adrian, I don't think she'd have said anything to me. We just didn't talk about those kinds of things, she was very… private.' He looked now at Slattery. 'Not too surprising really, when you consider what they went through.'

'Oh?' Slattery said, but he knew that no words were needed. Gains was going to tell him anyway.

'You know who she is, don't you?' Gains gazed up at a painting behind Slattery's back. Slattery, hardly an art lover, had spotted it when he'd come into the room. It was a huge canvas, big enough to fill an entire wall of Slattery's grotty little flat – if he'd been a man to hang a picture. Of course, Slattery's flat was still just a flat, even after a couple of years he hadn't managed to make it into a home, probably never would, but it didn't keep him up at night.

Gains studied the canvas now, a mish-mash of darkened oils, with a splash of wild flowers painted across the melee. 'She's Anna Fairley.' He looked at them both now, waiting for some kind of recognition. When none came, he moved forward a little in his

chair. 'The Baby Fairley case – it happened back in the eighties…'
he waited. 'The Fairley baby was Anna's sister – they never rightly
got over it. Anna couldn't talk about it at all.'

'The Baby Fairley case?' Iris said and tried to pretend that it
meant something.

'That's right, they never found her, people said she was dead
before they even called in your lot, but that didn't make not
knowing any easier. It always kind of hung in the air about the
place out there, can't imagine why she'd have wanted to go back,
to be honest.'

Slattery rested his back against the leather chair, took a sip of
tea from the small cup set before him. Let the words settle; he
wasn't quite sure what this meant for the case, if anything, but he
was sure of one thing, once the newspapers got wind of it, they'd
have a field day and it would be ten times harder to get anything
done with a posse of reporters on their backs.

CHAPTER 3

'He was smooth,' Slattery said when they sat back in the car.

'You say that like it's a crime.' Iris tipped the indicator. 'We're bloody lucky not to get a ticket here,' she said half under her breath.

'I'd like to see them try,' he snarled, and she had a feeling any traffic warden would think twice before tangling with Slattery. 'Anyway, I never said it was a crime, but being a fancy-pants solicitor doesn't automatically make him innocent either.'

'He was fond of her,' Iris said as she swung the car into heavy evening traffic along the quays. She caught a glimpse of the river beneath them, pewter dark and unforgiving.

'He was bloody in love with her, whether he knows it or not.'

'You're not seriously going to suggest they were having an affair.' Iris glanced across at Slattery. He was sweating now, a glossy film across his forehead.

'I haven't said anything of the sort, but if it came to a beauty contest… well, maybe it gives the grieving widower more of a motive.'

'You're clutching at straws.' They were pulled up, waiting for the traffic lights to change and Iris knew there was a question hanging in the air between them, like a shard of something deep and penetrating; it was the one thing that set them both on edge.

'Go on,' Slattery grunted.

'You go on,' she said. She would not be goaded into playing out the conversation in her mind again. 'Well… do you remember it?'

'Aye, I do, but it's a long time ago and I was hardly in the door of Corbally, just a uniform picking up nuggets from the big boys back then.'

'It was never solved?'

'They never found the kid, if that's what you mean.' Slattery cleared his throat, a rattling empty sound. 'I wouldn't get too excited about it yet,' he said, staring determinedly at the water beneath them.

'Do I look excited?' Iris said tonelessly.

'Good, because all that's going to be is another complication and if we end up following a lead that went cold thirty years ago, we'll miss what's in front of us while there's still a chance the trail is warm.'

'No harm looking it up, though – we're not all prehistoric on the team,' she replied as she pulled the car into a parking space at the rear of the station.

Corbally station. Iris sighed. It was the last place she'd have imagined herself working. It was over a hundred and fifty years old, built originally as a commercial bank, based on a design by Francis Johnston. It was an impressive building, although to accommodate its current occupation, many of the grander rooms were subdivided to cater to the demands of smaller office space. The corridors were long and high, with floors of marble and walls of stone, painted white mostly, but in some places an unfortunate sanatorium green. Voices tended to rise upwards to the high-domed ceilings, so that any commotion on the bottom floor boomed throughout the whole building, echoing long after the fracas was at an end. Locke didn't trust her own voice in the place, particularly in the larger open areas, like the stairwell, the foyer and the hallways. Still, she would have to make the most of it. Tonight, it was just a question of putting to bed what they'd learned for the day. Perhaps, if they were lucky, someone may have hit on a vital strand to close up the investigation quickly.

It seemed wrong to be heading out to dinner at her parents' house when there was so much more that they should be doing in the Murder Team. Grady had hung a roster for every member of the team on one of the whiteboards that lined the walls about the incident room. There was a skeleton shift on duty from midnight until six in the morning. People with families were expected to show up at home and everyone else seemed to be heading to the pub. He had partnered her, for the most part with Ben Slattery. Iris couldn't make up her mind if that was a decision based on their ranking or because he wanted them to keep an eye on each other. After all, she was an unknown quantity and she had a feeling that everyone had a measure of Slattery, for better and for worse.

Iris had no real excuse not to turn up at her parents'. It wasn't as if she didn't enjoy these evenings. The meal would be excellent. Her father was a big man who'd always loved food and being in charge of some project. Her mother wafted about and let him get on with things while making noises that might be appreciation or they might be offers of help she never expected to be taken up.

Iris drummed over the case on the drive out to Woodburn. She hardly noticed familiar landmarks on her way as she considered what they'd learned so far. Already, it was getting under her skin. She couldn't be sure if that had as much to do with the fact that there was something so familiar about Anna Crowe or that annoying bugger Slattery or something quite different. She'd felt a nerve pull inside her when she'd looked at the photograph of that little family. It was more than sadness; perhaps, she reasoned, it was the injustice of it all.

Woodburn was a sprawling old house that was as much a part of their little family as any of them. It sat in the Limerick countryside overlooking the Atlantic far off in the distance. Only half a dozen miles outside Limerick, but it couldn't be further away from the bustle of the city in terms of its ambience and charm. Tonight, perhaps more than ever before, Iris understood how important this place had been to her father. It was everything that Corbally station was not. Jack Locke had served his time before her, working his way up eventually to superintendent before retiring with a near perfect record. She knew his colleagues called him Nessie, but that had more to do with his bark than it had with any bite.

She drew her car up over the loose gravel stone, circling about to the back of the house so she could slip quietly through the kitchen door. On her way she passed by her father's old wellingtons, standing to attention for his early morning tramp across the fields. The kitchen was littered with used dishes and saucepans emptied and left to stand; the mess was out of character from her parents' typical order. Iris twisted the copper cold tap on. Its familiar noise grounded her, making her feel as if she'd left the atrocities of the day behind her in some indefinable way. She filled a large glass with fresh water and drank it thirstily. She stood for a moment, catching her reflection in the uneven glass before her. Outside the garden was in darkness. Her eyes strained to make out anything in the glass beyond her own reflection and the familiar kitchen around her. In the room beyond, she heard her father tell a joke he'd told a thousand times before. It was new enough to his guests and so they laughed wholeheartedly when he delivered the punch line.

Tonight's get together was in honour of distant relations who were visiting Ireland from the States. It might have been an all-day occasion, but Iris had cried off dinner promising to arrive for dessert. The truth was she knew tonight was not the night to tell her father she'd joined the Murder Team. She couldn't do that to him, not yet.

'Yes, the image of her mother,' Jack Locke pronounced proudly when Iris arrived into the dining room. She had missed pudding, but she helped herself to a glass of red wine and settled down at the corner of the dining table, fending off offers of food that she couldn't face even if she wanted to.

'Really?' An elderly grandaunt who'd last been in Ireland fifty years earlier peered at her over thick sparkly framed spectacles.

'Oh, yes,' her mother chimed in proudly, 'she's just like me when I was young.' It was enough to admit that she was following in her father's footsteps, Theodora was not letting him have all the credit for their daughter.

'I am indeed,' Iris agreed and sipped her drink lost in her own thoughts of the investigation while the party went on around her.

'Penny for them,' her father said later when everyone had left. 'You've been in another world all night long.'

'Oh, Jack, leave her alone. Isn't Iris allowed to have thinking time without you wanting to know about it?' Her mother bent and kissed her on her forehead. 'I'm off to bed, dear, long day, you know.' She smiled wanly and drifted towards the stairs.

'Night, Mum,' Iris said automatically.

'Come on, night cap,' her father said then, dropping a fat glass of brandy into Iris's hands. 'You can tell me all about your latest exploit in community policing.'

'Oh, there's not much to tell, actually…' Iris couldn't meet his eye, it was one thing not telling him that she'd joined the Murder Team, but quite another to actually lie about it. It was funny, really; any other parent would be delighted to think that a child was following in their footsteps. Jack Locke wanted Iris as far away from the Murder Team as it was possible to get. Much better, in his opinion, if she had any job that didn't bring her into contact with murderers and Ireland's criminal underworld. Iris wasn't sure that he'd be any more enthusiastic about the Limerick Murder Team than he had been when she'd mentioned Dublin Castle to him before she'd taken up the post in undercover.

'I ran into some people who knew you, back in the day,' Iris smiled. It was one way to distract her father from whatever he wanted to know.

'Really, did they call me Nessie too?'

'I don't know, hardly likely to tell me anyway.' She smiled at him now; his eyebrows seemed to be growing into each other these days and she wondered whether they had always knitted so closely together.

'So, who was it?' Jack asked her now, pulling her from her thoughts once more.

'Coleman Grady, he's…'

'With the Murder Team, still, I suppose?'

'Yes, has he been there long?'

'The only one longer than him is old Ben Slattery, but the less said about that chancer the better.' Her father shook his head.

'Slattery?' Part of Iris wanted to ask him all about her new colleagues. But it wouldn't take five seconds before Jack Locke would put two and two together and she had a feeling he wasn't going to tell her anything she didn't know. Ben Slattery was a walking cliché, a detective who had long since lost his moral compass – perhaps he'd seen too much. Iris had a feeling that even though he didn't like her, she probably shouldn't take it personally. He seemed like the type who didn't like many people anyway. One thing she was sure of, wherever he went, trouble would never be very far behind. Grady was a different kettle of fish. He had a quality to him that she couldn't quite place, but she had a feeling it fell somewhere between his broad shoulders as honour. It was, she thought now, a little sad that it marked him out among the many colleagues she'd worked with over the years.

'Grady, though, he's a good detective, so long as they don't try to bury him in some admin job.' Jack looked at her again, as if studying her for something she might say. 'He's a good bit older than you, probably well into his forties…'

'Oh, don't worry, I just ran into him, I'm not planning on eloping with him.' Iris shook her head, she knew her father would love to see her settled down, married and producing an army of grandchildren for him.

'Probably just as well, he's hardly the settling down type,' her father said, but he was watching her closely all the same, a whisper of some unsaid words passing between them.

'Look at the time,' she said to change the subject as much as anything else.

'Well, is there anything else?' He smiled at her now, perhaps hoping to hear that she had something to tell him that was a million miles away from the police and old memories.

'Not a thing,' she said, getting up and kissing his soft white hair. 'But, I'm on early shift in a few hours, so…' she left the hardly touched glass of brandy on the table before heading back to the city.

*

Slattery always seemed to pull the short straw when it came to post mortems. He sighed, perhaps he'd been on too many cases? Kilgee would be swarming with every uniform Grady could lay his hands on today; for once, Slattery wished he could have been one of them. At least when he got back to the station, there'd be some bones to chew – the younger officers were all eager to impress, it seemed everyone wanted to be on the Murder Team.

Sometimes, depending on the death, depending on the coroner, you could just attend the post mortem for the opening and closing. Not this time. Slattery and Iris arrived at the autopsy suite; both in their own way braced for what lay ahead. Slattery glanced at his well made-up colleague, with her soft wool coat and high-heeled boots. He was tempted to tell her it wasn't fashion week she was attending. Well, perhaps that was a bit of an overstatement. After all, Slattery counted it as a personal triumph if he managed to find matching socks and both clean. All the same, Iris Locke was a bit too high and mighty for his liking. Then again, anyone who'd had their picture across the front pages of the papers was bound to get up his nose. Didn't get her very far in the end though, did it? That thought warmed Slattery in some small way. He hated the idea that she had been foisted on them, probably just because she was Jack Locke's daughter.

Professor Rafiq Ahmed met them as they made their way through the cool corridors towards his office. It was hard to see where he'd put in an all-nighter. A three-car smash two days earlier meant he'd hardly left this place since. It meant the Crowe family had had to wait their turn. *It was just as well murder victims never complain*, Slattery thought. Ahmed looked as though he'd just stepped out of a Hollywood blockbuster – perfect hair, skin and teeth – and greeted them warmly. To be fair, there was worse out there than poor old Ahmed. Gay as a Christmas tea towel, of course, Slattery thought. Sometimes it seemed as if this country was running away from him with how PC everyone was meant to be. Still, he liked Ahmed. He was hardworking, good at his job and in Slattery's opinion that said enough about him.

All of the preliminary examinations had been done. Slattery wondered how they could get anything worthwhile from the charred remains he'd seen at the cottage in Kilgee.

'So, d'ye find anything?' Slattery shuffled into green scrubs that were never going to conceal his abundant girth.

'Ah, Detective Slattery, this is science, not alchemy. We will see what comes back from the samples we have taken,' Ahmed said, but his voice gave Slattery hope that maybe there was something small that might help.

'What are we hoping for exactly?' Iris asked from beneath a gown that was obviously built for a bigger physique.

'Nothing in particular really and everything at the same time.' Ahmed welcomed Iris as if she was booking into a hotel. Slattery could see she had warmed to him immediately. It didn't surprise him, but it scratched away at that growing irritation she was bringing out in him. 'We examine the skin, the hair, the outer orifices – like the ears and nose. It is interesting what the body picks up, more so if there was a struggle involved.'

'But the fire, surely it means you don't get so much?'

'Maybe, but you'd be surprised at what survives. Now, we need to put on masks and caps.'

The bodies didn't look quite so badly burnt to Slattery as he had expected. Perhaps it was the bright light, or the fact that their hair and burnt clothes had been scraped back. Slattery developed a pale sweat on his forehead despite the low temperature of the operating room and cursed the heavy scrubs and bright lights overhead.

Ahmed began the first incision, a long T wound that opened up Anna Crowe's torso from neck to pubis. Slattery watched and listened while Ahmed went about his work, explaining for an unseen recorder his every action, his every finding. After a while Slattery began to zone out; they could be here for six hours, between the lot. The only way to survive it, Slattery had realised a long time ago, was to use the hours to go back over the case in his thoughts. It kept his mind off the drink, or other things that were likely to make him bad tempered. Outside, he imagined he could hear the rain falling down, sheets of it across the city. They'd had two unseasonable good weeks, but the forecasters had gloomily announced there'd be payback for the next two. At least it didn't look like snow, just rain, rain and more rain. Slattery thought about Alan Gains, the Fairley baby and the thirty-odd years of history lived out in that cottage. Why would Anna Crowe want to go back there? Why would she bring her kids there? Surely, her life was not so unbearable that it drove her into the hands of a killer?

Or maybe, just maybe, she thought she was moving away from one.

CHAPTER 4

Iris thought that Adrian Crowe had the kind of job a detective might have envied. It would appeal to anyone who'd emptied themselves out and learned the hard way that it all counted for so little in the end. By comparison, engineering was clean, well-paid and didn't cause you any sleepless nights. It hardly mattered if you gave a damn or not, so long as you did what you were paid to do, you left the place at finishing time with a clear conscience. ABA Technics was based at Shannon Airport, a fifteen-mile drive from the Crowe family home, just twelve miles from Kilgee. Not that Iris was counting exactly. Crowe had his own office and worked mostly from there, a cubbyhole at the far end of a draughty hanger. Normally, he was on stand-by, called only if there was a problem the regular mechanics couldn't figure. He worked mainly on CAD, drawing up and designing small technical replacement parts, commissioned by various airlines around the world. Truth was, though, once he'd clocked in, he could legitimately be anywhere in the hangar – or ten miles away, the only way of contacting him was by mobile phone. His alibi, whatever his colleagues might say, wasn't worth a fig to them.

'She was a lovely girl, the lads here are shocked.' Bill McFadden offered to show them around. 'He never mentioned a thing about moving out into the sticks, though; quiet fella.' McFadden was pensive. He was a big man – a man who'd eaten too many steaks, drunk too many brandies. 'He's been here… must be ten years now, and I'd say I know as much about him now as I did on that first day.'

'Did he pal around with any of the mechanics?' Iris had her notebook at the ready.

'No, he really did keep himself to himself. I knew *she* was an artist, they'd a couple of kids, but that was it – he just comes in, does his work and goes out the door again.' He leaned in closer to Slattery, lowered his voice. 'Between ourselves, he's a bit odd. There was no reason to work nights, but he said he'd rather have the peace and quiet.' He shook his head then, as if he was still trying to figure it out. 'Still, a lot to be said for it, I can tell you, I'm not even sure that he's in the union.'

'Mind if we hold onto this for a day or two?' Iris held up the work mobile Crowe had given them earlier in the day.

'Not at all, keep it as long as ye want, I don't suppose Adrian will be back for a while yet?'

'No,' Iris looked up at McFadden, 'he's in a bad way, as you'd expect.'

'Oh aye, as you'd expect, can't imagine what it must be like, the wife *and* the kids, bad enough one… but… doesn't bear thinking about.' McFadden shook his head.

'Can we take a quick look at his office, while we're here?' Iris asked.

'Sure, but you won't find anything there, bar drawings and log books.' McFadden got up from his desk, sighing as he did so. 'Terrible do.' They walked slowly across the huge hangar. A wolf whistle sounded from somewhere out of sight. Iris stopped herself from throwing a dirty eye in the direction of the mechanics at work beneath them. She could feel Slattery watching her and so she tightened her expression into an unreadable neutral. She suspected he would enjoy her unease and she had no intention of giving him the satisfaction of that. On the floor there were two small carrier planes. Iris figured that space wise, the place could take something far bigger.

'How many have you working here?' Slattery called out to McFadden above the sound of wind and machinery.

'Forty. We had more, but the way things are now… well, you can't afford not to run a tight ship.'

Adrian Crowe's office was as bare and empty as his home. There were no photographs, no kids' drawings, nothing personal. It was as if he just spirited himself in and out of the place each day. Even now, Iris would have assumed the man had tidied up forensically, if he'd ever been here to start with. There wasn't so much as a coffee cup or an open folder left on his desk. Everything put away neatly – even his pencils sat in a company mug, heads down, eight General's Kimberly drawing pencils, perfectly sharpened, left ready for use.

'Is he an army man?' Slattery replaced a pencil he'd picked up to inspect.

'Yes, actually, he came to us straight from the air corps. Did his apprenticeship with them and then the few years he had to. Sure, there's no money in it. He was glad to get in here, I'd say, and he's done well for himself. He's good at his job. I'd be hard pressed to find anyone as good – shown him too, with regular bonuses.'

Iris nodded; it explained something, although she was not sure quite what. Certainly, it accounted for the neatness, maybe for the remoteness too. But there was something else about Adrian Crowe that didn't quite fit. Something niggled Iris and she knew that she'd have to get a better handle on the man before she could figure out quite what that was. Iris had spent sufficient time in undercover to know that her gut instinct wouldn't let her down. She had been a detective long enough to know that if you sit back and wait, people generally show themselves for what they are sooner, rather than later.

Slattery scanned quickly through the drawers, but there was nothing there. McFadden shook hands with them as they were leaving; telling them to be sure and let him know if there was anything else they needed help with. Slattery said they'd be sending two detectives out to talk to the mechanics and the rest of the staff. By the time this was over, McFadden would be well sick of the sight of them.

*

Slattery looked disdainfully down at his mug of tea. It was almost five o'clock, time for something stronger, but it would have to wait. For now, he sprawled on the flimsy office chair that had been his for too many years to count. Grady wanted a report on the day's investigation and that meant another hour here listening to teachers' pets doing their best to make something of the nothing they'd managed to collect after a full day on house to house.

'She was a schoolteacher, lives now just in the centre of the village…' one of the floaters was saying.

'She sounds like a proper old news bag to me,' Slattery couldn't help himself, 'on neighbourhood watch is she?' He knew the type: old dears, living out in the middle of nowhere with nothing but the television for company all day long. As soon as a policeman knocked on the door they were so helpful they could hold him up for hours imparting tea, biscuits and every bit of tittle tattle they'd ever heard or made up.

Grady shot him a look, which went some way towards quietening him, and so he angled his gaze through grimy windows towards the streets below. The reports droned on and Slattery could almost feel the life being sucked out of him, this was a waste of time. They had nothing. Maybe, he felt, they didn't know how to ask the right questions, but the fact was that even if they did, they probably wouldn't know what a lead was if it smacked them in the face. They were too young, too enthusiastic, too hungry.

He felt his gaze slide towards Locke, they'd have to wait and see if she had the makings of a half decent detective or if she was only fit for grunt work. No matter what they thought, Slattery knew, you can't make a good detective and there were plenty of second and third generation guards around that should have considered their career choices more carefully. Then, suddenly a name invaded his thoughts and it perked him up with curious keenness. Veronique Majewski.

That name was enough to make him gulp back the last of his cold tea, grab his jacket and head for the door. He hated writing reports anyway.

Slattery had left Iris back at the station typing up their day's work; figured she was as relieved to see the back of him as he was of her. He'd told her he had to visit the dentist. It was years since Slattery had been to a dentist; never ceased to amaze him what a youngster would swallow. Instead he'd made his way out to Kilgee.

Veronique Majewski and he had crossed paths a couple of years earlier. Veronique didn't care much for guards, didn't much care for anyone unless she could see a direct way of benefiting from them. They had history, she and Slattery. He had saved her life, so now she would have to put up with him, only because they both knew she owed him.

'You want coffee?' she asked when she opened the door, her Polish accent thick and heavy. If anyone recognised the sound of a hangover, it was Slattery. He nodded at her.

'Black and strong.' She handed him steaming coffee and Slattery figured by the aroma that it was as cheap as you could get. She sat in a chair opposite him, fixing her peroxide hair with a shaking hand. Slattery would have been hard pushed to put an age on Veronique, but he'd guess not yet thirty, although the dark circles that slumped beneath her eyes gave her an added decade. Her shape was good and she held herself like a young woman in her prime. Slattery figured that if she dumped the skimpy clothes and high boots, she could look quite classy – or classy to his mind, at least. But he knew that there would be no change for Veronique, no change at all.

'So, what is it that you want, Sergeant Slattery?' She eyed him as if he was a predator.

Slattery put his cup back down on the table; a sip was enough, any more would just be out of habit or by accident. 'Routine enquiries, Veronique.' He nodded towards the door. 'The fire across the way; we're doing a house to house, see if anyone noticed anything out of the ordinary this last while.'

'One of your guards was here already, asking me this.' She raised her hand theatrically in the air, as if all of this nasty business had managed to seep into the very fibre of her home. 'I told him everything I could think of then.' Veronique's English was improved since last time Slattery had met her, but she was still faltering, still grappling between her native and adopted languages.

Slattery looked around him. The kitchen was small and cramped with far too many empty vodka bottles piled up in a dark corner that had once been home to the dog's bed. It now lay swamped beneath them – pity the dog that had to sleep there at night. The whole room was cluttered with timeworn, cheap furniture and a wall of unsightly wooden kitchen units that had seen better days. A selection of game – owls, a fox and something that was either a weasel or a stoat recently trapped and stuffed – sat watching with lifeless eyes from a cut-rate reproduction sideboard. The only pictures on the walls had been placed there by a generation long gone.

'Did you know Anna Crowe?'

'No.' Veronique looked into her cup. 'They'd only just arrived. I saw her in the village a couple of times.'

'And your partner?'

'What about Ollie?'

'Did he know her? They both grew up here, didn't they?'

'Why?'

'Just trying to get a better picture of her, you know. We want to talk to anyone who knew her, even vaguely…' Slattery took another sip of the coffee out of habit, he regretted it immediately. It was cooling now and its bitter taste had taken on a tarry flavour. He grimaced as it hit the back of his throat.

'Not up to your fine standards.' Veronique nodded at the cup. They both knew he'd rather be drinking something a lot stronger.

'No it's fine.' He said the words automatically, avoiding her eyes. He needn't have bothered; she had no intention of doing anything to improve its taste.

'Ollie knew her years ago, thought she was a bit, how do you say it… stuck up? I don't think she had much time for many of the locals, and they didn't bother with her.' She looked up at a kitchen clock on the wall behind her back. 'You can ask him yourself if you stay here long enough.' Her body language belied the offer. She wanted him gone and that was fine with Slattery.

'I'll be gone soon enough. Veronique, you were her nearest neighbour; it's not all that long ago since you were on your own. Surely, there's something you can tell me about the woman. You must have noticed something.'

'Sergeant Slattery, in case you haven't noticed, I'm not the kind of woman who befriends other women. You might say that is half my problem. Even if I'd met the woman, I wouldn't have had anything to do with her.'

Slattery knew she was telling the truth; she just wasn't a woman's woman. Most women would see her as a threat, and they'd be right. Women like Veronique took what they wanted regardless of the cost to others. He sat back in his seat, as though settling in for the day. The movement had the desired effect; it unnerved, or at least irritated Veronique.

Veronique sighed. 'There is a… a tramp… he lives near the village, I think. He has a house, or a bit of a house, close to the church, but he spends a lot of time around her cottage. Ollie says they would all have been at school together, but this man… Pat Deaver? He was a bit… how do you call it? Slow, maybe? She always had a soft spot for him. Ollie says… we should have nothing to do with him.' She looked down at her shaking white hands, lowering her voice to a whisper. 'He burns things.'

CHAPTER 5

Her reaction had taken her by surprise. The woman in the photographs looked different to the one she remembered. Iris wasn't sure if she even knew the woman who stared down from the whiteboard across the incident room at her. But, there was no mistaking Anna Crowe in the later shot. She'd had her hair cut into a pixie style, must have been just before Iris met her, she decided. The tip ends were dyed a golden blonde; but the roots held a tarnished brown. *Anything to cover the grey.* It was unlikely that their meeting that day was connected to her death. It was just one of those random encounters and Iris played it back in her mind now, as she stood before the case board. She could hear Anna Crowe's voice as if she stood beside her.

'Oh no,' came the disappointed groan. Her accent had been Limerick, but not the city, it was much softer than that.

'You too?' Iris said, looking across at the woman opposite who'd obviously returned to damage on her car also. 'Welcome to Limerick,' Iris smiled.

'Ah, no, why on earth would anyone…' She was almost in tears and Iris knew she couldn't just get in her car and drive off, so she walked to the far side of her own Audi and around the little Mini that had been perfectly parked within its allocated box. They'd been scuffed either side, some yob in a car too big for its space, or maybe just a careless driver who made off without realising the damage he'd caused.

'That's rough,' Iris said, taking in the long gash, she traced along it with her hand.

'Oh dear God…' The woman looked to where her hand ran along the damage and then slowly back to Iris's face again. 'Oh dear, I feel…' Iris stepped forward to grab her before she almost collapsed against the car. It was then she took in the pale colouring and the glassy look about the woman's eyes, as though all the blood had flooded from her face, emptying her out of any kind of fibre that might keep her together.

'Come on, you need a decent cup of tea,' Iris had said, half carrying her and pulling her along to the car park exit and into the little coffee shop that was tucked at the very last corner of the shopping arcade. She ordered a pot of tea for two and shoved the woman onto a low sofa before either of them had time to introduce themselves.

'Thank you,' Anna Crowe said once she had sipped her hot sweet tea.

'Don't mention it, you looked like death warmed up back there,' Iris said, watching the woman now, she was beginning to come back to herself. 'Are you all right? I mean, apart from the car?'

'Oh, yes, I'm just… oh, probably doing too much.'

'Well, it looks to me like you'd have been better off plumping for a good rest instead of gadding about the place, if you don't mind me saying so.' They smiled at each other now. Iris thought of the six months she'd spent in Domestic Violence when she'd been made into a detective. She'd met countless ordinary women who would have died rather than go home and tell a violent husband that they'd scraped the car – of course, not one of them would admit as much to some stranger in a car park.

'You're very familiar,' Anna Crowe said. 'What did you say your name was again?'

'Iris Locke.' Iris stuck her hand out to introduce herself for the second time, she had a feeling the name had floated right over Anna's head before.

'Well, it's very nice to…' This time, Anna fainted right back into the sofa and Iris bounded across to her to pull her up, make her comfortable and put into practice as much first aid as she could think of.

'No, no, I'm okay, I'm really.' She looked down at her hands, then reached across and took Iris's in hers. 'I'm really glad to meet you.' She held her hand for a long moment, and Iris thought that perhaps she was going to faint again.

It was almost an hour later when they emerged into the car park and some of the cars had emptied out. 'Shall I drive you home and you can pick up the car later?' Iris asked. She really wasn't sure how well Anna could have rallied with just a cup of tea.

'No, no. I feel much better now.' She looked at the damage to the car, then laughed lightly. 'I don't know what came over me; in the greater scheme of things, it's only a car,' she said shaking her head and Iris decided that she really liked this woman.

'Perhaps we'll meet for coffee again?' Anna said, holding her hand now.

'I'd like that,' Iris said, 'coffee would be good.' They exchanged numbers, even if Iris had a feeling it would be one of those things she'd never get around to doing. Still, she followed the little Mini out of the car park and watched as Anna Crowe drove off towards her middle-class suburban life which was, Iris had no doubt, a million miles away from the world Iris knew.

And that was it – just one small interlude, quite by accident in a car park in Limerick. It didn't actually connect her to the victim, although as she looked up at the images on the board before her, she could admit to herself, it made this case more personal. Iris knew she should probably say something, but the resistance she felt from Slattery was enough to let her know her place on the Murder Team was far from secure. She had it all to prove. So, she'd keep her mouth shut and she'd work her backside off; she'd make a difference if it killed her, for Anna Crowe more than anyone else. Then, she'd do her damnedest to get into the Murder Team in Dublin Castle.

She checked her reflection quickly in the bathroom mirror. None of the other women wore any make-up; the uniform of the day seemed to be slacks, jackets and flat shoes, the uglier the better. There was no doubt she probably stuck out a bit from the rest. Her hair was copper, long tendrils of curls falling gently around her face. If she could just manage to lose a couple of pounds, she'd be happy. The other female detectives she'd seen were all well into their thirties and above, their shapes already falling like opened potato sacks and their faces tired and grey from too many worries, probably at home as well as at work. She threw her shoulders back before she stepped out into the hallway; the action gave her more confidence than she actually felt.

Corbally station was the oldest in Limerick. Iris thought she could hear the voices of ghosts bouncing off its high ceilings and bare walls as she walked through its halls. It was an overwhelming sensation; perhaps it was her father, part of him still lingering here, while the greater part of him lived a far more leisurely existence on the golf course. In some ways it felt as if his life as a superintendent was a dream she'd had long ago. But here, surrounded by the same fabric he'd spent his working life in, he loomed up large and intimidating before her. She couldn't stay here forever, she knew that; he was just too significant, too influential. He still filled up this place even though he'd left it to retire a decade earlier. 'Better to build your own ship,' he'd told her. He understood that she was proud to be his daughter, but maybe she was just a little too like him. She wanted her own success and for as long she was in Corbally, she'd always be his daughter. It was why she loved Dublin; not because of the streets, not the city, not even the people, if she was honest. What she loved was the fact that she was just Iris; there was no legacy, no history, and no great expectations.

She made her way quickly to the incident room, where she spotted Grady leaning across June Quinn's desk. Their conversation was hushed, their bodies close to each other. Maybe they were a couple? She'd never have put them together. He was an attractive man for his age, tall and muscular, with the brooding dark looks of a Mr Darcy, while June was well on her way towards being the classic Mrs Bennett shape. It was more likely, she figured, that they'd just worked together for a long time, had developed a shorthand conversation where sometimes you didn't need to say anything at all, just a nod, a wave of the hand. She'd seen it often enough in undercover. Detectives who worked together for years developed relationships that sat somewhere between reluctant friendship and a sibling bond, that survived more aggravation and irritation than any mismatched marriage. Sitting in a car, together night after night with nothing but the Tetra radio to keep you entertained, forged relationships better than boot camp, better than any marriage ceremony.

Iris strode over to Grady with far more assurance than she felt she had any right to.

'Okay,' she said and then peered at the desk they were both crouched over. Four pages lay in a line in front of them. The initial techie report had arrived. More would come later, pages and pages of analysis data, matching fluids and prints, but this report was detailing the most obvious and disturbing finds the forensic team had made so far. June Quinn, or maybe Grady, had already highlighted a couple of paragraphs and Iris's eyes were drawn to these first. After a moment she spotted it, said, 'No sign of a struggle.' She looked up into Grady's face. 'So she knew her killer?'

'Looks that way, or maybe she was killed in her sleep.' Grady turned to get his coat and Iris watched as he walked away.

June Quinn invited her for a drink with them when they were winding down for the night. Iris couldn't face it, said she might be there later. When they'd left, taking their friendly banter with them, she felt like crying. The most ridiculous thing occurred to her; she didn't know why she was crying. Perhaps it was this whole sorry case, nothing got to her like kids for some crazy reason. Perhaps it was the thought of Anna Crowe, dead on a mortuary slab – she hadn't known her well, but she'd known her. They'd shared a pot of tea, exchanged phone numbers. They might have been friends, given half a chance. There was a connection, and somehow that connection meant something. It made this case, her death, more personal. Maybe she just missed being part of a team. She'd been isolated in undercover – twelve months is a long time to spend pretending to be someone that you're not. In the end, you're out there on your own; even the unit you're working with feels remote – they're there for back-up, not for friendship. Iris suspected that it might be a mixture of all of that and something far shallower. Part of her knew she didn't want to face that, didn't want to front up to the fact that she wanted to be top girl – not in an ambitious way, but because she wanted to be the best. Corbally had made her feel she had to prove herself. God, there was so much about that thought that she didn't want to consider any more.

Iris was glad to have the place to herself. It gave her a chance to think; she rubbed her eyes and pulled her long copper hair back from her face, settling down before one of the PCs on a nearby desk. So far, they had nothing, not really. She knew it was probably her own morbid curiosity, but she wondered about what had happened all those years ago. There'd be no connection. It was just a horrible coincidence, one sister taken, another murdered – but still, Iris found herself typing in the name Fairley. The majority of the older files had been transferred to the F-drive now. It meant that, depending on rank, you had varying degrees of access to most cases on file.

When Iris typed in her PAC, her personal access code, the system rejected her request. She tried several times, assuming it was some kind of broadband failure. She accessed a case she'd worked a few years earlier. No problems there, access granted immediately. She tried the Fairley case a few more times. There was nothing. She looked at her watch. *Note to self, check file archive first chance you've got.* There'd be no one on duty now down there. Admin and anyone who wasn't front line would have gone home not long after five. She drummed her fingers on the desk, decided to try it one last time. Same response, access denied to the Fairley case files. She sat for a moment looking at the screen. The only information it was giving her this evening were two names and one of them was close enough to home to put a smile on her face. The officer in charge had been Superintendent Jack Locke.

The following morning, Iris was one of the first to arrive. She set down coffee, hot and strong, on the desk she had bagged up front on her first morning on the Murder Team. She hadn't slept, but when she looked around at her colleagues, she knew neither had anyone else probably. Slattery looked even worse for wear today than he had the previous day. She set up her notebook and connected to the station broadband. It took only minutes to get her F-drive up and running and then she had access to all the Gardaí databases she was entitled to use by virtue of her rank. A shadow falling across her desk brought her attention back to the incident room. McGonagle, when he circled her desk, looked as hungry as she was; she could see it in his eyes.

'How did you get on yesterday?' she asked. He was new; a reserve waiting for the recruitment ban to get lifted.

'I was on door to door, y'know, just seeing what the neighbours had to say.' His eyes were bright and she remembered her first investigations where just wearing the uniform and being taken into people's confidence was enough to make her feel like a real guard. 'It sounds like Slattery might have a lead, though.' He jerked his thumb to where some of the hard-core detectives were gathered around a desk at the back of the incident room. She looked towards them, glancing long enough to take in their number, but not so long as to seem interested in what they had to say. Slattery was leaning on the side of a desk, holding court with a couple of hard men – loud guffaws meant that whatever they were discussing was probably inappropriate.

'Some old tramp… she was looking out for him… sounds a bit dodge…' McGonagle's eyes were bright; this was probably the highlight of his career to date.

'Good for him, maybe he's managed to crack it single-handed,' she said lightly, but she caught McGonagle's eye and perhaps they both knew it wouldn't be that easy. Iris tossed her head, shading her face with her long copper hair; he was dismissed. She listened to the banter at the back of the room, the usual joking that passed between old men who wanted to avoid getting down to business for as long as possible.

'So, who's this guy?' Westmont finally asked.

'Me to know and you to find out, Sherlock,' Slattery said.

'Come on, is he known to us or not?'

'Ah, well, he might be known to the guards out in Kilgee, but he's small fry – Pat Deaver,' Slattery said self-importantly. 'He's never come up on my radar,' as if that meant he didn't figure.

'Oh, well,' Iris said with heavy sarcasm, 'I suppose we can all go home for the rest of the day now.' She'd got what she'd needed. All the same Iris wondered how he'd managed to catch this lead. She opened the F-drive, typed in *Pat Deaver, Kilgee*. Bingo. It looked like Slattery wasn't going to be the lone star of the show after all.

*

Grady stood in front of the team. They were an unfamiliar bunch with only three or four faces that truly belonged here. Right up front, like an over-eager school girl, Iris sat and waited. June was at her usual desk surrounded by tissues, family photos and customised mugs. Slattery reclined in a chair at the back, a self-satisfied grin on his red face. Grady cleared his throat, too loudly, and the room fell into an expectant silence. He nodded across at June, she set down her coffee cup and drew her glasses further up her nose before beginning.

'Okay, I've spent my time here. You asked me to look for anyone recently released from prison or spotted in the area that might have form… nothing strange reported to us, at least. Everything out in Kilgee seems to be as usual. But… then I started to take a look at the release database. Six months ago, a guy called Darach Boran was released from Arbour Hill Prison. He's spent two years inside for attempted murder.' June searched through the pages before her again.

'Is there a link with Kilgee?' Iris asked, without raising her attention from the small laptop in front of her.

'Not exactly, but, there may be a connection with our victim. I have a little more digging to do before I'll know for certain.' June looked up from her notes. 'This guy sounds like a sleaze bag; he's spent most of his career lecturing in various art colleges around the country, where he had a habit of developing inappropriate relationships with his students. There's been more than one complaint made against him over the years for harassment. A couple of years ago, he was employed in a private art college in Dublin and apparently seeing one of his students. When she'd tried to break off the relationship he'd gone to her flat, drugged her and threatened to set the place on fire. The girl was lucky enough to have her brother staying with her and when he returned home after work, he knocked six shades of shit out of Boran before calling the guards.'

'So, the link?' Slattery asked, tipping his chair forward, suddenly interested. Grady knew Boran sounded like the kind of suspect Slattery could relate to – well, if beating six shades of shit out him was relating. Slattery believed in getting confessions the old-fashioned way and Grady warned him through narrowed eyes, there was to be no funny business with any suspects on this case.

'The link, as far as I can see with Anna Crowe was that he was lecturing at the National College of Art and Design when she was a student there. I still have to connect Anna and Darach Boran, but…'

'Good work, June. Westmont, did you get a chance to look at footage from Traffic?' Grady nodded towards Westmont, a six-footer with a shock of blond hair and a ruddy complexion.

'Yeah, nothing worth looking at. We ran a tracer on the husband's car. If he was in the area, he didn't take the motorway. But sure you know these little villages, there's a thousand and one ways to get to them without ever being spotted.'

'What about some of those company vans we saw in the car park of ABA Technics?' Iris asked while still typing furiously on the notebook before her.

'We've run them all, even the plates for any of the other lads on shift with him. Nothing. If he travelled out from work we haven't picked him up on Traffic, but that doesn't mean much, there's a handful of back roads that tack together so he might never show up anyway.'

'Okay.' Grady raised his voice. Some wag had just shared a joke with the hard men at the back of the room. 'Crowe did his apprenticeship in the army – can we find out if he might have had access to rifle training?' He nodded towards Iris.

'Sure.' She noted the direction down efficiently. 'Just a thought… working out at Shannon, would he have any contact with the American planes that drop by occasionally?' US Marines landed in Shannon regularly to refuel. No one knew much of where they were headed, but often the soldiers were unloaded and given an opportunity to stretch their legs around a closed-off lounge. There shouldn't be any communication or possibility that Crowe could get his hands on a military gun there, but there was always a chance he could – wasn't there?

'That's another one for you to check out so.' Grady was moving on; it was a remote connection, but one that would have to be looked at all the same.

'Slattery?'

'We covered the PM. That just confirmed what we'd known unofficially. The three victims died of gunshot wounds. The timing confirms their deaths were close to the estimated time that the fire was started. It looks like our man did the dirty, torched the place and did a runner as quick as possible.' Slattery cleared his throat loudly. 'Nothing else of great note showed up. There are more tests to be run, toxicology and all that, but otherwise we have what we have.'

'Slattery turned up the name of a local tramp – Pat Deaver – seems like he spent a bit of time up at the cottage. Anna Crowe looked out for him; he's probably worth talking to,' Grady told the room. 'So ye're going to follow it up?' Grady nodded back to Slattery, he was answered with a cynical nod.

'He's got form.' Iris raised her head. 'This Deaver, he's been in and out of institutions of various types for most of his adult life. Mainly psychiatric services, but he's done time too.'

'So, what's he been in for?' Grady asked.

'Torching his council house, bang smack in the middle of Kilgee,' Iris said. It was all there on PULSE – police using leading systems effectively – if Slattery had bothered to check. Still, Grady looked at her. She was eager, he'd give her that, even if it wouldn't exactly ingratiate her with Slattery.

CHAPTER 6

Slattery slugged greedily from the bottle. He loved and hated the sensation of the whiskey as it stung the back of his throat and glided down his gullet, warming his chest, and then settling; a familiar balm in his raging stomach. He hated that he needed this remedy before the day had even started. He could blame this case, but the truth was, it was every case – or at least every case that reminded him of the one he couldn't solve. That case, well, it wasn't really a case at all. His sister, found strangled in the flat she shared here in Limerick – it happened before he was old enough to join the guards and it loomed large when he worked a case like Anna Crowe's.

Somewhere behind him a door slammed. Slattery was only vaguely aware of the noise penetrating his fuggy brain. All the same, he tucked the whiskey roughly beneath his jacket. The disused hallway was home to illicit smokers, stealing a moment away from the job. The open window reeked of fag ends and Slattery had long since convinced himself that they weren't all his. Either way, he'd never spotted anyone else here; unless you were lost or a loser like Slattery, there was nothing else to bring you here. He stuffed the bottle deeper into his jacket and made his way back to the incident room.

Slattery wasn't sure if he could even call Pat Deaver's place a house, never mind a home. It was, as Veronique had said, nestled close enough to the local church, down a small lane that may once have led somewhere, but now was hardly wide enough for the Ford Slattery had taken from the car pool. He didn't expect Deaver to be inside, for many reasons. Chief among them being the house could barely qualify as having an inside. At some point in its tragic history, it had managed to lose its front door and a number of windows. The roof only covered half the structure and what was left open was clearly covered at a lower level, the original tiles had been left where they'd fallen. Someone didn't want Deaver here, whether it was the council or his neighbours, and no one had bothered much to see if anything could be done to make it just a little more habitable.

'Mr Deaver,' Slattery called out the name, fancying that nothing much beyond birds and mice would be able to hear him. All the same, he stepped warily from the car. The track beneath was heavy with mud and his shoes gave a satisfying squelch with each step he took nearer the cottage. There was no answer, but he began to walk the perimeter cautiously, peering into the dead windows as he passed each one. The rear of the house was slightly better than the front. Here at least, two windows had survived, their lace curtains smoke damaged, but the rooms, from outside at any rate appeared to be sealed. Slattery pushed in the back door slowly, calling out that he was there at the same time. It took a moment for his eyes to adjust to the dark and he blinked them shut tightly for a second. He'd arrived in a room that was serving as an all-purpose living area. A fireplace held an old kettle, and a table heavy with all sorts of knickknacks stood grumbling silently beneath a tower of empty food cartons. Meals on wheels? In the corner, Slattery just about made out the form of Pat Deaver. He was a bundle of grey coats and shaggy hair. An English sheepdog of a man, but a man all the same. If Slattery had the will to inhale now, he knew he'd smell the rancid odour of living death.

'Mr Deaver, Pat.' Slattery bent down, shook the man awake. For a minute, he thought Deaver must be dead. Then, there was a moan; a vital sign of his continued existence – whether he liked it or not, his drunken reverie had been broken.

'What the…?' He looked up drowsily into Slattery's eyes. He wasn't used to being woken; maybe he wasn't used to having anybody near him at all. Maybe it was a place anyone could drink themselves into very easily.

'It's all right, everything is fine, Mr Deaver. I'm a guard. I wanted to talk to you about Anna Crowe.' It seemed for a moment as though Deaver had fallen asleep again, and then his body began to shudder.

'So, it's true?' Deaver said finally from beneath his uneven breath. 'It's true, she's gone?'

'I'm afraid so,' Slattery said and he wondered at how this wretched man could feel any pain at all for another soul beyond his own sorry state.

It took almost an hour to get Deaver from the cottage. Slattery knew that he had to bring him to the station. They had to get him sober first and from the looks of him, that could take days. Slattery lifted him; he was a corpse of a man, rotting from the inside out. In the car, Slattery opened the windows, but it was no good. He was retching from the smell before they reached the end of the driveway. Where was this man's family? Who really gave a shit about anyone when *good* people could live nearby and someone was permitted to exist like this? And, maybe worst of all, he wondered, if he wasn't a guard, would he be much different?

*

Grady told Slattery he would question Deaver with him. Iris knew that she shouldn't take it personally. After all, they were both at the same grade, both sergeants, only Slattery had twenty more years' experience and a blind man could see that he and Grady were as tight as rashers in suction wrap. Iris sighed. She'd get her chance; all she had to do was hang back and wait. Slattery would mess up sooner rather than later, the old guy was lucky to have hung in this long.

Grady had just set her a paper exercise, something to cross off his list. Well, she was going to show him what she was made of. She'd spent most of the morning being shunted about various army extensions trying to get anything she could on Adrian Crowe. 'This is a murder inquiry, for heaven's sake, a woman and her children are dead,' she'd finally shouted down the phone. Then as if by magic, she'd been transferred to a helpful corporal.

'I remember him,' Corporal Huxley said, as if he was conjuring before him a vision of Adrian Crowe. Huxley sounded as if he'd spent fifty years sitting at a desk, buried somewhere deep in military bureaucracy. 'He came here straight from school. Great worker, but he had no interest in the army – he was all about the planes. I'd say he wanted to fly, but he didn't make it into the cadets.' He said the words as if they were a common malady and his world was divided into the fliers and the ground bound whose dreams had been crushed early. Iris didn't have to guess too hard to know which category Huxley belonged to. ''Course it was a long time ago now, must be ten years, at least.'

'Yes, about that, your memory is good.'

'Well, I'm here a while, I had a bit of a run-in with a land mine over in Iraq. Peacekeeping. That's what they call it, anyway.'

'Sorry,' Iris said, worried this guy could talk all day. 'Should I apply somewhere to see his file?'

'I wouldn't bother, I have it here, give you anything you need, considering the circumstances, it's the least I can do.' Huxley sounded as if he was flicking through pages. 'Now, he was a worker all right, but he only stayed for the minimum. Got his qualifications and he high-tailed it into the private sector. Handy with a gun, though…'

'How's that?' Iris felt her stomach fill with butterflies. Part of her didn't want to think of Adrian Crowe cold-bloodedly shooting his family, but she wanted someone to pay for this more than she'd ever expected she would on a murder case. And Adrian Crowe had a drop of something in him that she didn't like at all.

'He's won prizes for shooting skills and for endurance tests. He's a tough bit of goods.'

'He hardly looks it.' Iris found it hard to think of the Walter Mitty figure she'd met having any resemblance to a soldier with a gun or being involved in any kind of physical testing.

'Ah, no, you don't see what I mean. The endurance testing he excelled at was psychological. He's a mind game man. Bet you'll find he's big into puzzles, Sudoku, anything that challenges him mentally.' Huxley began to stammer, then he barked abruptly, 'Maybe you should make an order for the file.' Iris could hear him closing up the pages on the other end of the line.

'Can't you tell me any more?' She was pleading; she had a gut feeling that there was something in those pages that might really help the investigation.

'I'm not sure I can. I think you'll have to go through the proper channels for anything more.' Huxley's voice had closed off; perhaps someone had come into the room and warned him to keep his mouth shut.

'Listen, Anna Crowe is dead, her two kids are dead, we're not dealing with a smash and grab here, we're dealing with a murderer. A cold-blooded murderer and he could murder again, so if you have anything there, anything at all that might help us to move a bit quicker, then please…'

Huxley coughed at the other end of the phone. Lowered his voice and seemed to move his lips closer to the phone, so it sounded to Iris as if he was whispering just to her. 'Look, you should order the file, have it removed from the records here; it's just a day's worth of paperwork, and I'd have it on your desk before the week is out.' She could sense urgency in his voice.

'Fine, fine, but tell me, off the record, do I have to worry about Crowe?'

'Off the record,' he lowered his voice further, 'now that I look a little more closely, I'd be very worried about him; his psych assessment is throwing up words like *obsessive* and *manic* – now, I'm no quack, but that sounds like he could be a bit of a nutter to me.' Iris hardly had time to say thanks; Huxley cut off the phone so quickly.

She looked around the incident room; if she had to leave today and head back to Dublin would she even remember this place? Would she remember Slattery, Grady and the rest? She'd remember Anna Crowe, she was sure of that. She'd remember Anna Crowe, who'd once sat opposite her, held her hand and taken her phone number and had two small kids that were the centre of her world. She'd remember what someone had done to Anna Crowe, cut her down, made her into a grotesque charred creature who would never laugh again. Anna would never paint again, never have another glass of wine, or a cup of coffee. When Iris looked down at the black coffee before her, she knew that she had to be sure they had the right man in for questioning.

She looked back at Dennis Blake, who was shuffling through the various reports already submitted. As the bookman on the case, it was his responsibility to make sure that everything tallied, that everything fitted into place. And she wondered, just for a second, how long he'd been around. Back when Baby Fairley had been taken, had there been a bookman? Had everything been recorded, or was there someone like Dennis Blake, walking about, knowing far more than he realised even now? That case was bothering her, as much because it seemed like a shadowy presence that slipped between them all. Grady wasn't taking it seriously as having any link to the present case and Iris knew, he was probably right.

Iris was itching to get her hands on that file. It would mean a trip down to archives. She'd been there once before, as a student; she'd done a turn in the large offices to the rear of Corbally station, just photocopying, making coffee, that sort of thing. Now, she knew, no real guard wanted to be anywhere near the place. It was the home of the bureaucrats in the southern region. Then, it seemed like the place to be. At seventeen, she'd snatched glimpses of files that quickly passed through her hands, armed robberies and domestic violence reports were as close as she got to the action, but it was too late by then. It was in her blood, she was born a guard, born a detective, no other choice, she supposed with Jack Locke's blood coursing through her veins. It was the last thing he wanted for her – the guards, Limerick, Corbally, and definitely Murder. Hard to please everyone. She'd soon have to tell him that she'd managed to land herself in all four. She still remembered the archives rooms – essentially a long vault, running the length of the old building, *probably built as a wine cellar*, according to the old guy who'd shown her around in those heady days. Everything had been stacked high, so much paper, so much time, too many lives and deaths, recorded here, a necropolis with no relatives coming to tend what remained.

'How come I can't access anything on the Baby Fairley case?' she asked Blake who was sitting opposite her, his desk a perfect fairy fort of piled papers, working their way beyond his chair, the stacked files insulating him from anything that might encroach.

'That's going back almost thirty years, back to your father's time…' He raised his reading glasses high on his craggy forehead. 'Give us a chance, you'll see that…' He gave a dozen quick taps on the keyboard before him, moved closer for a moment and dropped the glasses down before his eyes once more. 'Hmmm, now let's see…' Iris moved closer to him. 'That's strange.'

'What's strange?' She pulled a seat in beside him.

'Oh, nothing, I'm sure it's nothing.' But Iris knew, the look on his face said it was far from nothing. 'Leave it with me, will you?' He no more wanted her watching him work than he'd have invited her to spend time with him in the jacks.

'Sure,' she said sweetly. 'Like me to get you anything from the canteen?'

'Ah, no, no, you're fine.' He wasn't even listening to her now. He was too wrapped up in figuring out why a case that was as cold as a toddler's toes in seaside Rossnowlagh would be restricted access at this stage.

Iris made her way down to the canteen. She picked up a cup of what seemed to pass for coffee in this place and headed back towards the incident room again. She was frustrated. She wanted down and into that archive room – and what was stopping her, she thought as she headed towards the stairs. After all, she was working on a case directly related to the Baby Fairley case – well, connected at least, right? Worst thing that could happen, they'd run her out of the place for not having clearance. She was new, just getting the run of things, she might actually get in there without having to go through the crap that was now basic procedure in opening closed files; these days, it was almost easier to get an exhumation order signed.

She took the two flights of stairs down into the basement where the first thing to hit her was an ominous smell of damp. Taking out her badge, she flashed it at the old boy who sat at a desk surrounded by files that seemed to have been scatted about him.

'I'm looking for the Baby Fairley case – it was 1990, should have been transferred to PULSE, but they want me to take a look and see if there's any physical evidence.'

'You'll be lucky,' the old guy said rubbing his eyes, but he got up slowly and led the way through what seemed like endless aisles of storage. He stopped, three quarters of the way along an aisle that had dates running through the eighties. 'Fairley?'

'Yes, that's right.' She stood back a little, surveyed the case names and numbers on each of the storage boxes.

'Nope, can't see anything here.' He shook his head ominously.

'Could it be…' She waved a hand about the catacomb of investigation files; it was unthinkable that anyone would be stupid enough to put an archive file back in the wrong place.

'No, no…' The old boy moved closer, peering at a small tab that had been stuck against an empty space on the shelf. 'Your file has been taken out…' He shook his head again. 'Bloody hate this, they've signed it out and never left it back.'

'But how?'

'It happens, old cases, some youngster is put on them to review them, it generally happens with cases that look as though they'll never be solved, where the lead officer has designated a file SO6.'

'SO6?'

'It's been reviewed at least six times and each review has led to the same conclusion. They may have known what happened to the victim, but it can't be proved.'

'I don't understand?'

'Like in the McCracken case,' he lowered his voice as if she could have forgotten, added, 'your old case in undercover.' The guard smiled at her. 'Oh, don't look at me like that, we all know who you are, Sergeant Locke, and we know as well that it wasn't your fault he got off, but the truth of it is, he'll never see the inside of a prison cell and there's no point thinking anyone's going to get him in there. That's an SO6 in the making.'

'Does that mean,' Iris nodded towards the empty space on the shelf, 'that the Baby Fairley case files are gone for good?'

'Unless someone comes across them here in the station and returns them to us, I suppose it could,' he said shaking his head. 'They didn't even sign them out under a name, so it must have been some time ago now.'

With that, Iris's phone rang, she thanked the officer and began making her way back up towards the incident room.

'Dad?' She pulled the phone close to her ear, moved away from the corridor that brought her down to archives. There were other ways to get what she wanted. She promised she'd call out to Woodburn later in the week, managed to shake Jack Locke off the phone and headed back to the incident room.

CHAPTER 7

If Slattery had thought about what Pat Deaver would be like, he wouldn't have been far off the pathetic sight that slouched before him in interview room number two on a cold and blustery day in October. Deaver was not an old man, but his face told the story of too much cheap alcohol and a diet consisting of the Irish staples, starchy white bread, spuds and more bread. Whatever life may have at one time danced behind his eyes was long since extinguished. This was the melancholy result of a health system more geared towards doling out anti-depressants than actually figuring out how to help people. He walked with a slight stoop and Slattery wondered if he'd been born to a middle class couple, would things have been different for him? Was there hope for more, someday, for people like Deaver?

'For the tape…' Grady took a seat opposite and Slattery knew his place was next to him. At the other side of the table, Deaver and the duty solicitor sat silently, tapping time, as if waiting for something momentous to begin. 'I'm Detective Inspector Coleman Grady and this is…'

'Sergeant Slattery.' Slattery tried to keep his voice as neutral and clear as possible. They had a game plan, but they'd both agreed as they watched Deaver through the one-way glass, they probably wouldn't need it.

'We're interviewing Mr Pat Deaver of Bishopsquarter, Limerick. Also present is Mr Clifford Kane-O'Neill, solicitor for Mr Deaver. You've had a chance to consult with your client?' Grady nodded towards the tape. It was all for the tape. Deaver had had a chance to sleep off whatever he'd taken last; he'd had a good meal and a packet of cigarettes. Kane-O'Neill had spent half an hour with him, satisfied himself that he knew as much as he needed to for this interview. 'And we have cautioned him in your presence.'

'Yes, indeed, you have cautioned my client, we have conferred,' Kane O'Neill, the polar opposite of his client said in juicy round vowels.

'Mr Deaver, you knew Anna Crowe?'

'Yeah, I knew her all right.' He looked down at his hands, they were dirty and worn. Slattery considered they probably hadn't been washed in years. The forensic boys would have a field day with him. 'Terrible do,' he offered to no one in particular.

'Can you tell us what you know about her death?' Grady asked again.

'Same as everyone else knows, I suppose.'

'Tell us anyway, why don't you?' Grady moved closer to the table, reaching a hand behind his left ear, mirroring the actions of the man opposite.

'Okay, well…' Deaver moved closer to the table. 'I'm not sure I know what happened rightly. I mean I know there was a fire, I saw the house afterwards. But, it was like one minute she was there and the next… well, she was gone. They were all gone.' When he looked across at Slattery, his face was completely clear. For all his years, and all of his cynicism, Ben Slattery would happily swear on a bible that this man was hiding nothing; probably wasn't able to hide anything.

'She looked out for you, didn't she?' Grady gently suggested.

'Aye, she did. I went to her house every evening; she always had a bit of dinner for me.' Deaver looked across at Grady now. 'I looked out for her too, have done since we was kids. She was always a timid little thing… especially after… well, you know.' He nodded awkwardly.

'After the baby was taken?' Slattery asked, his voice unusually quiet.

'Aye, after that.' He couldn't quite say the words. 'Never the same after that, she wasn't.'

'Can you tell us anything about that time, Mr Deaver?' Grady asked the question. Slattery could have told him, this man's brain was almost drowning in alcohol. All that remained now were distinct impressions; maybe a still picture that occasionally passed before his eyes, but details would be blurred. In the not too distant future, he wouldn't know his own name, he'd probably find it hard to remember his birth date.

'Aye, never the same again.'

'Did you bring her flowers?' Grady's voice carried with it a warmth, an encouraging friendliness and Slattery knew that he needed to stay quiet. If he was required later, he wasn't going to be the nice guy in the room.

'I did, for a while, but then…' Deaver seemed to drift off, into a world that Slattery couldn't see; he wondered if Anna Crowe was in this far-off land.

'Did you stop bringing them?' Grady pushed gently.

'She had so many.' Deaver looked as though this was the most reasonable answer in the world.

'How do you mean?'

'Well, I just saw, inside, one of the days. All my wildflowers, she'd kept them lovely, in small glass jars, here and there. Meant something that… to me, anyway.' A small tear escaped from Pat Deaver's eyes. 'But then I knew there were too many flowers, flowers are supposed to make you happy. I think they made her sad, though.'

'When did you stop bringing them?'

'I don't know… sure how would I know that? One day's the same as the next to me.'

'It's just she still had them…' Grady's voice was low, gentle. 'She still had them; they really *did* mean something to her.'

Slattery watched as Pat Deaver's world crumbled before him. He could hardly remember what he'd been doing, or where he'd been on the morning that the cottage was set alight and Anna Crowe had been murdered. The man probably couldn't remember what he'd had for breakfast or indeed if he'd even had one for the last year. Drink is a dangerous thing like that; and Slattery discarded the thought immediately. Deaver said he couldn't remember where he'd heard about the fire, but he'd gone to the cottage, to see for himself. At that stage, there were a few people there, men in white suits, a guard at the entrance. He knew he wasn't wanted, so he'd set off again.

'Would you be willing to provide us with a sample, to eliminate you from our enquiries?' Grady asked him, looking across at Kane-O'Neill.

'How can you eliminate him, the man has told you he's been in the cottage? I really don't see how I can advise him to…'

'Not like that.' Grady smiled knowingly at the brief. Deaver's life meant nothing to the solicitor, but the last thing he wanted was his law practice suffering with news of an easy conviction. 'We are looking for traces of gunshot residue. If your client would submit for forensic examination of his hands and clothes, and it shows up that he hasn't fired a gun in the last few days, he will effectively have ruled himself out of our enquiries.'

'I'll need to consult with my client for a few minutes first.' They all knew that he would ask Deaver if he'd fired a gun, not necessarily if he'd fired *the* gun. That, in many ways, was irrelevant to Kane-O'Neill. On the other hand, it would be more than enlightening for the investigation. If Deaver refused to co-operate, he would look as guilty as sin, and if he consented? Well, at least he believed in his own innocence and that meant either he was blameless, or he was booking a one-way ticket to the central mental hospital.

*

'How very convenient,' Veronique spat at Ollie Kerr before he even managed to shake off that greatcoat that was dripping with the day's rain.

'And what's that supposed to mean?' he barked at her.

'You've just missed the police – they were here, looking to talk to you, been watching the place, have you?'

'I've no need to see them or avoid them, Veronique, not as long as you keep your drunken trap shut.' He hated her now, hated that she knew so much, he wanted her gone, maybe as much as she wanted to get away. Ollie turned his back once more on Veronique. He knew that if he looked at her now, her eyes wild, spittle coming from her mouth as she insulted his mother, his home, his life, he could throttle her.

'And as for your… that woman…' Her voice lowered now. She was clever enough to know exactly how to push his buttons, but she still couldn't manage to stretch her vocabulary in English. He could sense her building up behind him, ready to volley a litany of names at him. That was the problem with Veronique – no respect for the dead, and in the end, when you didn't have that, what were you worth?

He'd only wanted Veronique to shove her in Anna's face, nothing more. They lived a stone's throw away from each other, but it seemed like worlds apart and after that baby went missing – well, he never expected things to be right after that. Veronique had come with perks, she'd also come at a high fucking price. He'd never had such grief in all his days. Now Anna was gone, and he still had this shit being thrown at him. *Maybe she'll drink herself to death?* The thought made him smile. He took the vodka from his mother's sideboard, filled her up again. Kill the bitch, let her be gone; he doubted anyone would miss her anyway.

'And don't think I don't know about your little secret…' Veronique had come up close behind him, whispered in his ear, a slithering poisonous snake. He could hear the spittle in her mouth rattle her throaty voice. 'Oh yes, I found your little box of papers…'

Words would not leave his mouth; his breath caught in his chest, trapping bile that had no connection to anything he ate, but rather to the venom this woman spat around her.

'Don't worry,' her words were lighter now, 'I've kept them safe, nothing will happen to them, but we wouldn't want the wrong person seeing those now, would we?'

'You had no…' He was going to say 'right', but then what right did he have to them, to anything now? He was meant to keep them safe: fine job he'd done of that. Anna had given them to him, finally, she trusted him and he had let her down on every front.

'They made very interesting reading, once I'd managed to put it all together.'

'You have no idea.' He kept his voice even; the last thing he wanted was to give her a stick she could beat him with.

'It doesn't matter now anyway, does it?' Her voice was playful and he wondered how much she'd actually enjoy seeing his pain if the guards ever came knocking on the door. Jail would kill him, she surely knew that, he couldn't take this house most of the time, much less a prison cell.

'You'd want to be careful where you go putting that big Polish nose of yours, Veronique. Safer keeping it in a vodka glass if you know what's good for you.' He pushed past her roughly before heading out for the night. He'd rather sleep with wolves than with this scavenger.

CHAPTER 8

Slattery watched as Grady pulled together as many of the disparate pages on his desk as he could. All case notes and reports would be passed along to the bookman, but Grady was a perfectionist and he double checked everything. It was always the same. The devil, Slattery knew, really was too often sitting buried in minutiae. Too many times they'd worked on cold cases where everything that was needed to solve the case had been filed away amongst the raft of paperwork accumulated over an investigation. So, Grady spent more and more time in his cramped office, straining tired eyes, behind his faux-pine desk. Slattery sat, staring out the window at the car park below, his approach to detective work very much at odds with that of the inspector. They might respect each other, but there was no question they were as opposite as night and day. A light tap on Grady's door broke their concentration – through the old glass Slattery could see the outline of June Quinn.

'Pat Deaver has just made it onto the six o'clock news.' June stood at the door. She wasn't fifty yet, but her shape was well and truly middle-aged. If Slattery noticed what June looked like, it was only when she looked rough – when she was coming down with some kind of flu or bug.

'Feck it, that's all we need.' Slattery blew out a long breath and Grady rolled his eyes at the expletive, but his brows had knitted into an acceptance of sorts.

'You really don't think it's him, do you?' June closed the door behind her and flopped down in the chair opposite Grady.

'June, if you saw him, you wouldn't think so either,' Grady said evenly. They had let him dry out as much as he ever would and with sobriety came a kind of placid innocence to him.

'He probably has difficulty tying his shoes. I'd say he's the type that would be devastated over a wasted kitten on the road,' Slattery said. It was true, Deaver, whatever he was like before the drink was what Slattery would call a bit soft.

'If not Pat Deaver then…' June said aloud.

'Well, it's back to square one, isn't it? We're looking at the husband, the guy from college…' Slattery paused a moment. Time was passing. If they didn't make an arrest soon, they'd be into a week, and then, for all his griping about the media, they'd lose interest, then people would lose interest, and Anna Crowe and her family would become just a tragic statistic. A case, like any other, that would be open for as long as the big wigs could justify it, but the trail was already cooling and he knew they needed something now.

'Darach Boran?' June tested the name.

'Yeah, him. He sounds like someone you'd like to lock up just for the heck of it, make the world a better place.' Slattery smiled across at June.

'It's hardly good news, but better to get it right now than spend a couple of days grilling Pat Deaver and maybe letting whatever trail to the real killer go cold,' Grady said, hardly lifting his head from the pages before him.

'Yeah, but remember in eighty per cent of homicides…' Slattery's voice was a monotone – they'd all heard it before too many times for it to be interesting anyway.

'I know, it's down to the spouse or a close family member.' June picked at a fleece of cats' fur that clung belligerently to her dark pants.

'What's he like?' Grady asked again. He would have been the one to question the husband if it hadn't been for Byrne and his bloody budget meetings.

'Crowe?' Slattery checked.

'Yeah, does he seem like the type?'

'Hard to say. At the moment he's in shock, but then let's face it, you never know.' Slattery looked out across the city, his thoughts catching off the familiar rooftops as his mind tumbled through that interview once again. 'Cold. I'd say he's a cold bugger, but I'm not sure he's got the level of depravity something like this would take. Again, though, would we know for sure?'

'You wouldn't rule him out like Pat Deaver?'

Slattery sat back in his chair, closed his eyes for a second, trying to picture Adrian Crowe. What he could see was a tearful, dazed man, who'd just lost not only his wife, but his two kids as well. A man who lived in a very tidy house, with a very tidy life. Would he be the kind of man who could kill his wife? Maybe. Kill his kids? Even to himself he couldn't answer this. Finally, Slattery opened his eyes and looked across at June. 'I don't know.' He said the words simply, but in his head, he thought of killing Anna Crowe and her two children and something just seemed to echo at the back of his brain. Killing the kids tied everything up. If Adrian Crowe wanted to be free of his old life, certainly the death of his whole family in one go was a neat and effective job. And, Adrian Crowe was a very neat man.

*

Slattery had heard the rumours; they'd been doing the rounds for a few days now. There was a new superintendent on the way, but no one knew who it was. There had been nothing more from Byrne, apart from the occasional bark that he had enough to be doing not to have to be bothering with running Murder, DV and Traffic on top of it. He stomped through the incident room on a daily basis, but Slattery had known him long enough for them to both know where they stood.

Today, they almost collided in the corridor.

'Christ, Slattery, what happened to you?' Byrne stepped back sizing him up. 'You look like shit, seriously…'

'Late night,' Slattery grunted.

'Nothing new there, but…' Byrne's eyes hardened. 'You can't come in to work in that state. Go home, have a shower and a gallon of coffee. Feck's sake, Ben, anyone could run into you here. The commissioner is next door this morning and you look like you belong in a cell rather than in one of our most elite teams.'

'Yeah, well, it's what happens when you're doing real police work. Just because we're not putting in for overtime doesn't mean we're not putting in the hours.' Slattery hated the idea of being brought down a peg, especially by Byrne – time was when Byrne and plenty more of the big brass had looked up to Slattery. Still, he knew, a shower, a shave and a change of shirt probably wouldn't go astray. Iris Locke had actually sniffed and moved away from him earlier in the incident room. Slattery smiled derisively at the recollection.

'Before you go, any luck tracking down Boran?' Byrne's mouth lifted in something that Slattery assumed was meant to be a smile; he didn't wait for an answer. 'Just the wife picked up a couple of pen and ink drawings of local landmarks for the lady president's prize.' Now Byrne allowed his eyes to drift into the more familiar territory, waiting for Slattery to join up the dots.

'He's based locally? Where?'

'That's up to you to find out, but, they're carrying his work in the Bridgend Gallery, down in Sarsfield Street – there can't be that many Darach Borans around can there? He has to be your man.'

'Mighty,' Slattery said, 'I'll pass that along, obviously.' He was thankful for the heads-up, but he'd have preferred if it had come from anyone but Byrne. June had reached a dead end in her search for Boran. Slattery assumed he'd left the country; he'd fulfilled the terms of his release conditions and walked away, free to start a new life. Now, if he had been living in Limerick for the past few months, Slattery had to wonder what kind of a new life he'd chosen. The death of Anna Crowe would suggest he was settling for more of the same.

*

Iris sat down with her coffee. Dennis Blake had vanished from behind his desk, an unusual phenomenon. She couldn't remember a time between eight in the morning and five in the afternoon since she'd arrived that he hadn't been sitting there looking harassed. Maybe he finally had to take a leak, had to happen once every couple of days, she figured, snorting into her coffee as she thought about it. She looked around her. Apart from herself only McGonagle and June Quinn remained in the incident room. Slattery had left his phone on his desk. From the corner of her eye, she could see it light up while it rang once more on silent. *Must be the sixth call in the last ten minutes*, she thought. She got up from her desk, planning to turn it face down. It was a distraction she didn't need. The caller was 'Angela' and she considered for a moment, wondering if maybe she should answer it. 'June,' she called across the room. 'Should we answer this?'

June Quinn waved her left arm; her face had a preoccupied expression as she continued to look at the screen before her. A mobile rested on her shoulder. At that, Slattery's phone rang off and Iris picked it up considering. Angela. It was hardly connected to the investigation – was it? More like a wife, ringing to let him know she'd wormed the dog and not to bother doing it when he got home. She held the mobile in her hand for a second, considering a name like Angela. The notion that Slattery might have any life outside the Murder Team seemed unreal. He was all detective and if there was anything left over, Iris suspected it had long ago been discarded at some bar counter.

She brought the phone across to June's desk and dropped it there. She looked around the incident room: the crack that rose up beneath the windowsill and continued on to the roof following its own trajectory – the window was no obstacle in its path; the worn-out floors, sanded down by officers long gone; the feel of the desk, old and battered and ripped through with the scratches of time and hours spent poring over cases that may have eaten detectives up as much as this one felt like it might devour Iris. This old desk had probably been in this building since her father was here, maybe for as long as the police had moved in. The place was becoming too comfortable too quickly. Even the other officers, Westmont, Quinn and Blake – it felt as though she'd been working with them for months rather than days. Slattery and Grady were different, though – giving her a wide berth? No, preoccupied with the case – that was probably it. The gossip among some of the men was that a superintendent was going to transfer in from the Midlands, but that was only gossip. No one had any idea who was coming, but there was no doubt the whole station was understaffed. A murder team without a super, especially for a case like this, well, it was unheard of. She wondered why Grady wouldn't put himself up for promotion; from where Iris stood, he seemed to fit the criteria perfectly – he was a male, about the right age, with an impressive career to date and the full team behind him and, oh yes, once more, he was male. She imagined that the thought of a newcomer would be enough to rattle some of the older boys. They had no names yet, but still, a new brush sweeps clean and it would mean change for everyone on the team. She shook the thoughts from her head. None of it made any difference to her. She wouldn't be here to see it, probably. No doubt, they'd ship her out as soon as they had a full complement; God knows, she'd done enough hinting that she wanted Murder in Dublin. It was the right thing too, *if* it could be arranged. It was hard to see how she'd ever slip out of her father's shadow in Corbally. Once more, Slattery's phone caught her eye. It was ringing again – without thinking Iris rose from her seat to answer it.

'Hi, I'm afraid Sergeant Slattery isn't here just now...'

'No, well, he wouldn't be, would he?' The voice on the other end sounded like a young woman, thirties, no more. Angela.

June Quinn looked up; perhaps it was the irate voice on the other end of the phone, but she stopped mid-sentence and mouthed towards Iris, 'Okay?'

'Is it urgent? Can I get him for you? He's interviewing a suspect at the moment.' Iris heard her voice, calm and reasonable.

'You might call it urgent. Perhaps you could tell him that his wife has been rushed to A&E after a car accident. If he can tear himself away, she's down at St Dominic's.' Angela sighed anxiously and Iris reckoned the girl was on the verge of tears.

'Of course I'll get him. Is there anything else I can do for you? Is she going to be all right?'

'I don't know how she's going to be, they won't let me see her. Imagine, my own mother and...'

'I'm sorry. I'll get your dad straight away. He'll be there before you know it.'

'You mean you'll tell him. God alone knows when we'll see him.' The girl hung up the phone, probably relieved that at least she'd managed to pass on the message. For one awful moment, Iris had glimpsed into another world. It was a world every guard carried with them; no matter where you ended up, at some point you had to give devastating news to a family and those moments never really left you. The loss or impending loss of others created a chasm so great it took in all around it like an enveloping and freezing fog.

'What is it?' June Quinn hung up the phone she'd been glued to for most of the morning.

'It's Slattery's wife. She's been in an accident. They want him down at St Dominic's.'

'Oh no.' June's eyes watered and then Iris knew that she had been fooling herself and she really wasn't anywhere near part of this team yet. For all her empathy, there were years of relationships built up around her – like a net she'd probably never manage to break through. Only problem was, as each day passed, she was beginning to wonder if maybe she did want to be a part of it, after all.

CHAPTER 9

Slattery turned over the box of John Player Blue in his sweaty hand. If Maureen were here now, she'd be doing his head in over smoking. Well, she *was* here, she was just beyond those double doors, through A&E, stretchered off as quickly as they could move her to an invisible part of the hospital. The operating theatres were behind locked doors. Even a detective couldn't get in there; Slattery couldn't flash his badge, bully or push his way through. Nor did he want to. Angela could see it. Angela had always seen him for what he was. A fraud. Even when she was a baby, she'd looked up at him, with her shrewd stare and she had him sussed. He couldn't relate to her after that; couldn't look her in the eye. So he'd spent a lifetime – her lifetime – avoiding her. Until now. Now, they both knew the time had passed and it was too late.

'Do you want to nip out for a smoke?' she'd said in a neutral tone.

He knew she didn't expect him to come back. She was giving him an out. Did she want him to go? Is that what she really wanted? Or did she just want this terrible time to pass? And, maybe, without him there, she could breathe, she could text her husband, her friends, maybe have someone decent come and support her in her hour of need. Slattery considered it for a while, for the full six minutes it took him to smoke his fag and light up another. His whole body felt as if it was being pulled away from this place with its sterile interior, alien beeping noises and strangers who for a brief moment in time were thrown together through misfortune and misery. He wanted to be gone, every fibre in him wanted to be sitting at a bar counter somewhere, silently nursing a pint and a chaser. Could he go? Could he just leave Maureen and Angela, and turn his back on them one more time? He stood for a while, opened the pack of cigarettes again, better than running for the hills anyway; he lit another fag.

'Slattery? Sad do, sorry about your missus, how's she doing now?' It was Vic Warren, ten years in the Traffic division and he still looked like a teenager. *Perhaps there was something to be said for it*, Slattery thought with a touch of bitterness. 'We came in with her and—'

'Any idea how it happened?' Slattery asked. If Maureen was anything she was a careful driver, too careful if that was possible.

'Well, the poor bastard in the other car isn't going to be telling us now anyway.'

'Shit.' Slattery offered his smokes. He didn't expect Warren to take one. When the younger man lit up hungrily, Slattery knew it had been a tough one.

'Yeah, they just lost him. He was only nineteen years old, just started in college this year.' Warren sucked in the night air, for all the good it'd do him.

'You stayed with him?'

'The family are driving down from Dublin; they'll be here soon, too late now, though.' He jerked the words out, looked towards the overcrowded car park. 'So, how's your missus?' His voice was quieter, maybe fearing the worst; he must have seen she wasn't in a great state coming in.

'She's had surgery. It's a waiting game.' Slattery dragged hard on his fag. 'But she's a tough auld bird, so…' He wasn't lying; she had to be made of serious metal to put up with his shenanigans all these years. Slattery nodded back towards the hospital. 'Does anyone know what happened?'

'Anyone there said she was completely in the wrong. Sorry.' Warren spoke softly, but he was talking to Slattery, he had to be straight. He knew the man well enough to know that he wouldn't thank him for anything less. 'It'll all be on camera, if you have the stomach for it, it happened just on the junction at O'Connell Street.'

'Shit.' The busiest corner in town, the only surprise was that more bodies weren't on their way to Rafiq Ahmed. 'So, what, she conked out, halfway?' A likely scenario, Maureen was as apt to start in third as opposed to first gear.

'Jesus, no.' Warren took a final drag, turned to face Slattery, his expression filled with genuine sorrow. 'Fuck me, Ben, she sat for three rounds of green lights, then took off like the clappers on a red; the boy had no chance.' He patted Slattery on the back. He had to go, there was only so much brutal honesty he could impart at a time and he still had to face a dead boy's family. 'You're lucky to have her, from what I've heard, Ben. Any of the witnesses there, well, they were sure she was a goner first.'

Slattery pulled a final fag from the packet. He hardly tasted the tobacco this time. Maybe he could smoke himself to oblivion right here. He stood for a while longer, thinking of all the times he'd missed over the years with Maureen. Times like birthdays, anniversaries, Christmases. He could say he was in a state of regret. They passed through his mind, a sea of broken promises. It had started with Una. Maureen and his sister Una had been great friends. They left Limerick together before they should have even left school, they were hardly sixteen with grown-up jobs in Campion's Tea House. Life must have seemed so simple then, until that terrible evening when Slattery's world had fallen through a crack so slender he'd never seen it coming. Maureen returned following an afternoon shift serving up fancy cakes and coffees to people loaded down with shopping bags. She must have expected everything to be the same as when she'd left only hours earlier, but she returned to find Una's body, in a strangled heap on the faded settee. That was when Maureen took to God and somehow, Slattery saw fit to take her under his wing. He still wasn't sure if there was ever any romance, but there had been some tacit agreement that led them to the altar and in due course to a marriage as filled with emptiness as it was with disappointment. Eventually the rows had stopped, until she expected nothing more from him. They had made it to their silver wedding anniversary under the same roof; the following day, he moved into a flat at the top of the Ship Inn – it was, they all agreed, a natural progression. The flat was meant to be a stop gap, before he settled somewhere properly. The place was a kip, but at least he could come and go without an argument at every turn. She was welcome to the house in return for a bit of peace and quiet – he had a feeling the arrangement suited her more than she'd ever admit.

He knew that going back into that hospital would make up for none of it. He was tempted to pull up his collar and disappear into the falling night. He stubbed out his cigarette, still in two minds. Something caught his eye, a reflection in the glass above. He strained his eyes to look closer, sure it was Maureen. He stood there for a moment, transfixed, was it all a terrible dream? Was she really patched up and marching around the hospital in one of her familiar grey cardigans? Then, something cold ran through him, as though ice had filled up in his veins. It was not Maureen, whatever he'd seen, or thought he'd seen, it wasn't his Maureen. He turned, back through the emergency doors, it wasn't too late to do the decent thing, and somehow, she'd managed to let him know that.

'Sorry, I took so long…' he said to Angela. She was still sitting where he'd left her, clutching two large handbags. He presumed one of them was Maureen's.

'It's okay; sure you're back now… I did wonder…' Her voice trailed off.

'Oh, yeah… well.' He couldn't look her in the eye, so he plonked himself down on the plastic seat beside her. It was going to be a long night; he had nothing to say to this stranger that was his own flesh and blood. But he was determined now to stay, even if it was in uncomfortable silence.

It was hours before anyone came near them. When a woman in her forties, wearing faded scrubs, came towards them purposefully, Slattery's heart lurched. He elbowed Angela beside him to make sure she was definitely awake.

'Mr Slattery, Angela.' She said their names as she pulled a chair from across the corridor to sit at an angle beside them. She looked then at Angela. 'Your mother is out of surgery. We've managed to stop the clot, but she's been well shaken up.' Her words were slow, deliberate. This woman was used to giving bad news, same as Slattery.

'Will she be okay?' Angela's voice sounded weak and worried beside him.

'We really can't say yet. I'm sorry. She's done well to get this far. We'll be holding on to her in a recovery room off ICU for the next few hours. Really, at this stage, you'd be better off going home.'

'Is she… in any pain?'

'No, she's still under; she'll be unconscious for the next twenty-four hours at least.' She was matter of fact, but Slattery could see, behind her lightly creased blue eyes a deep compassion. She looked as if she too could have a family at home. Her ring finger, naked now, was usually home to a stack of heavy bands, judging by the pale skin, taken off and probably left safe while she went about her work. 'Look,' she smiled now at Slattery, perhaps recognising he was the less emotional of them both, 'better if you go home tonight. She's stable for now. If there's any change we'll give you a call. But going in there, well, it just increases the risk of infection for her.'

At that Slattery felt Angela let go a heaving unsteady sigh, defeated. They were going home.

*

Grady scheduled the press conference for four o'clock and he asked
Locke and Westmont to flank him at the top table. It was fairly
obvious neither June nor Slattery would feel slighted, neither of
them exactly had a face for TV. He had chosen the youngest and
most attractive and if it was somehow not very PC, well, Iris wasn't
going to complain at least. He'd warned Westmont to keep his
mouth shut, nodding as sagely as he could manage was the most
he was allowed to do. Iris had a strict agenda. Her topic was the
victim. Grady opened the conference with a set piece he'd already
prepared. They wanted to convey that, although they were still
pursuing a number of lines of enquiry, they had not made an
arrest at this point and any additional information could really
help them over the line.

'So, Pat Deaver is not your man, then?' A reporter from one
of the red tops stood up with an anger that betrayed his avarice
for a scoop.

'We had a man help us with our enquiries, but that was all.
He's not a suspect at this time in the investigation.' Grady was
cool; he was carrying the pack of cards after all.

'So, are ye near making an arrest?' Another red-top reporter
thrust a microphone nearer Grady's face.

'We are following several lines of enquiry at present and we are
asking the public to come forward with anything at all that may
be of help. I would like to stress that no matter how small it may
seem to people, sometimes what appears like the most insignificant
detail can be invaluable.'

Iris knew they were taking a chance on every curtain-twitcher
in west Limerick ringing the station, but it was a chance they
needed to take.

'So what are you looking for exactly?' Bill McMahon, a reporter
with the local paper, poked a familiar face through the crowd.

'The usual stuff, Bill. If anyone was hanging around, anybody who knew anything about the victim...' Grady looked across at Locke, giving her the cue to take over.

'Anna Crowe and her family kept themselves to themselves for the most part. We're interested in talking to anyone who knew her, anyone who can give us an idea if there was something worrying her of late. We are interested to hear if she'd been bothered by anybody hanging about the cottage. Even if, as Superintendent Grady has said, it seems foolish to ring up, we're urging people to pick up the phone.'

Locke pointed to the numbers that covered the wall behind her back. In large blue font were displayed the local station number and a Crime Stoppers national number. When she finished there was a sea of camera flashes. She knew she had the additional potency in this room of being known to the media – it couldn't hurt Anna Crowe to keep the press interested for as long as possible. There were a few more questions, but Grady called proceedings to a halt quickly. They got what they wanted. Last thing they needed was the general public to go off the boil. The trail would only be warm for a short time. After that, they were depending on what people had seen or heard; sometimes information came in second- or third-hand. Often, soft information was the only lead they had and at this stage, Iris knew they would take anything they could get.

The phones started to hop as soon as the conference went live. TV West aired a newsflash. The killer of the family of three had not been arrested; a murderer was still on the loose, or something to that effect. By eight o'clock June's complexion was almost grey. She had been answering calls all afternoon since the press conference. The first call to Iris's phone had been from her father – well, she'd been expecting that anyway. She fended him off with background noise and promises of catching up when she called out to Woodburn.

In the evening, Iris dragged a heavy chair next to June and planted a strong take-out coffee on the desk for them both.

'Anything?' Grady asked, pulling another seat alongside June's desk.

'On the Crowes?' Iris asked.

'On anything at all…'

'Sweet damn all worth writing up, and less to follow up – just the usual cranks and weirdoes. Maybe tomorrow, yeah?' June yawned.

'Maybe.'

'Any word from Slattery?' June's eyes were filled with the kind of concern that comes from working with people for a long time, even if it appears you may not like them very much.

'Nothing,' Grady answered shortly.

'Well, that has to be good, hasn't it?' June was grasping at straws; Iris had caught it on the air that they all knew Slattery's daughter would not have called him unless it was very serious.

'Does it?' Grady said. 'We should have sent him in a car, shouldn't we?'

'Maybe, but it was all too fast,' June said. 'Anyway, we're not his keepers, Grady – he's got to do this on his own.'

'Yeah, but—'

'Will he?' June finished off his sentence.

Obviously, she'd known him long enough to know what he was thinking now and again, Iris supposed.

'Have a little faith,' Iris said lightly and she lifted up a small glass angel from June's desk. 'Sometimes it's all anyone can hope for.'

'I think, Iris, if you believe in all that palaver,' Grady paused, 'maybe you're one of the lucky ones. You might have to have faith for all of us here as long as it's not knocked out of you in Murder.'

CHAPTER 10

Slattery knew it was time to get back to work; he needed to, and maybe he knew Angela needed him to be gone also. There was no change for Maureen. The next doctor, a fresh-eyed youngster, spoke with the energy of one just coming on shift. He was hardly old enough to have finished school, in Slattery's opinion. They would keep her sedated for the next few hours at least. Angela would stay by her mother's side until she regained consciousness. That she was going to be a martyr like her mother was as pre-ordained as night after day.

Corbally station was nearly empty when he made his way back into the incident room. He'd been tempted to head straight to the pub. God knows, he felt entitled after the last few hours. Only the thought of those two kiddies and their mother burnt in their beds had propelled him back into the station.

'You all right?' June asked. Of course, they both knew what she meant was, *how's Maureen?*

'As well as can be expected.' His words were gruff and he knew that he sounded as if he somehow blamed the woman for her stupidity. June knew that wasn't how it was, though.

'Anything we can do… you know that, Ben.' She placed a hand on his shoulder, just for a moment and it made him stop. No one touched him any more. Even at the hospital, Angela didn't reach out – it just wasn't who he was.

'Nothing anyone can do now,' he said absently, but he looked at June and winked, 'not unless you fancy rhyming off a few novenas for us.'

'I'd have a go for Maureen, but let's face it, Ben, you're just a lost cause.' She sat back in her seat again, rubbing the tension from her neck. Good luck with that, Slattery felt like saying, but the words for a change did not fall from him.

'Anything new?'

'You heard that Deaver is out of the picture?'

'Yeah, I figured he would be anyway, but Grady let me know before it was on the news.' He rifled through some loose papers on his desk. One of the younger uniforms had been busy; he'd marked up as many of Slattery's notes as he could make out from the scraps of paper lying about his desk. He managed to capture quite a lot, since the investigation had begun. Being decent, the youngster left them for Slattery to give them the once over. Smart kid. 'Any calls when I was gone?'

'Anything that came in…' June looked over the rim of her reading glasses, 'should be filed somewhere on your desk. McGonagle's been doing a good job of keeping your corner warm for you.'

Slattery flopped into the chair and pulled it close up to the desk. The lad certainly had left the place ship shape. He pulled out a pile of Post-its. Calls he had to make, messages left and dead ends confirmed. 'Did I hear right we might have a new chief on the way?'

'That's what Grady says.' June avoided his eyes. 'It's Anita Cullen.'

'Christ, tell me that's just a bad joke.' Anita and he had what others would call history – one bad case that she still blamed him for losing on her. 'Is she still on the gargle?'

'Not so's you'd notice. They say she managed to clean up when they sent her to Templemore.'

'Shit or bust time, I suppose.' Cullen had been in line for a commissioner's job, until word had got out about Slattery roughing up a suspect – it was a shame, because the bugger got off and Cullen missed her promotion. If there was anyone he could do without having around now it was Anita Cullen and he knew she'd feel the same with bells on. 'Hopefully, it'll be just a temporary arrangement,' Slattery said, digging deep to find his inner optimist. He switched off the light on his desk, knowing that somehow things had just managed to get worse for him and he'd have to suck it up. 'Where's everyone, June?' he asked, eying the cheap digital, that had lasted much longer than it should have, on his wrist.

'Grady has us all following up new leads.' She pointed to the whiteboard, filled with the names of each detective and their duties for the day. Slattery squinted towards it, made no difference to him. He'd nip into Coleman Grady's office, see if there was anything specific needed doing, but chances were, he knew that Grady would have discounted him for the foreseeable, and that suited him just fine for now. It would give him a chance to follow his own nose and that still worked no matter how much the whiskey pocked away at it.

June looked across at him. 'Ben, no one expects you in yet, go home, go back to Maureen and sit with her… this,' she waved an arm around the incident room, 'this will still be here when you get back.' Of course, she was right, but when had he ever done anything that was right.

'Grady about then?' He dropped his eyes from hers as he asked the question.

'You're a grade-A prick, Ben Slattery, you know that?' June flashed her temper rarely, but she was one of the few Slattery could take it from.

'I know that.' He spoke quietly. 'And you know that I can't help what I am.' He got up from the desk and walked towards the door.

'You do know that's bullshit,' she called after him and he knew she was right. He stopped for a moment, nipped into the men's toilets and swigged the last of the small bottle that sat nearest his heart. Then taking a deep breath he looked in the mirror. He knew everything about him was shit. Anything decent he might have had he'd managed to fuck up. He looked into the dead eyes of his increasingly unfamiliar face. It seemed to him that he was ageing far quicker than he could keep up with. Perhaps he could do some good; perhaps there was some way for him to redeem himself. He snuggled the empty bottle deep into his inside pocket and headed for the third floor – Traffic division.

*

'So, you're still about the place.' Kathy Tarpin nodded towards Slattery from a bank of screens that kept watch over Limerick city drivers night and day.

'Just wondering, Kathy, can I have a look at an accident that took place yesterday?' He had no time for small chat now, things to do and this was just one of them.

'Of course, Jesus, I nearly forgot, your wife was involved in a crash, wasn't she? How is she?' Tarpin got up from her seat, and moved a second seat beside it, making room for Slattery.

'Ara, she's in hospital, they can't tell us a lot yet, but it was a bad auld smash.'

'Right, when and where?' She'd blanked one of the screens, her fingers moving fast across the keyboard.

He gave her as much as he knew, as much as they needed to know and within seconds he was watching Maureen's little Fiat in a line of cars waiting to pass through the O'Connell Street junction. She moved with the snaking line of traffic, slower to start than the rest, holding up those behind her for two changes of green to red. She was top of the queue. The camera position changed and he could see her face quite clearly behind the wheel. He watched as she sat, her expression blank, staring straight ahead into nothingness. Then the lights changed and she did not move. The cars on either side took off quickly and sped past her, through the junction and on towards their destination. Angela had told him she was on her way to a doctor's appointment – having an ingrown toenail lifted. He looked at the screen wondering, was she thinking about it now? Was she thinking about where she would park? What the doctor would say? If it would it be painful? Her expression said she was thinking of absolutely nothing and he wondered for a moment if perhaps she wasn't experiencing some kind of absent seizure. Then the cars around her came to a halt. It looked for a moment as if she'd turned to her left and spoken to an invisible passenger. If right was right, there should be three more changes of lights before it was Maureen's turn to sail off into the sunset and abuse the doctor with a long list of medical complaints.

But Maureen didn't wait for three changes of the lights; she didn't even wait for two. Instead, she waited until Peter Hynes drove into the yellow box before her in his battered old Ford Fiesta and then she took off like the clappers so when she rammed her bonnet into the driver's side of his car Slattery thought he could hear the collision. He imagined he could hear young Hynes thud against the steering wheel, then his head thrown back violently so his neck snapped in one loud crack. Even if the internal bleeding hadn't killed him, he'd never have walked again. He'd never have forgiven Maureen either and Slattery knew that Maureen lived with enough guilt already. She carried with her the divine mixed blessing of being so thoroughly devout. The last thing she needed was to know she'd killed that boy by manslaughter as surely as if she'd taken a gun to him in the heat of her worst temper. The tape was still rolling twenty minutes later. He watched but only half saw the ambulance crews arrive on the scene, recognised some of the faces. He watched Warren taking down details, directing the scene so that the whole sorry mess caused as little disruption to Limerick commuters as possible.

'I'm so sorry.' Kathy Tarpin handed him a very strong cup of tea. He drank it mechanically. 'I couldn't imagine having to watch that if it was…' She looked into her own chipped mug for a moment.

'You couldn't not watch it either, love.' As he said the words, he knew they were true. They were both cops, long-timers; they always had to know the worst.

'Do they think she might have had some kind of attack?'

'I haven't even asked them that yet. Couldn't get my head that far around it.' He still wasn't sure he had, but now, as he sat here, little things were coming back to him. Things like missed phone calls he'd returned and she couldn't remember why she'd rung him. Things like no card or call for his birthday this year. The small things hadn't bothered him at the time, he wasn't even sure if he noticed on the day, but now, somehow it seemed ominous. Maureen never missed a date. Never missed an occasion. Everything, even the cat's birthday, had to be commented on, they had to be marked. *Life is too short, Ben Slattery, as some day you'll find out.*

Maybe that *someday* was coming quicker than he'd expected. He drained the cup of tea and left it on the desk before him. Kathy had returned her attention to the remaining screens. He mumbled something as he left, it counted for thanks, see you and goodbye. Kathy wouldn't expect much more, not at this stage. He pulled his anorak closer as he made his way out into the overcast afternoon. He had things to do.

*

Anita Cullen was built like a twin tub. She'd probably been taller in her youth. You had to be at least five-six then to get into the guards if you were a woman. Now she was hardly five-three and she stood as tall as she could. Years of sitting at a desk probably made you settle into yourself swiftly. Her hair was grey, her skin was grey but her eyes were quick and when she spoke, Grady had the impression that she'd thought long and hard about her words, although they fired out of her so quickly you had to listen hard to make sure you hadn't missed anything. She probably had little more than ten years on Grady, but he knew that she'd seen and endured more in her career than all the commissioners put together. There had been no fast-tracking for Anita Cullen. She'd made the grade when they didn't want women there. She'd made it despite them, not because they needed her to fill a narrow quota. She'd headed up some of the most high-profile cases in the history of the state. Grady liked her immediately, not just because he admired her professionally, but she had an easy manner and he figured she'd be well able to handle Byrne. From the look on Byrne's face, he knew that too, and it wasn't sitting well.

'I'm not so sure that I'm all Byrne was hoping for.' She chuckled.

'I hear you requested to come here?' Better to change the subject than get caught up in gossip.

'Not exactly. I'd have had to go somewhere, better to pick than be chosen, I thought. So when I heard ye were looking for someone...' She drew out a desk drawer, surveyed the contents for a moment. 'I started out here, long time ago now; it was one of my first bases as a detective. Sure, in many ways it's like coming home.' She smiled. 'Ah yes, the good old days when they moved you every couple of weeks. It tended to weed out the men from the boys, and the women entirely.'

'Not completely, it seems.'

'I'm a resilient weed, difficult to prune.' She smiled at Grady. What was there not to like? 'So,' she sat back in the leather swivel that had recently been her predecessor's, 'what's the story?'

Byrne had already appraised her of her duties at Corbally station. She'd be overseeing Domestic Violence and Traffic as well as Murder, but the deaths of Anna Crowe and her two children were top priority. Now Grady told her everything to do with the investigation to date. He'd finally got an address on Darach Boran and even now, he had sent his best officers out to question him.

'I could get used to this...' She smiled across at Grady. 'If you didn't mind...'

'Hey, you're welcome to it. I like what I do, I'm just glad you're here; lets me get on with running my team. I can't be doing with keeping everyone sweet, when I'd rather be leading this investigation.'

'We'll make a good team so.' Anita Cullen extended a pudgy hand across the table and when Grady held it, he hoped they'd struck gold.

CHAPTER 11

Iris thought everything about Darach Boran's cottage was small. The doors were narrow. The windows were beady eyes, and the rooms cramped, as if Boran had crammed every stick of furniture into two rooms. It seemed to Iris that when she and Westmont entered the tiny living room, their proportions were gigantic compared to everything around them, including Darach Boran. Westmont jostled between sideboard and sink then perched on what looked like a piano stool. Iris settled for leaning against a gaudy kitchen unit. The room was dark and Boran managed to blacken it further with a ubiquitous miasma of cigarette smoke. If fumes differed or resembled each other, there was something familiar about the smell of Boran's fags – or at least that's what Westmont suggested when he sniffed the air with an appreciation others might save for aromas more pleasant. She almost missed Slattery. While they sat there in silence, Boran managed to smoke his way through three cigarettes. Each burnt slowly, gently growing into grey caterpillars, in separate ashtrays around the poky room. Boran was an electric eel of a man, long and reedy, jumpy and giddy; with deep-set eyes that Iris supposed might set him aside as an artist, or in Iris's line of work, a player.

'Yes, I know who you mean, impossible not to, when her face is splashed across every paper in the country.' His accent carried a northern undercurrent, hardly detectable. Iris would lay bets he was south of the border, just, Donegal perhaps.

'We believe you knew her before this… tragedy.'

'Why would you say that? Because she was an artist, of sorts, and I am an artist?' Boran lit another cigarette, dragged on its thin body and exhaled loudly.

'Do you remember her?' Westmont stood a little taller, leaning towards Boran. Truth was, they didn't want to intimidate him, not yet at least. Always better to move softly at first. They had Slattery back at the station if they needed to run the tough-guy routine on him.

Iris leaned backwards again, allowing her face to relax a little. 'She attended the National College of Art and Design, same time as you lectured there, late nineties to 2002.' She managed to soften out the dates, knew that here, the tone was as important as the words.

'That's a fairly tenuous gambit.' Boran smiled sardonically. Somehow the expression was incongruous with his nervy body language, but in that smile Iris could see how first-year girls, up from the country, could easily fall for his charm. His name was Gaelic, but Iris would bet Boran was upper-middle-class Irish protestant, probably educated across the pond. The accent had stuck only just beneath his northern lilt, delicately fondling most of his words.

'You think?' Westmont reminded them he was there, watching everything, his bulging eyes on stalks, taking in Boran, taking in all.

'Detective, I've taught in more colleges around this country than your dog has found lampposts. Even if I remembered half of the people I met along the way, I couldn't tell you when or where I met them.' He dragged on his cigarette. 'You might say I've forgotten more girls than you'll ever be likely to know.'

'Yeah, well, I'm sure they haven't forgotten you.' Westmont sneered and Iris caught his eye.

'My colleague is right; we've seen some of the reports against you, Boran, it all makes for heavy reading.'

'Unfortunate misunderstandings, that's all.' He dragged deeply again.

'With matches and a can of petrol? I don't think there was any misunderstanding there, now do you?'

'That was different.'

'Oh?' Iris tried to keep her face neutral, her voice even.

'I wasn't well. At the time, I wasn't well at all.'

'And tell us, Mr Boran, how were you feeling last Friday night, the night that Anna Crowe died? Were you feeling *well* then?' Iris waited for what seemed like an eternal minute. Boran didn't smoke, didn't move, and didn't blink. Only the tick tock of a small travel clock somewhere amid the chaos toned out the seconds. In that stretching silence, Iris caught her breath and she half expected a full confession when Boran finally opened his mouth to speak.

'I'm very sorry about the girl, sorry about her children too. They shouldn't have died.' He dropped his eyes, searching for some elusive pattern on the faded floor cover. 'It's a terrible tragedy. None of them should have died, not like that.'

When Westmont cleared his throat, Iris thought that Boran might jump from his skin and slide easily down the nearest drain. Instead, he looked towards the bare kitchen window. When he spoke next, his words were a whisper, a conquered undertone. 'I suppose I'll need a solicitor for this?' And although he'd asked a question he was already taking out his mobile and scrolling down through a short list of numbers.

*

The rain had been steady all evening and that suited Slattery perfectly. He liked the predictability of it; you knew where you were with rain and there was no onus on a man to be doing things he had no interest in doing. He liked, too, the familiar smell of cold and wet settling along the window ledge beside his desk, the damp aroma of coats drying and umbrellas pooling across the incident room.

'You look pleased with yourself,' June said and he figured he'd never seen her look so worn-out. 'Considering…' There was only the three of them in the incident room now and it was hard to be sure if Iris was even awake, she'd been staring fixedly at the computer screen before her for so long.

'Yeah, well… there's nothing like the welcoming of the early evening and knowing that you're going to be heading off for a pint in an hour or two to make any man feel he's settled into himself for the day,' he said cynically.

'You'll be going to the hospital first,' June said.

'I'll be doing what I have to do… I hardly need you to tell me how to…' he spat at her, but something in his voice must have alerted Iris and she stirred enough for him to know she was listening.

'I'm just saying,' June said, but she was staring determinedly at the papers on her desk.

'Well, bloody don't,' he snapped. It was bad enough that Grady had handed his lead on Boran over to Iris Locke without a by your leave; assuming that Slattery wouldn't be here, indeed. 'That's the trouble with you lot, everyone just says and assumes when it's not your place.' He grunted then.

'Bad time to ask if you've ever noticed this fella about the place.' Iris swung her chair about and popped a grainy picture of Darach Boran before him.

'How did you guess?' Slattery shoved the printout off to the side – there was a photograph of Boran already, hanging on the board; the image before him now looked ten years older. There was something about him, but it was fleeting, one of those people you pass by on the street maybe twice and they stick in your memory. He pulled the photograph closer again. 'There's something familiar about him, but, no…' He shook his head, he remembered every face he'd ever put away – it wasn't always a blessing. 'No, I've never done this fella for so much as a parking ticket. That doesn't mean much, though.'

'I have a feeling about him… it's more than just…' Iris sighed.

'If you ask me, in this case, you could have a feeling about anyone – we're so far off having anything concrete – just do me a favour and don't have any feelings about me, right,' he said and decided it was time he got out of here. He headed towards the exit with only one destination in mind and it wasn't the hospital.

*

It seemed to Iris that Satan, her father's cat, eyed her with a certain amount of wariness when she arrived at Woodburn. The old cat scrutinised her for a moment, shook himself out insolently before burying himself further into the deep cushions of the weary sofa that ran opposite the timeworn stove in the shadowy kitchen. The house was warm and welcoming, and her dad had managed to stretch his culinary skills to coffee and his own hot buttered scones. She knew she was honoured, she knew too she had nothing to be proud of. She hadn't lied to him about joining the Murder Team, but omitting to tell them was every bit as tactical.

'Come on through,' he said neutrally, walking ahead of her; he always preferred the front of the house, overlooking the long avenue that held back the village life beyond. Her parents had moved here when they first got married, long before they'd even thought about having a family. Jack and Theodora were young and in love.

The house had been a gift to Theodora from an elderly aunt. Iris had always assumed the inheritance had weighed heavily on Theodora's shoulders, *guilty conscience, we'd fallen out with them all beforehand, the old girl was dead a week before anyone realised.* The Murder Squad gave her father a level-headedness Iris always hoped she wouldn't inherit, as she seemed to have so much else of him.

Woodburn hadn't always looked like it did now. Even when Iris had been growing up, the place resembled a building site for many of her formative years. *Old houses, never finished*, he'd said it a million times. It looked now like he was wrong. There was nothing more to do here except play golf like her dad, or perhaps wither slowly away like her mother.

'So, how is everyone in Corbally?' He was balancing his cup on the seat beside him, moving a pile of magazines and holding onto his scone with his hands. He'd done well not to grill her before he'd brewed the coffee, she knew.

'I'm sorry, Dad. How could I say anything when I knew how worried you would be?'

'I'm not a child, Iris,' he said thickly, with as much irritation in his voice as she'd ever heard. 'Seeing you on the evening news with Coleman Grady is hardly the way I wanted to hear. You should have told us, I mean, how long have you known? You must have applied for it some time ago.' His tone turned soft and she could see the hurt behind his eyes, the idea that she had been so duplicitous.

'It wasn't like that at all. Please, Dad, they moved me in just for this case. I may not even have a place on the team when it's all wrapped up. They were short of bodies and you know how these things work...' Her voice petered off.

'Well, that's something I suppose,' he said grudgingly and she wasn't sure if he was pleased because her term might be short or it was a measure of her honesty with him. Better that she'd lied for a week rather than a month. 'So, you've been on this case since the beginning?'

'Almost,' she said, sipping her coffee. At least she could pretend that she'd only come to visit, rather than make amends.

'Out of all the cases they could have put you on.' He shook his head sadly.

'Dad, just because it's the same family as you investigated all those years ago, doesn't mean there's a connection. Grady hasn't even looked at that old case…' she offered, but of course, in her gut, she knew there had to be a link; lightning doesn't strike in the same spot twice, does it? Well, not unless there's a pretty ready conductor.

'Well, of course not, the Baby Fairley case – well, there was no case, not in the way the papers tried to make out.'

'Well then…' she said, but she laid down her cup and waited for what he could tell her.

'No, you don't understand. That case, it was never about not solving it.' He shook his head sadly. 'It…' A tear glistened in his eyes and his thoughts wandered from her, searching the darkness of the gardens outside. 'It all happened when you were so small. Your mother…' he shook his head, 'I think that it contributed to the way things turned out for her. You know with the…'

'Post-natal depression?' It wasn't a secret exactly that her mother had taken almost two years to pull herself from a darkness that had hung about her after Iris was born. Jack Locke had always blamed her drinking on the depression. Iris had long thought the blame should probably be apportioned the other way round.

'So, that's it anyway, you finally got into a murder team, just like your old man.' Jack Locke tried to smile, but he wasn't fooling Iris. He would worry about her even more now.

'Well, for now, it's all press conferences and desk work,' she lied.

'That's something, I suppose.' He'd seen too many women chewed up by Murder; it gives you nightmares, he'd told her once. But she knew that wasn't really the problem. His biggest fear was that she'd end up in some kind of danger, danger that was too awful to contemplate. He was quiet, gathering his thoughts, but his coffee had been placed on the floor, the scone abandoned on a nearby table – it'd likely choke him now, she knew. He ran a hand beneath his open shirt collar, for once it wasn't checked. Since he'd retired it seemed to Iris he'd worn nothing but checked shirts. As though he was making up for a lifetime in plain blue and then white, he'd taken to small printed cream-and-beige patterns as though he'd lived in them forever. Funny, they'd worried he'd never survive without Corbally. Now he wanted nothing to do with the place.

'Well.' He finally took his eyes from the avenue beyond. 'And are you enjoying it?' His voice was as even as he could manage it. If she wasn't his daughter, she wouldn't have recognised the emotion that was filling it up.

'We both know it's not what I wanted, I'd have preferred the east coast, but…'

'The times that are in it eh? You have to go where they send you, I suppose.'

'I could be waiting a long time to get into Dublin Castle…'

'Well, I'd like to be happy for you, but there's no use pretending, you know how I feel… it's dangerous for you there, too many people; they haven't forgotten who I am, Iris. There are nasty feckers out there, still wanting to hurt me and by God, but if they hurt you, well… I don't know what I'd do.' It was as honest as he'd ever been with her. She couldn't ever remember hearing him using foul language before, not in the house at least. 'I can only wish you luck, but you know what I truly wish for.'

'I do, Dad, of course I do. But, I have to take my chances; it's no different to what you'd have done yourself.'

He knew she was right; he didn't come up the ranks without grabbing every opportunity that came his way.

'Of course, but things were very different then. Even now, I know all you young girls are liberated, but…'

'How's Mother?'

'Oh, you know your mother, waiting for the next great cause.' He winked at Iris; she knew he wouldn't want to talk about Corbally any further. She'd leave it for now, so they spoke about the garden, about her mother's newfound interest in bridge. 'Anything is better than her pains and aches. I swear someone should ban that Google, it's the worst thing that ever came into the house. You should hear herself and Judy Battle, anyone would think they were finished their internships at the Mayo clinic. I think it's migraine today, but I've no doubt she'll be up and running for her game of bridge tomorrow.' He smiled. Iris knew that he was truly fond of her; even if their relationship had grown into something that more closely resembled carer and child than husband and wife over the years. Iris had always supposed that it would be very hard to be his equal. He was a protector by nature. Even now if anyone should hurt a hair on her head, he wouldn't rest until they'd paid a heavy price.

They sat for ages, watched while the struggling sun dipped beyond the clouds, casting shadows through the trees that dotted the damp lawn. Eventually he turned to her. 'There's something else too, isn't there?' he said, his blue eyes watery pools, the whites they sat in almost permanently bloodshot these days.

'The Baby Fairley case.' She watched as regret flickered across his eyes, just for a second.

'I thought you said they weren't connected?' He was almost talking to himself now and Iris wondered, when he read about the current case, had he turned over the possibilities in his mind? Imagined himself in Grady's job? Suddenly she was glad she was in Corbally, glad she was on this case. Damn it, she'd hate to miss a minute of this, hate to leave it behind someday, but worse, know what you might have done and never taken the chance.

'No, we're pretty sure they're not, but of course, it's early days.' Better have a safe conviction than a fast one. 'Anyway, I've been trying to access the files on that earlier case, Dad…' She could see he was miles away. 'Dad?'

'Sorry.' His dark brows had drawn so close together it looked as though they were one. He was pensive, preoccupied with a world long gone and one that he'd never be part of again. 'Brings it all back, you know?' He looked away from her again, towards the darkening garden beyond. 'I wouldn't bother if I was you. That baby was well gone before we got there. I've always blamed the mother. She told the kid – your victim – told her not to look in the pram. It was post-natal depression, as bad as any woman could get it, she wouldn't have known what she was doing. They called it the baby blues back then. Just lucky she didn't take the other daughter as well. There but for the grace of God, I'd say.' He lowered his voice now. 'Doesn't do any good raking these things up… going back.'

'Maybe. But isn't it strange that I haven't been able to access it electronically?'

'Really?' He looked at her now, perplexed. 'I thought all of the murder files had been transferred over? Yes, I'm sure they were. Every single file was, and then we had the almightiest bonfire you could imagine. Had to hold onto some bits, obviously for DNA testing, what have you, but yes, all of those files should be on PULSE now.' Her father had been there for the setting up of PULSE, he would have overseen the transfer of many files like the Fairley case.

'So the originals are probably gone?' That explained Blake's reaction when she'd asked him to check it out at least.

'Maybe not.' He chewed on his lip for a second, shook his head sadly. 'Probably though, probably.' He didn't offer her any more coffee or scones. Neither of them could face a thing to eat, but they sat side by side, he holding her hand, tracing the lines that were fading now as evening drew in.

By the time it had got dark outside, she knew she'd have to leave. Jack Locke threw two large logs into the open fire. He was greeted with a volley of shooting spits. As she left Woodburn, she was filled with loneliness. Her father had hugged her close, as though he didn't want to let her go, afraid that the world beyond might take her from him. And after her visit, she was none the wiser, was she?

Although maybe she was. After all, her father had led out the investigation. He'd rarely been wrong in his career. There had never been a conviction called into question and she knew that his humanity would overtake all else in a case like the Fairley case. If he thought the mother had, out of some sort of desperation, killed her child, Iris knew without any doubt, that her father would feel nothing but compassion for the woman and give her support in any way he could. Maybe she knew more now than any file could tell her.

CHAPTER 12

Darach Boran's solicitor was halfway across the country representing some nut job who'd taken a gun to the local primary school and frightened a couple of teachers witless with an empty rifle. Grady felt Iris Locke had made the right decision when she said she would expect to see them both at the station within the next twenty-four hours. Detaining him now would only eat into the time they could question him for later. Grady liked that there was no way she was doing anything that wasn't by the book – so far she seemed to be the complete opposite of Slattery and that was a good thing for the team.

Grady had just sat at his desk with a mug of over-brewed coffee when he picked up a message on his pager from Anita Cullen. She was headed towards the incident room for a look round. *Timing couldn't be better*, he thought. Most of the team were out of the place and she wanted to have a look-see. This would be quick.

'Don't worry, just getting a feel for the incident room,' she said nonchalantly as she swung her ungainly frame into a precarious-looking wooden swivel seat. 'Corbally station – they don't make them like this any more,' she directed her comment towards June.

'With good reason too,' June laughed. 'You should be here when the winter sets in and the heating freezes in the pipes and if you need to run to the loo the nearest one is across the yard in those fancy offices that we otherwise avoid like the plague.'

'They're not that bad, are they?' Anita Cullen would know more of the big brass based in the adjoining regional headquarters than she did of the team she was assigned to.

'Aren't they?' June snorted. 'Unfair of me, I suppose; I wouldn't know since they're far too high and mighty even to acknowledge us most of the time.'

'They're busy people, I'm sure,' Cullen half apologised for them.

'No one is that busy,' Grady said, but his voice was too flat he knew and he raised a hand to pull an errant dark lock of hair from falling across his eyes.

'Aye, you're right, I don't know why I'm making excuses for them – and if they are, well, they'll find out some day that maybe they shouldn't have been.' Cullen's eyes strayed off into the distance. Grady figured that she wasn't noticing anything beyond the old Victorian windows that framed a view of the impressive opera house opposite.

'So, what's your story?' She turned on the youngest officer in the unit, McGonagle.

'Me, ma'am?' McGonagle looked surprised. He'd been sitting against a radiator, taking in the woman who would run not just this department but two more also. 'I'm just a rookie… hoping to get my foot in the door if they ever let me.' He smiled a heavy, long grin that managed to pull not only his mouth, but also his eyes, ears and forehead higher than Grady would have imagined possible.

'You're McGonagle so?'

'That's right…ma'am.'

'It's Cullen… better that than what some of them call me, and I've no interest in being your mammy, sonny, so we'll keep it nice and civil, yes?'

'Of course M—Cullen, that's grand.'

'How are you getting on here, do you think?' She eyed him now, with the gaze of a hawk, assessing him. Would she double check his answers later, make sure he was telling the truth? Grady felt sorry for the lad. He had the makings of a good guard and a fine detective, given half a chance.

'I love it,' he said, flushed with enthusiasm. It was true; standing next to him, Grady wondered if he couldn't charge his phone off the excitement that seemed to be running through the lad. 'Like, I mean, it's very sad, you know, what happened to Anna and Martin and little Sylvie, but for me… well, to work here, with the Murder Team, you can't imagine what a buzz that is.'

'Oh, I think I can, McGonagle, I think I can.' Anita Cullen crossed her stocky legs, ran her hand through her cropped hair and said softly, 'Don't cod yourself, McGonagle, we were all like you once, hungry for it. If we hadn't had that, we wouldn't still be here. Careful, though, because I've seen youngsters get eaten up by it. It manages to consume some, so they have nothing else.'

'Are you here for long?' June asked.

'Long as ye'll have me; honestly, I'm delighted to get out and do some real police work again. You get stuck, you know.' Cullen nodded towards Grady and walked towards one of the full-length windows. 'So, everyone else is out, yeah?'

'You picked the wrong time, I'm afraid,' Grady said and picked up a file from Iris Locke's desk. He thumbed through the first few pages. It all seemed to be meticulous; perhaps she was extra careful after the McCracken fiasco. Grady suspected she'd be thorough anyway; if the fault in the McCracken case was on their side, it had probably not been on the part of Iris Locke. There was nothing personal on her desk, apart from her notes. Not even a calendar or a photograph. Perhaps she liked to keep things separate; that was what undercover taught you.

'Big into paperwork, this one, isn't she?' Cullen was at Grady's elbow. She took up a report. 'Locke? Nothing to…'

'His daughter.'

'Christ.' The word escaped her softly. 'So little Iris is a detective? He won't like that.' She spoke over her shoulder, to no one in particular, and moved quickly along the next desks.

Grady left down the notes, watched as Cullen made her way around each desk, picking up a page here, a photograph there. She stopped at Dennis Blake's desk, flopped in his chair and pulled out a copy of the inventory that categorised everything so far collected in the case.

'That's Dennis—'

'Blake,' she cut him off before he had a chance to finish. 'I know, don't worry, sure we go back a long way.' Anita Cullen's voice was low and friendly. There was no doubt, she probably knew every other guard in the country, she'd been around long enough. That she'd remember them all was a tiny miracle, but there again, Grady reminded himself, she was sharp as a buzz cut. She sauntered over to Slattery's desk. Moved around the pages cautiously, opened the top drawer, only slightly, but enough to pull out a pack of Slattery's fags. She murmured something about Customs and Excise under her breath and in that moment Grady had a feeling that all might not go so smoothly in his team after all. 'Who sits here?'

'Well, I've been...' McGonagle started.

'No, I mean, who has had his arse planted in this seat for the last five to ten?' Her eyebrow rose only slightly, alerting McGonagle to the dangerous ground upon which he might be walking. He looked towards Grady.

'That's Ben Slattery's desk.' He kept his voice clear, his eyes straight on her.

'No reason, just getting a feel for the place... and the people.'

'Sure, well, he's around as long as I am, a good detective.' Grady wouldn't add the horror story of Slattery's career as a guard. He didn't have to, not to Anita Cullen at any rate.

'Ah, well.' Cullen lowered her voice. 'Change is as good as a rest, isn't it?' She smiled sweetly before moving on to the next desk, but Grady could feel June beside him stop breathing and he wondered if she'd managed to stop her heart beating also, so dead and quiet had the room become.

*

'Don't you think it's a bit of a coincidence?' Iris Locke was standing in front of Coleman Grady's desk, her long copper hair catching the light. The flecks of gold that flashed in her green eyes gave away more about her passion than any words could. She'd caught a scent of something and nobody, certainly not Coleman Grady, was going to stand in her way.

'Yeah, I think it could be just that, a coincidence.' He looked at her now, met her eyes and perhaps they both knew that given a few short years, she could be his equal, and someday, in the not too distant future, she would probably outrank him. 'They do happen, you know; just because he won prizes a long time ago, doesn't mean he's going to keep his skills up by murdering his entire family in one go.'

'But the psychological report…'

'Which we still don't have here.' Grady lowered his voice. 'It means nothing, not until it is verified, not until we have it in black and white and double checked by someone with more letters after their name than *screw you too*.'

She walked to the window that looked out on the incident room. 'We have to start really looking at him. I think we should bring him in for questioning.'

'Well, since it's not up to you who we bring in for questioning, it looks like we might stick to gathering evidence first, like real detectives.' Grady took a deep breath. He looked tired, they all were.

Now, for a moment, she regretted coming in here, after all, they probably all felt the same, needing something to move, something to break so they could see a result. She wasn't a wet week in Murder and already she was attempting to call the shots. 'It's just…'

'Yes, and a few days ago you were dying to get your hands on the Baby Fairley files.' It was an offhand comment, but it threw her a little, she hadn't expected him to hear she'd been snooping about.

'Well, I'm covering the bases, nothing wrong with that, is there?'

'Of course not, it's highly commendable.' He raised his head to look at her again now, lowered his voice. 'Whatever you'd found out, which I suppose was a big fat nothing, you never reported back at a briefing. If you want to be taken seriously, you need to remember you're part of a team.'

'You know I couldn't have found a lot anyway, the computers are playing up.'

'I have IT on it, but just so you know, they're not hopeful of unlocking the Fairley case any time soon. It wasn't the only one affected by whatever kind of bug has eaten in to them, but it seems to be the worst affected, which is just shit luck for us.'

'So, you checked too?' she said softly, not in an effort to create some kind of one-upmanship, but as she didn't like coincidences, perhaps Grady felt the same. The truth was, she was divided between the past and the present, but there was no getting away from the smell of something shady about Adrian Crowe either.

'Look, Sergeant Locke,' he used her title neutrally, but it served to remind her of her relatively junior rank, 'I appreciate that you've worked really hard on the case and I'm going to spend some time going through your notes to date, but…' He watched as her shoulders tensed now. 'If you want us to pull in someone for questioning, you have to give me more than your gut feeling. I'd say your best bet is to sit out there in front of that CCTV footage and see if there's anything to put Crowe near that cottage when he shouldn't be. Okay?'

'Christ, but we could get as much if we just brought him in… I'll get McGonagle to look at the CCTV and…' she looked at him now, 'there's something not right here, and you know it as well as I do.'

'It doesn't matter what we think we know – we need to be sure before we bring anyone in. Or, haven't you noticed the line-up of reporters just outside the station? Last thing we need is another false promise. No, we hold tight, you give me something, something worthwhile to go on. In the meantime we keep digging.'

Locke turned on her heel, her silky hair swishing insolently behind her. Anger and disappointment made her walk with even more cockiness than usual, but it was only on the surface, deep down she wanted to get a result and she wanted to get it now.

'Oh and Locke,' he waited while she closed the door, 'go through the CCTV yourself. McGonagle is going to be working with Slattery now he's back. He'll benefit from Slattery's long experience on the Murder Team, I think.' Iris just caught Grady's smile as she banged the door behind her. The message was loud and clear, there was a pecking order and he was telling her where she stood in it. *Know your place.*

CHAPTER 13

Veronique sighed. She hated this place now and she hated Ollie Kerr. She had only come here to escape her old life. Outside grey clouds canopied the fields blotting out any hope of sun. It seemed every day was wet and depressing in this overcast village. Still, she'd been glad to come here a few months earlier, anything was better than the streets, and Veronique knew that from experience. If she had hung around Limerick much longer, the welcome she'd almost worn out would have forced her back into a life that she swore she'd never fall into again. Now, as she stood looking out through faded net curtains that smelled of turf smoke, she wondered what was the difference between sleeping with Ollie Kerr in exchange for a roof over her head or taking her chances turning tricks when she needed extra cash.

The difference she knew was simple – here, in this godforsaken place, she was safe. Ollie Kerr had the table manners of an animal, but he had never hurt her. She had assumed, until Anna Crowe was murdered and Slattery had arrived out here, that Ollie wouldn't hurt a fly – now she was not so sure.

All the same, she took a deep breath, because the memories of men she'd met on the streets wouldn't leave her, no matter how much vodka she drank. She shivered, walked to the window and pulled back the curtain; it was cosy here, but some memories always made her cold.

Slattery. God, she hated him, not that he'd ever... well, he probably hadn't had a woman in thirty years. No, not that, but she owed him. Veronique wouldn't admit it to anyone else, but she knew that Ben Slattery had pulled her from the grip of a life that wouldn't have been worth living if her last pimp had managed to catch up with her. Veronique had had pimps before, she knew she was lucky to get out of that situation. Slattery had saved her last time from falling back in. She should have told him everything she knew, that was what owing someone meant in her world. There was a code, the least she could do was try to keep on the right side of it. Be straight with him this once and then maybe the debt would be paid.

Mind you, it wasn't that there was anything she could tell. Not really. After all, she didn't know who had killed the Crowes, did she? It could have been Ollie, but there again, it could have been anyone. She looked up at the door that led out the back of the cottage. It never locked properly and before Anna Crowe had been murdered that hadn't particularly bothered Veronique. After all, she had slept rough for much of her teenage life and when she came here first she was just grateful to have a roof over her head.

No. She couldn't tell Slattery what he wanted to hear. She couldn't tell him who had murdered Anna Crowe. She couldn't tell him that it wasn't Ollie, because she really wasn't sure. But there was plenty she could have told him.

She could have told him that there might have been a reason for the woman's death. She could have told him that there was one man who might have wanted Anna Crowe wiped out so she didn't ask questions that he wouldn't want answered. She could have told him that there was one person who had every reason to want Anna Crowe dead. The only thing was, Veronique had a feeling that this person might pay handsomely for her to keep quiet.

She bit her lip now, taking out her phone and thinking of the box of papers she'd found stashed in the back of a wardrobe in what had once been Ollie's mother's bedroom. One phone call, that's all it would take and she could have enough money to get out of Limerick altogether. This could be the winning lottery ticket she'd always knew she'd find one day.

Veronique had been tumbling the possibilities of this over and back in her mind for days. Ollie didn't want her here any more. He had no reason now and it dawned on her that before, when Anna was alive, she had a purpose. Veronique, just by being here had made him look normal, as though he was not forever alone. Now, the hard reality facing her was that she had nowhere to move on to.

She pulled out her mobile and keyed in the man's name, taking a deep breath she waited until his name showed up in her internet search. A giddy rush of excitement bubbled in her as she came closer to searching out his contact details. This was going to change her life, she was certain of that.

*

Slattery stared glumly at the board behind Grady's back. June had already filled in their tasks for the day. Again, it was another day, when they hadn't expected to see Slattery and so, Grady had left him floating. Slattery shook his head, you'd think that after all these years Coleman Grady would know better than that.

'It's not a lead, Iris,' Grady said flatly.

'How do we know that until we check it out?' She blew a stray strand of hair from before her eyes, meeting Grady's with equal steel.

'Look, Anita Cullen remembers that case, she worked it all those years ago in this station. It wasn't a case at all, as far as she remembers it. They had it cut and dried within a week and I don't need to remind you that they had some of the best detectives we've ever had here working on it.'

'Still…' she said.

'What would you have us do? Conjure up the old files?' Grady was livid. Slattery couldn't remember when he'd last seen anyone get under his skin so badly.

'But that too – I mean, how can files just disappear into thin air? There's not so much as a sample left.' She was standing now, coming dangerously close to crossing an invisible line that everyone else in this team knew was drawn out in front of Grady as clearly as if he'd marked it with chalk.

'I'm not sure what you're trying to insinuate, but I would suggest it would be more in your interest get on with the work of this investigation. You've been asked to get a file from the army and we're still waiting for that – never mind about trying to dig up old cases and we all know why...' He let the words hang and Slattery watched as Iris Locke's colour drained.

'I only want to solve this case, same as everyone else here in this room and if you're suggesting for one moment...'

'Ahem,' June coughed meaningfully from the other side of the room, saving Iris from herself and maybe doing them all out of a good old scrapping match which Slattery, for one, knew would end up with her getting a reputation to match his own. Iris flopped into her seat, suddenly the air expelled from her and it felt to Slattery at least as if the tension from the room went with it.

'Right, so it's back to today...' Grady was saying, although no one was really listening to him now, rather, every officer in the room was filled with one question... what was Grady suggesting? Of course, Slattery and June knew only too well what, but they weren't going to share that with anyone else in a hurry.

*

Iris Locke walked past her desk. To say she was livid was an understatement. That bastard, he was a typical, country bloody bumpkin guard. Old school. She was angry with Grady, fractious with the Murder Team and mostly frustrated with the whole investigation. She decided to head out of the station for a walk. There was a briefing scheduled for later in the evening, so she grabbed her coat from the hook on her way. A quick walk around the city should clear her head. God knows, if she waited here any longer she'd either kill someone or cry. She wondered, as she made her way down the noisy corridor, if perhaps she wasn't premenstrual. It was just one of the many thoughts zooming around her brain when she almost ploughed into Anita Cullen.

'You in a hurry?' Cullen, like everyone else in this godforsaken place probably knew her only too well from the coverage of the McCracken case in all the papers. She was a minor celebrity. A poster girl for an organisation packed to the core with fat men and old bitches. In a way, she knew they'd used her image to the max when it had come to putting a spin on the whole McCracken debacle, for all the good it had done her in the end.

'Oh, no, I just need to get a bit of air.' Iris heard the words trip lightly off her tongue – that's what undercover did for you. She could lie at the drop of a hat now, didn't knock a stir out of her. Maybe she'd always been good at it.

'Mind if I join you?' Cullen said, falling into step beside her. There was something comforting about it. She had a solidity to her that you didn't often find in women. Cullen was old school, but she was female and that made her quite the anomaly. 'It can be hard, starting out… trying to prove yourself…'

'Might be, if I was actually stationed somewhere permanently… I don't know. I think I want to crack this case more than anyone here, but it feels as if it's going nowhere.' Locke kept her voice low, glancing around her as they walked. She never fully trusted this building where whispers carried up through the stairwells when you least wanted them to. She kept her conversations low and her thoughts to herself.

'I can't believe you're still a floater.' Cullen pulled her jacket closer as they stepped out into the cool Limerick air.

'They offered me a post in Fraud. A desk job.'

'The way you say that, I guess you're a girl after my own heart.' Cullen chuckled, a deep satisfied noise that invited you to laugh with her. She made it hard not to like her. 'Listen, we're both outsiders here, if there's anything I can do for you…' Cullen stopped and Iris wasn't sure if she was meant to say ditto or tell her all of her problems. Either way, she wasn't saying too much for now.

'I appreciate that,' she settled on, eventually. 'Thank you.'

'You're welcome; we girls need to stick together, right?' They were turning into Athlunkard Street. 'Fancy a decent cup of coffee?'

'Murder one!' Locke said. It was no harm to keep this woman on side; she was very well connected, and anyway, she was easy to talk to. Iris felt like she'd known her all her life, reckoned that the day would come when tales would be told to young women joining the force about Anita Cullen, and, who knew, perhaps she'd be the one telling them.

They picked out a seat at the back end of a self-consciously trendy coffee shop. It was all lattes and cappuccinos and expensively aromatic chocolate.

'So are we both looking to get into the Murder Team in Limerick?' Cullen asked, making her way through a chocolate muffin.

'I don't know. I'd have said no before I came here. Even yesterday, I'd have taken the train out of here without looking back, but I've been finding myself thinking, the team are okay and I like the city, my family are here, so…'

'Lucky girl, what's not to like so?' Cullen was stirring brown sugar into her coffee.

'Maybe I've too many connections with the place. It's complicated.'

'Yes, your father?' Cullen tipped her head to the side. 'I knew him, knew him well, he was a great detective. Big shoes?' Cullen cast her eyes towards the door for a moment, a lifetime of watching, perhaps it never left you. 'But, Iris, remember he had to start out, too, and from what I hear, you're going to be every bit as good as him.' She smiled now. 'How can you not be sure, like father, like daughter, right?'

If her father had known Anita Cullen, he'd never mentioned her to Iris. Then again, who did her father not know in the guards? Iris lowered her eyes for a moment, attempting to hide the disappointment that there was someone else who'd judge her on her father's sterling reputation. When she spoke again, she plastered her *you got me, thought I had you fooled, but you got me* best smile across her face. 'Yep, he was a big man, as you say, very large shoes to fill.'

'You be sure and tell him I was asking for him, and your mother, too, won't you.' Cullen sipped her coffee, and Iris was certain that she was drifting back in time, to conversations with the great Jack Locke, rather than being here with the slightly less enigmatic daughter. And wasn't this half the problem – her half at least. The footprints set before her here in Corbally, in Limerick city, maybe even in the southern region, seemed far too immense to fill. If her father had been just a bit like Slattery, she might have had some hope, but he was so bloody perfect, she hadn't really a chance in Limerick.

'And Grady?' Cullen moved in closer, smiling across her coffee. 'He has a bit of a reputation for the ladies, or so I hear.'

'Has he?' No doubt, he was attractive, in a brooding kind of way – but Locke figured you could put that down to the sense of power he had about him. There was a strength there that Locke hadn't really seen in any man she'd ever met before. She suspected, though, that if they clashed – which they'd come very close to today – well, there'd be a few casualties as a result of it. 'I honestly can't say I noticed.' The lies really did just fly off the tongue after a while.

'Ah well, just be careful, that's all I'd say to you.'

'Well, he's safe enough around me, that's for sure.' Iris sipped her coffee, and then she told Anita Cullen about her conversation earlier with Grady. Cullen nodded agreeably while she spoke and in the end, when she left down her cup, somehow Iris felt much better.

'Bit of advice to you, Iris.' Cullen leaned closer to her. 'Learn from him; he knows what he's about, eat the bit of humble pie, prove yourself. You could go a long way, provided you don't decide you need love, or babies or any kind of life outside of the guards. Up to you, my dear, but if you haven't set your mind on anything yet, my best advice is, keep your options open.' She winked across at Iris and leaned still further into the table. 'All of your options, that is.'

CHAPTER 14

The station had been inundated with crank callers since the media appeal – it was par for the course, but that didn't make it any more endurable. The crazies set everyone on edge and Slattery knew that it only added to the tension he was already feeling piling in on him between Maureen and Angela, the arrival of Anita Cullen and dealing with a team that were for a large part wet behind the ears on a murder investigation.

He dug in close to his desk now, crouched over a chipped mug half filled with strong tea. This morning, even being here felt like it might be enough to push him over. Most of his colleagues were savvy enough to give him a wide berth and the only people who came near him were either stupid or brave enough to know his bark was ten times worse than his bite. He had spent almost half an hour studying the grey street traffic below the window that ran alongside his desk. Today, he noticed the years of ingrained dust, thinking idly that Maureen would love to be let loose on those frames for just a few hours – there was no doubt in his mind that his wife got as much satisfaction out of scrubbing a thing clean as he did out of a long cold pint of Guinness.

A weary sigh pulled his attention back to the incident room where Iris Locke was standing with her mobile stuck to her ear. All dressed up and nowhere to go – that's what his father would have said years ago to Una. Today, Locke was being sent off with Westmont to talk to Darach Boran again – Slattery figured you didn't need a fancy suit and shoes to get answers from scum like

Boran, all you needed was fat fists and a menacing glare. From the sounds of him, Boran was used to taking charge of women. Slattery smiled then, realising what Grady had maybe spotted immediately. Iris Locke was not a woman to be buffed about the place – good luck to Darach Boran with that one.

'What?' she rounded on him now. 'What's so bloody funny?'

'Me?' he said with mock innocence, realising that he'd been grinning in her direction without noticing that she had hung up on the call that had been causing her such grief only moments earlier.

'I suppose you think it's madness too? Trying to track down files for Baby Fairley.' She stalked over to his desk, stood towering over him, and suddenly he was immersed in an overpowering aroma of heavy perfume that made him want to catch his breath and clear the fumes from his body.

'I never said that,' he said quietly.

'So…' She looked around the incident room, suddenly aware that they'd become a floor show. She smoothed her hair back from her forehead and dropped to the seat opposite him. 'Look,' she said quietly, 'look around you… this place, they're all just chasing shadows. Every time a phone rings it's another lunatic talking about aliens or gang members.' She put up her hand to stop him saying anything. 'We both know this wasn't gang-related, this was personal.'

'It seems to me it might be getting a bit too personal,' Slattery spat.

'What's that supposed to mean?'

'You being here, day and night, trying every way you can to track down what happened to that baby all those years ago when you know full well the one who can best answer that is your own father – he led out that investigation and he's not different to any of us now. He'll have more stored away about that case than you'll ever find on a case file, even if one has survived.' He grunted then, maybe he wasn't angry with Iris, probably he was just angry with the whole world, for the mess he'd made of it, for the sister he'd lost and for family that he'd as good as thrown away because the guilt of one seemed to filch the good of the other. 'The truth is, Iris, your father was one of the best detectives this station has ever seen, he was a good man and a brilliant superintendent and it's as plain as a rich tea biscuit that all you want to do is pass him out. Well, let me tell you something for nothing, solving that case from all those years ago isn't going to make you any better than him.'

'It's damn well not about that…' Her words were low and menacing. 'Am I the only bloody one here to feel there has to be connection between the two cases – seriously, Slattery, tell me now, how often do horrible coincidences happen in a murder case and they're not linked?'

'Well…' He hated to admit it, but she had a point. 'Maybe,' he settled on, because it wasn't giving in, but he had to admit it *was* a bloody big coincidence that one sister was stolen and the other was murdered. 'Here's a thought, though, rather than chasing about here trying to catch your tail – why not go straight for the horse's mouth? Why not just go and ask your father – if anything I'd say he'd enjoy reliving the glory days.'

'Hmph.' It was a strange noise at odds with her usual composure. 'If you must know, I already have…' She looked about the incident room gloomily. 'He says that there was no crime. Mrs Fairley had post-natal depression, even if they couldn't prove it… he's pretty sure she was the one to blame.'

'Jesus.' It was all Slattery could manage, but when he glanced back at Iris he knew that terrible and all as it was, she still wasn't convinced. He moved forward turning his back on the window outside. 'Listen to me now, think about this, can you really see someone coming back after all this time to finish off the sister? Even if that baby was stolen, whoever took her would be lying as low as they possibly could for the rest of their lives. The last thing they'd want is any kind of comeuppance with the law – don't you think?'

'I know, that all makes sense, even my father's explanation makes a lot of sense, but I can't shake the feeling that somehow that baby has something to do with all of this... it's not even something I can put into words.' She shook her head now, smiled with a wry sort of movement to her lips and Slattery wondered if maybe – beyond all that gloss and the obvious ambition – she might be half all right to work with, given a chance.

'Yeah, well be careful not to get too hung up on it, you know cases like that... they can haunt you, if you let them. In here,' he nodded towards the incident room behind her, 'you have to keep moving, don't let it get personal because as soon as you do...'

'What, I become like you?' She inclined her head slightly, it wasn't said in a mean way. 'I think that's one of your few redeeming features, by the way, the fact that you *do* take it all personally.' She cocked her head then, and stalked away from him before he could answer.

*

Slattery decided to start at the beginning. It was actually easier to track than he'd imagined and if he'd given it too much thought, he might just have wondered why no one had thought to do it before.

'What can I take?' he asked Billy Henry, a cadaver waiting to happen, some might say a mirror image of himself, only blond-grey hair and arthritis problems instead of gut ones. He'd long since taken to a desk job and most people felt that the streets of Limerick were no less safe as result. Now he was in charge of every item in Corbally station. Everything from paper clips to vehicles. If you wanted it, Billy was the man to talk to.

'You still alive, Slattery?' It had been a while since Slattery had done any major amount of paper clipping.

'Yeah, I'm waiting for you to go first. Probably be the first thing you beat me at.'

'You're still hilarious, just a laugh a minute. Heard 'bout your missus, sorry 'bout that. Tough one.' It was as near as the likes of

Slattery or Henry would ever get to displaying a sensitive side – rumour had it, though, Big Billy cried like a baby at the smell of gin. Gin just sickened Slattery, but there you go – it was a woman's drink anyway. No man, unless he was a right old ponce, should go near it, in Slattery's opinion.

'Yeah. Tough one.' He nodded towards the lot. Not much choice out there. 'I'll take the blue one.' It was an older model Ford, small, not too obvious, just perfect.

'Is what I hear right?'

'What's that?'

'Anita Cullen is up there lordin' it?' He raised loosened eyes to heaven that threatened to roll completely round in his sockets, so watery were they against his lax skin.

'Aye.' Slattery didn't have time for small talk. 'Old girlfriend of yours, was she?'

'Are you all right? She nearly got me kicked out back in the day. Long time ago now, but I'd say she's same as ever.' He looked around him, as though invisible ears might collar his next few words. 'Rumour has it she's looking to catch you out, Slattery, better watch yourself. That one, she's a hairy bit of work on a bicycle, take it from me. You watch yourself up there now.'

Slattery grabbed the key from the hook. Yeah. Yeah. Who had the time to listen to this old lady talk? He managed something almost affable as he slammed the door behind him.

*

In Slattery's experience, every town, village or street had one. It was a matter of finding that one person who knew what needed to be known among all the other reams of useless information that an investigation picked up. Often, too, it took little more than a sympathetic ear and knocking on the right door at the right moment. Of course, it also took knowing which questions to ask.

'A nosey old cow,' was how Veronique had described Bridgie Brennan under her breath as she'd shown Slattery to the door. And for as much as he might outwardly be pinning the deaths of Anna Crowe and her two kids on her husband, the only thing that niggled him was that missing baby. Maybe, even if they got a full confession from the bloke that wouldn't be enough for Slattery. That was just how it was with him. So he left the station and headed back towards Kilgee.

Mrs Brennan's house had what Maureen would have called *notions of grandeur*, way beyond its entitlement. A small bungalow, it sat nestled amidst a garden of privet, yew and trumpeter roses that had seen better days. It was, Slattery considered, surprisingly private for one whom he assumed took a great interest in the comings and goings of the village around her. She showed him into what he supposed was the *good* room, the smell of damp marked it as one not often used, and when she produced china cups and saucers he knew he was getting best.

'Of course, *he – Fairley himself* – worked on the lighthouse. He'd be gone for weeks at a time, that's the way they worked it. Come back then and do what had to be done, gone again. Some women, I suppose, are able for that.' She left her cup down on the sideboard to her left. It was heavy oak, old and waxed fervently over the years.

'And was she, was Mrs Fairley… able for it, do you think?' There was a selection of biscuits at his elbow; obviously Mrs Brennan thought a big fella like him needed feeding.

'No,' Bridgie Brennan said quietly. 'No, I'm afraid she was not. She was a delicate woman, never had much to say for herself. We all wondered at the time what he'd seen in her, to be honest. No doubt she was a beauty, in her way, but to the rest of us, it didn't look like there was a lot more to her. The daughter, Anna, she looked a little like her, except the hair, of course, but sure that's young wans for you now, it's dark today, bright tomorrow.' She sipped her tea again, thoughtfully. 'I don't think any of us round here will ever forget that time. Your lot were very good, very... sensitive. I think we all knew, really.'

'What's that?'

'Well, I'm sure there's a record of it somewhere. Sure even the way they kept coming back, keeping an eye on her.' She leaned closer now, and Slattery could see in her eyes she was not a bitchy woman; if she liked gossip, she didn't take any pleasure in other people's misery. 'I'd say they knew it was her, from the first day. It was all too much for her, a young girl like that, with two small ones and no man about the place. We were wrong, too, we should have seen it. If she'd been here... in the village, well, who knows, it might have been different.'

'And they kept coming?'

'Oh aye, say what you want about social workers, but they never let a week go by, but they weren't knocking about the place. Up at the house, down at the school. *He* gave up the job after. I wouldn't think they ever had much of a life. Sure, in the end, I think they had to sign her in. How does a woman live with that? Drove her mad in the end – the guilt of it, probably.'

'But the baby was never found. You can't know for certain that she did kill it.' Slattery kept his voice low.

'No, the baby wasn't found, but sure, maybe there are currants for cakes and raisins for everything.' Bridgie Brennan joined her hands together.

'What do you mean?'

'Sure it was back in the days when the priests and the guards ran the country, Mr Slattery. I'd say even if they did find the child, they'd never have said. Sure what good would come of putting the poor creature away for the rest of her natural? No. No. They did the right thing; they left us all to get on with things, kept an eye on the child that lived and maybe hoped that someday we'd all forget Baby Fairley.'

'So where do you think the child was buried?'

'Like I said, Mr Slattery, it was between the priest and the guards.' Bridgie Brennan moved towards the teapot now, a lavish affair of flowers and gold leaf. 'You've hardly touched your tea.' She topped up his cup and he sat back into the cold velour of the cushions at his back.

'There were no winners there, so,' he said thoughtfully as he looked at the electric fire that gave an occasional rattle to let the room know it was labouring away.

'Aye, no winners, but the important thing for you is that there are no losers left about the place now.' She nodded at him and he knew she was right. The people who'd lost out in the Baby Fairley case were all gone now and Slattery had to wonder what that meant for the Anna Crowe investigation.

CHAPTER 15

'For the tape, Mr Darach Boran is being represented by Nathan Cosgrove, Senior Counsel, with particular expertise in murder trials,' Iris said loudly. She had read Boran his rights, clearly and slowly, enunciating every word so crisply that everyone knew the nuns had done themselves proud by her. Grady had chosen interview room number three, the least comfortable of the rooms available to them. Not that the others were all that much better, but this was by far the most cramped, with no window and no air conditioning to speak of. It wouldn't take long to draw sweat from a guilty man inside its putrid green walls.

'I don't think that has relevance or bearing on your current investigation.' Cosgrave was in, quick as a flash.

'Well, unfortunately, Mr Cosgrove, we can't strike it from the record here – it's not as easy to wipe our tapes clean as it is to make sure a smear of DNA doesn't see the light of day,' replied Grady.

Locke looked across at him. *What the hell,* her eyes silently screamed, *and they told me to tread softly?* Iris took a deep breath, reached for her water and looked across at Boran. He seemed much calmer now than he had been earlier, which was in itself unusual – Iris would have laid money on him shitting himself in the intervening days, thinking about this.

'So, we're here to ask you about Saturday the twelfth of October – can you account for your whereabouts between five and seven on the morning in question?' she asked.

Boran shifted in his seat, leaned forward, his breath sending a rasp of earlier inhaled stale tobacco across at Iris. When he smiled he bared even, yellowing teeth that probably hadn't truly smiled since childhood. 'Yes and no is the answer to that question.' Boran sat back then and began to examine his long fingernails. Iris couldn't help but notice they were very clean. Not the fingers she would imagine of an artist. She looked across at Nathan Cosgrove who nodded silently at him. 'I... and a group of some fifteen others, from the local Women's Institute travelled to Donegal on Friday the 11th. The plan was, with a bit of luck, we might catch the Aurora lights – they've been particularly visible over the last number of weeks – you may have heard.' He gave a withering look towards Grady. 'But then, perhaps not. Either way, we set off, early afternoon, about three, I'd say, left Limerick, headed for Donegal. Booked into a very nice hotel.' Cosgrave slid a single sheet of paper containing the hotel address across the table so it sat in the no man's land of the middle. 'We stayed there until the following day, returning home sometime after a light lunch in the bar of the hotel.'

'So these women, the WI ladies, they can account for your whereabouts right through?'

Boran looked once more at Cosgrove, who nodded much too sagely for Iris's liking. 'Well, they can tell you that we sketched and photographed the Aurora lights together. It's up to you to figure out how I might have managed to transport myself in the time frame it would have taken to make it halfway down the length of the country.' His expression turned to self-congratulatory. Iris knew, that for now, at least, they had nothing much else to ask Darach Boran.

After all that, it seemed they had nothing. His alibi would be checked, but of course, he wasn't stupid enough to give an account that wouldn't stand. For the first time since undercover, Iris needed a drink. The incident room was emptying when she texted Slattery.

*

Slattery was waiting when she arrived at the Ship Inn. He called drinks for them both. He looked like shit, but then, he did have more on his plate than any of them now.

'Things any better with your wife?' she asked, knocking back a measure of the whiskey she hadn't asked for, but Slattery had placed before her anyway. It almost winded her, but she was glad of it all the same. Suddenly she felt emptied out, perhaps it was just this case, it felt as if there was something personal about it; still it was road blocked.

'Same,' Slattery grunted into his pint, obviously not the reason for his newfound inner joy, then. 'I spent the afternoon out in Kilgee, met a very chatty woman called Mrs Brennan.' He was adept at changing the subject to suit himself. He smiled at Iris, a strange rearrangement of features that had long since set in bitterness. If his eyes were anything to go by, Iris reckoned he'd been in the Ship Inn for too long, getting well oiled-up.

'Oh?' She settled her fingers around a glass of larger that had arrived as soon as the whiskey shot glass was taken away. She wiped the damp from outside her glass, her moving fingers steady and deliberate.

'I think you're right, if it's any consolation,' he slurred.

'How's that?' Iris asked, leaning a little closer.

'Well, there's no such thing as a coincidence in a murder case.' He shook his head, looking up as June arrived beside them.

'Anita Cullen was asking for you today.' June slipped in the far side of Slattery.

'Well, be sure to tell her I said hi, with bells on, won't you?' Slattery sneered at June. Iris leant back; she didn't want to be in the way if these two exploded at each other. 'Ah, feck it,' he said then, moving off to the far end of the bar to wrap his mind around his worries.

'I'm sure it's an emotional time for him,' Iris said finishing off her drink.

'He doesn't give a flying donkey for Maureen, and we all know it. That's not natural, whatever you say, that's not natural at all.'

'Has he always been the same or is it just me?' Iris asked, not entirely sure she wanted to hear the answer.

'No, don't worry, he's been like a cactus as long as I've known him. They used to say he had a soft underbelly once, but I've never seen it myself,' June said staring at her glass of soft drink. 'The thing is, Iris, everyone in this job gets fucked up. Slattery can blame it on the drink or the sister he lost all those years ago…'

'The sister?'

'Oh, it's all ancient history now, but back when Slattery was hardly ready to finish school, his younger sister was found murdered in a flat here in Limerick. Someone told me once that Maureen found her body and after that, well, none of them were ever quite *right* again.'

'Maureen – his wife?'

'That's right, so then, they got married and I suppose something like that, shared between a couple… well, it's only going to fester, isn't it? Then Angela came along and apparently, she's the spit of her aunt Una with the spirit of her mother and Slattery just went off the rails; he's never quiet managed to get back on them again.'

'Christ.' Iris let out a long sigh. 'And I thought my life was complicated.' It was no secret in Corbally that Jack Locke's wife was delicate nor that she was a drinker and, now, it had to be fairly public knowledge that his daughter was doing her best to emulate her father rather than her mother. Freud would have a field day at their Christmas party if they joined up with the Slatterys.

'Anyway, I'm not making excuses for him, he's a prickly bastard, but he's a damn fine detective when he hasn't got his nose stuck in a pint.'

'Can't be easy, though, you know, with the accident and everything.'

'No.' June sighed, a long low sound that seemed to come from deep in her soul. 'No. But just so you know, it's not love that made a mess of him, it's guilt and not being able to forgive.' She sipped her drink.

'Forgive?'

'Maureen, Una – and probably himself most of all – he's eaten up with remorse and the only way he knows how to deal with it is to work and to drink.'

In the corner at the far side of the bar, a man who had been tuning up his guitar for what seemed like the whole night began to strum out some seventies' number that June had long forgotten and Iris never knew.

'Time for me to be getting back,' June said, looking at Iris's drink. 'You'd be better off leaving sooner rather than later too, you don't want to get stuck into this scene… it's…' She looked across at Slattery who was staring blindly into the drink before him.

'Yeah, you're probably right,' Iris said, taking up her coat. She looked along the bar counter at Slattery, feeling just a little sad at such a terrible story, she could almost feel his pain now. 'Still, I think I'll hang about a little while longer,' she said and walked over to Slattery, slinging her coat across the bar stool next to him and sitting beside him for the next half hour in almost complete silence. She was about to order them both another drink when she spotted Grady watching them from a group of detectives who had spent the evening standing around in a circle discussing the case in a quiet, increasingly drunken whisper. Instead, she knocked back the whiskey and headed for the cold night air.

Limerick, with the rain sheeting down and the river Shannon barrelling along its banks, is probably the most brutal city in Ireland. Even on a sunny day, there is a backdrop of history and it's visible no matter where you cast your eye. Tonight, Iris was struck by its beauty. King John's Castle, lit up in the distance, fired out of the blackness of night, it had stood overlooking that water for almost a thousand years. It had watched over clans and clashes, stood stout against invaders and warriors and, even now, Iris felt its sturdy presence, a levelling force that stood for no nonsense.

They would solve this case. They would find answers. But, she wondered as she admired the crouching walls, if it would be solved because of their efforts or in spite of them.

CHAPTER 16

'Grady, he's a piss head, you know it, I know it, and everyone knows it.' Anita Cullen was eyeballing him and if she was a good ten inches shorter than him, it certainly didn't feel like it at the moment.

'He's a good detective, Anita.'

'His wife is in ICU, and he's here, like nothing has happened. He's a bomb ready to blow, that's what he is.'

'They've been separated for years; it's not as straightforward as it seems. He's been to the hospital, spent the first day there, but he can't do anything for her, and he feels he's of more use here.'

'Yeah, I bet he does,' she said drily. Grady thought Cullen wasn't a naturally vindictive person, but she had her sights set on Slattery. If she scented even a hint of him stepping out of line, she'd be down on him so quick he'd be reeling afterwards. Already she'd made buddies out of most of the team, she knew too much about the connections that had taken years to build. Grady reckoned that by now, she knew who had slept with whose wife, and who knew about it. 'You just tell Slattery, I won't be made a fool out of. I'll be watching him, and now that he's getting the heads up, the consequences will be severe if he steps out of line.'

He needed to have a look-see at whatever Slattery *was* up to. In Grady's experience, it was never good when the old man went too quiet. He was up to something; he seemed on edge. A bit like Iris Locke; he sensed something was a bit off with her today as well. For a moment, he felt like he'd missed a step. He'd watched them as they'd sat together the previous evening in the Ship Inn. They really were an incongruous pairing. Idly, he wondered what they'd found to talk about. Probably the case – Anna, Martin and Sylvie Crowe and perhaps Adrian Crowe too. He wondered if they'd talked about the earlier Fairley case. He'd lay his last euro that missing baby lingered between them, even if she had no connection to the death of her sister. Slattery hated loose ends; Grady suspected Locke would be the same. The Fairley case was old news, an unsolved case that would remain open well after they all retired. You win some, you lose some. That child was dead and gone long ago, probably buried somewhere deep in the countryside, many miles away from where hundreds of people had searched for days and probably weeks after the disappearance.

Anita Cullen took a deep breath – onto other things. 'So, what's this about the victim's husband not being where he says he was?'

'The phone trace has thrown us this little nugget: he left the factory for over an hour. As far as the mobile is concerned he drove directly to his house and stayed there the whole time.'

'But…'

'Well, if he went home, he had to have a reason, so why not tell us…'

'Fear he might lose his job?'

'Maybe, but this is a murder investigation, he's not a stupid man, he has to know that we'll be looking at him as a suspect. Why lie, if there's nothing to hide?'

'Why bring the phone at all?'

'Maybe it was a mistake, maybe he hadn't meant to.' Grady looked out the window now. Cullen's office had a view upriver towards King John's castle. 'Perhaps he wasn't going to kill her, frighten her just, try and get her to leave the cottage and come home?'

'Costly mistake,' Cullen said, checking the near-empty coffee cup before her. 'There was nothing at the house, no smell of petrol, nothing at all when you visited there on the day.'

'Not a thing and it's the kind of thing you'd notice, right?'

'So, somewhere along the way, he'd have to have a shower, change his clothes, yeah?'

'We had a look through the house on the morning, didn't see any clothes. We went through the place from the attic down to the bins, if there was anything dumped we'd have it by now.'

'Okay, so you'll have to look at the factory.'

'There's no way he had a shower there. Slattery got the grand tour when he went out that first day. The showers are used for storage, and they haven't been used properly in years. No, I say we get the forensic boys out to the house, let them take apart the drains if they have to. He'll have dumped the clothes in someone's wheelie bin along the way, they're well gone now.' Adrian Crowe was smart, if he killed his wife, he'd have all the bases covered, but Grady knew that wasn't always enough. One scrap of rogue DNA, that was all it took and he'd haul Crowe in and throw as much at him as he could to get a confession from him.

'Right, call out the forensic boys, and Grady, get those phone records traced right back. Get someone to cross reference where he was every night he was on shift, right back to when Anna Crowe moved out to that cottage.'

'Sure,' Grady said, halting for just a moment. 'I'd like to search his house too…'

'Right, right… well, you know what to do,' Cullen barked.

*

'We have a warrant, I've divided the team into two.' Grady was standing in the centre of the incident room. It had taken just over a day to convince a judge to sign an order so they could pull apart every fibre of their suspect's existence. It could take two more days to examine every crack and crevice of the Crowe family home and ABA Technics just to try and find one small chink that might open up the case.

The news of a warrant injected a new wave of optimism into the team, as if somehow they were about to take a giant stride forward and that belief was sometimes as much as any team needed to break a case. Grady shuffled his papers back into a neat pile and Iris knew he felt her watching him. He turned towards her desk wordlessly.

'I don't think Crowe is our killer.' Iris spoke softly, but when Grady looked at her, she knew he was listening, interested in what she had to say this time. Somehow, she couldn't put into words how she knew that their killer was still out there and he might just strike again.

'Why's that?' Grady asked.

'I don't know, something doesn't quite seem right about him, I can see that, but I don't think he killed his wife and children.'

'Is iad na muca ciúine a itheann an mhin,' Grady muttered beneath his breath. Iris recognised the words. *Always the quiet ones.*

She tilted her head sideways gathering her hair to let it fall down her back. It was something between a nod and a stretch.

'Sure there's nothing else?' He probably asked the question more out of routine than any sense she might share her thoughts with him. Perhaps he figured she was getting a taste of what it was to hold people's lives in your hands. If they charged the wrong man, more than just Anna, Martin and Sylvie Crowe would have lost out.

'No, why would there be? It's just a feeling, that's all.'

'Sometimes,' Grady's voice was gentle and low and when he leaned towards her she caught the light scent of his aftershave, musky and male, 'sometimes, Locke, things are too difficult to see. No one wants to believe that he could kill his own kids, the wife he married all those years ago. We've seen the photos. It's inconceivable, but it does happen.'

CHAPTER 17

A chill wind was beginning to blow north, up the Shannon, sweeping past King John's castle, winding its way through the narrow side streets of Limerick and finally funnelling great gasps along the main thoroughfares. He'd known the weather would change; it was time for winter. He could feel it setting in around him, no bad thing. He liked the darkness, craved it like a friend, long lost, little valued by most. For him it was a time of abundance. His prey came out – foxes, badgers, owls. He'd trapped for years, made a few bob on it too. Supplemented the social welfare nicely, wouldn't want to lose that now. The animals were a select market. He had a pal, up in Liscannor, did a little taxidermy for him. He asked him once if he did crows, he didn't catch the joke.

He pulled the collar of his army jacket closer, there wasn't a lot of heat in it, but it was a barrier to wind and rain, and really he needed nothing more. He'd wait here for hours if he needed to. He knew that. He'd once spent four days after a stag. Twenty points. They said he wasn't real and it had taken all his wits to shoot the animal. Quite a feat, he reminded himself now – the beasts had been in the country for over ten thousand years, perhaps from the end of the ice age, for all anyone knew. He'd lain in mud, eaten grass and worms, pissed himself and all the time waited.

Once or twice now, he caught the eye of a guard, coming or going from Corbally station, but they wouldn't really take any notice of him. If anything registered, he looked like little more than a street bum, getting over his methadone fix from the clinic down the road. Guards'd see plenty of them round here, he figured.

It didn't take long. In the end, she walked through the doors after little over an hour. Some red-haired youngster keeping up with her. She was all elegant hair and expensive clothes, but beneath all that sophistication – he could smell it. He could smell her, as if she was an animal, waiting to be tracked. He whistled a low, toneless tune between his yellow teeth. He ran a coarse hand through his rough beard and began walking behind his prey. Some two hundred yards down the road, they turned left, then left again. He knew they were headed towards the car park at the rear of the old station. There was no point following further for now. He could wait, it wouldn't take forever. He was very good at waiting.

*

Veronique Majewski straightened her jacket around her. She had managed to get a lift to the village; it was benefits day and she felt like splurging. She passed by the convenience store where she normally stocked up on cheap spirits and headed instead for the pharmacy. She parted happily with twenty euro for new make-up and nail varnish. She had plans. Big Plans.

Finally, she'd managed to make contact with her mark. A few days earlier he wasn't interested in what she had to say, at first, but then, the more she persisted, drip feeding him what she knew, the more she could feel she was reeling him in. She walked from the pharmacy, her cheap shoes making a tic-tac noise on the pavement in the empty street. Soon, she would be leaving here, not to return to her old life, but instead to start somewhere new, somewhere better than this godforsaken dump.

Now that she had dangled the carrot she knew she had found her prey. Maybe he *had* killed Anna Crowe and her family, Veronique didn't know for sure, but she knew enough to know he would pay to keep her quiet.

He had agreed easily to five thousand euro. Later today, she would tell him what else she wanted. She was careful, not letting him know where she lived or how she knew. She wouldn't take any chances. Living on the streets had taught her to be wary, to protect herself as far as she could. No. She would tell him what she wanted and she would meet him in the village, in that little coffee shop that always seemed to be closed before. Funny, but what is it they say, every cloud has a silver lining. Veronique smiled. She was not the only person in Kilgee benefiting from the death of Anna Crowe. The coffee shop had never done such a roaring trade before the tragedy. Anna Crowe and her murderer had put the village on the map, it seemed.

Yes, she would call the man today. She would set a time that suited her, a time when she could walk out of that coffee shop and straight onto a bus headed for Dublin. She walked across to the dreary bus stop. It was little more than a green pole, leaning skewed where someone had reversed into it and, obviously, Kilgee did not figure highly enough to straighten it out again. On its side, a peeling notice told her that the next bus to Dublin was in three days' time. She crossed back to the phone kiosk.

'Hello,' he answered immediately, as if he was waiting for her to contact him.

'Yes, it is me, have you organised the money?'

'I have,' he said and she caught something in his voice, perhaps it was a smile, perhaps he was glad to think that she would be paid off with this small sum of money.

'Fine, I will meet you.' She looked back over her shoulder, to the left of the phone box, an expensive car was parked facing the opposite direction, its windows blacked out, something about it made her shiver. 'In Kilgee, in the coffee shop.'

'Shall we say the day after tomorrow?' he supplied smoothly.

'No. The next day is better, say three o'clock,' she said crossly. She hung up the phone quickly.

She could wait. She'd had enough of this place, there was nothing to be gained from waiting about any longer, but she had to be practical.

She turned on her heels then, headed towards the village shop. She would buy enough vodka to last her the next few days and then she would leave this place behind and never look back.

Veronique crossed the road, hardly noticing the heavy car that had crawled away from the phone box and parked just at the end of the village. It passed her later, slowly as she turned up the narrow track that brought her to Ollie's cottage. She cursed as its wide tyres threw up mud on her faded jeans. Still, she didn't notice the eyes that took in everything about her quickly in the rear-view mirror as the car sped off into the distance.

CHAPTER 18

Iris shivered. The cold feeling that had overtaken her in Kilgee was still chewing laconically on her bones and she knew that there was no coat warm enough to cover the chill. She would be glad when this day had closed in on her and she could convince herself that they were moving nearer to some real answers.

Alan Gains's office had all the trappings of fading wealth, a Victorian three storey, tastefully converted. In the outer reception rooms the furniture was antique and polished to a shine, the rugs were old, but still sumptuous. The receptionist was young and quietly glamorous. When Locke looked around, she figured the cleaner probably didn't call as often as she once had, perhaps the heating was a little lower and the waiting room less packed. Maybe the admin staff spent more time now searching through accounts for bills that might yet be paid and less lodging documents with the Department of Land Registry. Sign of the times – people remembered the recession, if you were lucky enough to survive in business, austerity still seemed like the wiser path. The man himself showed similar tell-tale signs of the learning curve of property crash and looming Brexit. His suit had been expensive a decade earlier, but now it looked crumpled and worn. His hand was steady though and when he spoke, he searched her face constantly with his own owl-like brown eyes, magnified by glasses that needed wiping. Alan Gains's eyes were intelligent and arresting, and probably his best feature. They sat in an oily face with a flat nose and mouth – too many years of expensive restaurant food and not enough exercise had wrecked his shape, so there'd be no going back.

'Are you any nearer to finding out who did this?' he asked when Locke and McGonagle were sitting with coffee in his well-appointed office. Last time round, Iris reckoned he was well shook and upset by the whole business. He was composed today, though, so that, to Iris's mind at least, gave less reason to suspect a guilty conscience.

'We're following a number of lines of enquiry at the moment.' Iris kept it brief.

'Well, it wasn't anyone who knew her anyway, that's for certain.' He blew out a resigned sigh.

'I'm afraid we don't know that yet,' McGonagle admitted quietly.

'Well, in that case, what can I do for you?' He joined his hands prayer-like across his desk, looked down as though inspecting them for a moment. It seemed to Iris that he was lost in thought. The coffee had been placed on a table to the side, but no one made a move towards it yet.

'Funny, isn't it?' Gains said. 'I've made a living, a good living, for the most part out of the law, and yet, when it comes to something like this, after all this time, it seems useless.' He closed his eyes for a moment. 'None of this,' he spread his arms out, a net catching the trappings he'd worked so astutely for, 'none of this, not the district court, or the high court, will bring them back. We'll have answers, but what good are they to you in the end?' He looked across at Locke.

'We're really sorry for your loss, Mr Gains.' Iris heard the words slip from her tongue, hoped that they didn't sound pithy, they weren't meant to be. She could see that Anna Crowe's death and the death of her children had deeply affected this man. Could be for any number of reasons, but chief amongst them was the fact that there had been a relationship there. Perhaps it was just friendship, mixed with a little business, but nonetheless, it had been enduring, more enduring than her marriage. 'How sad,' she'd said the words aloud, hadn't meant to. Gains bowed his head, a quiet agreement.

'Anyway, you didn't come here to grief counsel me, right?' Gains made his way across to the coffee pot. 'What is it that you want to know about Anna?' He poured three cups of steaming coffee, sat behind his desk and smiled an even-toothed smile across at them.

'We're interested in anything you can tell us.' Iris sipped her coffee. 'You dated her briefly, when you were younger I believe.'

'Oh that, that's old news, I'm afraid. There weren't that many kids in the parish. If you didn't end up dating someone in your class…'

'And then things changed?'

'Well, yeah, don't they always? Adrian headed off for the army. A year later it was our turn. By the time we were heading to college, we'd both set our sights on a big world beyond Kilgee. Anna dreamed of being an artist, living the bohemian life in Paris or what have you. I thought I'd be walking straight into a John Grisham movie, all good deeds and massive pay-outs.' He laughed now. 'I ended up specialising in tort law and I've made most of my money out of the property boom.' His voice was hollow, a decade, if not wasted, perhaps not taken for all it was worth.

'So how did Anna and Adrian end up…?'

'You'd have to ask him that. We'd kept in touch the whole way through, me and Anna. I suppose for a long time, I thought she was the one I'd marry, just never quite yet. Then she up and married Crowe and that was that. One of those things, I'd say. They weren't five minutes married when young Martin was on the way…' He held his palms up. 'When she told me they were getting married, I don't know, I felt she was marrying the wrong man, it was all so fast in the end.' Gains was quiet now.

'You lost someone very special,' Iris said.

'We all did.' Gains sipped his cooling coffee and looked across at the large oil painting that hung opposite his desk.

'The separation…' Locke leaned forward in her chair slightly. 'There seems to be no reason that we can find.'

'I'm not the right one to ask on that score, I'm afraid. We kept our marriages out of most conversations, kept it civil; she'd tell me about Martin and Sylvie. I'd tell her about my girls.' He nodded towards a framed photo of two small girls, pink cherubs with massive curly heads of white blonde hair and pretty strawberry mouths. 'Like their mother, thankfully.'

'Is it possible that Adrian Crowe might have been having an affair and Anna found out about it?' Locke queried gently. She watched as Alan Gains's face moved from surprise to pensive and then to something she thought might be close to resignation.

'Adrian? I wouldn't have thought so, but,' he spoke slowly, sadly, waited a moment, 'then, isn't anything possible?' he asked, as though they might be able to answer the unthinkable.

*

It took less than two hours to get the search organised. A record, of sorts, but Slattery knew it was a combination of the high-profile nature of the case and the amount of clout that Anita Cullen pulled when she wanted something badly enough. They would have preferred if it was the strength of the case that had swung it so quickly, but then this was Ireland and still cronyism and cover-up went much further than fact or truth. The forensic boys took another hour to get organised. Slattery and Locke reviewed the case book, while they waited, as Grady had directed.

Slattery knew the case book would be meticulous, like Blake himself – a small, neat, fastidious man. In all the years, Slattery had never met his wife, didn't know where he lived, and didn't know much about him beyond the fact that he brought his own skimmed milk to the station for his daily cuppa. If he was to guess, though, he'd say Blake had a wife and two point three children. He probably drove a Toyota and mowed his lawn each Saturday morning – waiting until the neighbours had opened their curtains before setting off the engine. Blake stood nearby while they read, occasionally drawing his glasses further up his nose, even though Slattery couldn't see how he could possibly raise them any more, sporadically grunting and nodding where he felt he'd got something spectacularly correct.

The forensic boys – or the techies as some of the newer detectives referred to them – worked the entire mid-region. Their area sprawled as far as the Murder Team's and then a whole lot further. Everything from burglaries to murders, it was the same deal: fingerprints and fibres, basically picking up anything that was out of place. They would work from the top to the bottom of the house, taking apart doors and windows if they had to.

If Adrian Crowe had been shell-shocked before this, he looked downright scared when Slattery and Locke arrived, produced the search warrant and explained why two large Gardaí vans had pulled up outside his house. The forensic boys were less like beagles on a trail and more like sniffing mice, taking over each corner, seeing cracks where they had been missed before.

'How long will this take?' Crowe asked as he stood in his neat kitchen that had suddenly become cramped.

'I'm afraid, it'll take as long as it takes.' Slattery's attempt at civility was limited. He would not leave Crowe's side while the search was in progress. If Crowe left the house, walked beyond the garden, Slattery knew that he'd be searching with the rest of the team. 'It might quicken things up a bit if we had anything to go on from you.'

'How do you mean?' Crowe looked at him now, calculating.

'I mean, the night your wife died, if there was anything you felt you might like to share with us…'

'I've told you everything you need to know. I'm not the heartless bastard that murdered my own kids, if that's what ye think you're going to find here.'

'I sincerely hope you're not.' Slattery turned from him and walked towards the window. 'It's a fine house, this…' He looked back at Crowe, baiting him. 'Very neat.'

'I'm a neat person,' Crowe said evenly.

'Yes, everything in its place and a place for everything. Isn't that what they say?'

Still Crowe stood silently, listening to the scratching, sounds of his home being systematically ripped apart one square centimetre at a time. Overhead, occasionally a floorboard would creak and Slattery knew that someone had leaned back, taking a look from a different angle at something. There would be no big steps; it was all nudging, slow, measured movements. In the attic, two officers called Wolver and Kennedy were working their way through the top of the house. They'd pull up insulation and take out water pipes before they had finished. It must be, Slattery had often thought, like having legal burglars, people tearing up your house and sanctioned by the state to do so, hardly taking anything, but the information of how you lived your daily life in the fabric of that most hallowed of sanctums – your home.

'Why did your marriage break up?' Iris asked the words low and deliberate. She had materialised from the hall, but Slattery had been aware of her, ghosting about. Her tone was soft now, not wanting to dig the wound deeper, but knowing that for Anna Crowe, they had to ask all the same.

'It had nothing to do with this.'

'How can you be so sure? Perhaps she'd met someone else, maybe… she just wanted to get away from you to be with… she was a beautiful woman.'

'She was a beautiful woman; if only I'd seen just how beautiful at the time,' Crowe murmured to himself, a regret-filled whisper that meant nothing now to Anna Crowe. 'But she wasn't like that; she'd never have done that to me…'

'It never ceases to amaze me what people are capable of, Mr Crowe.' As Slattery said the words he watched the other man. In a moment he'd turned and grabbed his jacket from a hook beneath the stairs. The noises continuing upstairs, broken only by the occasional sound of a camera flicker across something that he'd overlooked, were a low drawl now, a background chorus of busy intruders who would not leave until they'd examined every fibre of this house.

'I'm going out; you can lock the door when you leave.'

'We'll be a few hours, at least.' Slattery didn't add, *that's if you're unlucky*; if they didn't find anything, Grady would keep the team going, checking and rechecking, until they had something more than they had now. Even if Anita Cullen hadn't said it, plenty of strings had been pulled to get them in here, Slattery knew, they couldn't leave without something to show for it.

CHAPTER 19

'So the dead have arisen and now they walk?' Maureen Slattery sat up in her bed, fixing her husband with a look that said she hadn't expected to see him any time soon. He took it as a good sign that she was back to her old self – nagging him.

'That's a nice welcome for your husband.'

'Not so flipping loud; I'm hoping they'll take me for a widow. I'm sure Angela's hoping the same thing.' Her voice was heavy, but her eyes smiled, probably just relieved to be alive. Slattery sat awkwardly in the chair opposite her, pulling his anorak close in around him, and leaning forward to grab a chocolate he knew she couldn't eat. 'They'll kill you too,' she said.

'Not as fast as they'll kill you, my sweet.' Slattery looked at her. It was a bloody vicious God that declared she should develop diabetes while he could throw just about anything into his belly with no greater penalty than an occasional bout of heartburn. Aye, someone up there had a sick sense of humour all right. Still, Maureen Slattery went to mass seven days a week, kept her rosary beside her bed and would remain married to him until the day she met her maker with a fixed scowl on her face. The expression of martyrdom suited her best, he'd always thought. Well, a broken arm, neck braces and a bit of internal bleeding would give her plenty of praying time.

'What have you been up to?' she asked him now, her eyes narrowing, to glimpse his soul perhaps, although she should know by now it had rotted years ago.

'Big case.' He grabbed another chocolate, to keep his mind off having a fag. 'Fire out in Kilgee, a woman and her two kiddies.' He kept his voice low, it never did her any good to hear about his work.

'That's not good,' she said, looking down into her hands; then she brightened. 'I met your boss today.' She nodded towards an expensive-looking arrangement of white roses. 'Anita Cullen, she seems very nice, very nice indeed.'

'Oh, she just popped in, did she?' Slattery could hear the words journey from his lips, a remote sensation as if they'd been spoken by someone else. What in hell was Anita Cullen doing visiting Maureen, and what the fuck had they talked about?

'Aye, popped in with those and the sweets.'

Slattery thought he'd choke.

'Wondering where you were, actually. I got the impression she thought you might be here.'

'Well, sure…' He tried to look as though he couldn't give a toss, but damn it he had to know. 'What did you say to her?'

'I didn't say anything at all. Angela though, Angela said you'd just popped home for a shower – honestly, she gets that from you.' She looked at him now, irritated. 'The lying – not from my side anyway, even if we're responsible for the flat feet.'

'That's grand so,' he said. He'd finished with the chocolates. 'Anyone else in to see you?' He wasn't really interested, but at least it gave them something to talk about for a few moments. While she prattled on, he could lose himself in thoughts of the case.

'And you know what I'd like…' She was still talking; it seemed to him she must have been talking for hours, but when he looked at his watch, hardly five minutes had passed. How had they stayed married for so long? How had they managed to give birth to a daughter and remain under the same roof for over twenty years? He wondered now as he looked at her. Not so much that he disliked her, it wasn't that. He didn't love her either, mind, but rather they had nothing of interest to say to each other. Had they ever? His sister Una had brought them together, but that subject was closed now, Maureen never mentioned her any more and Slattery stopped asking. 'You're not listening to me, Ben Slattery…'

'What would you like?' A lifetime of keeping one ear open still paid off.

'I said, I'd like you to find out who it was that made mincemeat out of me little car – not to mention what they did to me neck – I'll be paying the price of that long after they've taken the plaster off, let me tell you, won't do me arthritis a lot of good either.'

'I'm sure Traffic are well onto it now, Maureen,' he said automatically, then sighed a long sigh; he'd have to tell her. He looked at her now, for the first time really, probably in years. She was getting old. His wife was getting old, and so what exactly did that say about him? He knew when he looked at her that someone should have told her by now. Someone should have told her she was lucky to be here, luckier than Peter Hynes at any rate.

'What is it, Ben?' she asked, her voice a low quiver.

He moved closer to her, all else forgotten. He had to tell her. He just didn't quite know how. He'd been giving people bad news for thirty years, always gave it straight, kinder that way, he reckoned, no point meting it out. But here he was, staring into the eyes of a stranger, and still the closest person in the world to him, and he didn't know what to say.

'I'm sorry, Maureen, but…' He watched as tears began to drop, fast and silent. He didn't need to say any more. Maybe she already knew and that, for so many reasons, made things a hundred times worse for her and so many more times worse for Slattery.

He stayed for – he didn't know how long after that. They didn't even hold hands. It wasn't what they did. Instead, she just cried. Great big whale breaths overtaking her body, it seemed like oceans of salty tears had flowed from her innocent blue eyes. And Slattery said nothing. There was nothing to say; they knew the score already.

'Suppose I'd better be off...' In the end, he shuffled uncomfortably in his seat, his square hands and large gut out of proportion with his skinny legs and arms.

'About time too...' she huffed at him, her eyes still red and tired.

He knew better than to lean in to kiss or embrace her in any way – at this stage it would be like hugging Westmont. Still, there was history; truth was, this woman, for all her gruffness was his next of kin. She was probably the only one who'd give a shit for him some day. Maybe the only one to give a damn for him today. Slattery tried not to think about that for too long. 'I'm glad you're... y'know,' he said awkwardly, not managing to meet her eyes, not managing to say the words he knew should be said.

'I know you are, Ben. I know you are,' she said quietly, and he knew she couldn't hold his eye either. They were some pair, no doubt about that, but at least they were a pair and it was more than some had at this stage.

He caught up with the doctor in a corridor, called her aside, *Just a sec, nothing to worry about. Not unusual to have concussion. Forgetting things? We'll run some tests.* And that was that. He could walk away from this. Couldn't he? He made his way to the car, all sorts of outcomes racing through his head. He knew that if he went back to Corbally station, next up was a team meeting. Well, he wasn't going in for that. A few more minutes here and he was off, down the Westward Ho for a swift one, then to the Ship Inn for closing time, hopefully there'd be no bloody guards there tonight.

CHAPTER 20

'All right, the sooner we get this over, the sooner ye're all out of here…' Cullen beat a notebook off a table. It let out a hard slapping sound that managed to quell the sea of deep voices filling up the incident room. Grady took in who was there. Noticed immediately Slattery was absent. That was the problem with having the same desk for a decade; everyone automatically knew where to find you – if you cared to turn up. Not that Grady would have minded Slattery taking time off, for Maureen. The truth was, he'd have applied for the leave for the old bugger himself, but there was no point. Slattery wouldn't miss an investigation unless he happened to be dead – even dying probably wouldn't keep him away. Grady looked across at Cullen. She was a woman who wanted out of here sooner rather than later this evening. She nodded at him to start.

'Grand.' He grabbed a legal pad, made his way to the front of the room and perched on a table, loosening his tie at the same time. 'Well, some of you have spent a good part of the day round at Crowe's house…'

'And?' Anita Cullen already knew the answer to this question, she'd known it since he'd decided to call it a day and sent the forensic boys home.

'There was nothing there. Fibres and hairs probably belonging to the victim, as you'd expect since she lived there for ten years, but nothing to point any fingers at Adrian Crowe. We checked everything, drainpipes, between floorboards, the lot. If he set that fire, he didn't return home to shower and change.' Grady felt his forehead pound. He had the start of a bad migraine on its way to whittle whatever bit of sleep he'd been hoping for between tossing the case around in his head into the early morning. He'd go for some fresh air, soon as this briefing was over. Clear his head; it was breezy outside, the odd shower, real soft weather.

'Well, he mightn't have, but our man wasn't what you'd call surprised when we suggested a possible affair.' Iris pushed her impossibly shiny copper hair away from her eyes. 'Alan Gains has remained friends with Anna Crowe since they were kids, probably the closest she had to someone decent in her life and he hardly batted an eye when I mentioned it.' She looked across at McGonagle who nodded enthusiastically at her, a golden retriever, eager to please.

'And we still have Darach Boran – have we ruled him out completely yet?' Cullen looked across at Grady.

'Well, he has an alibi, but he's as dodgy as a two-legged stool down in the Ship Inn. June?'

'I had a chat to a couple of the ladies in his art group; they're all vouching for him. Trouble is, none of them saw him after twelve and he didn't surface the following day until late. No one can say they had breakfast with him; no one can say there was any sign of him before midday. I'd say, if they could at all, they'd be lining up to give him an alibi. Whatever his charm, he seems to have won all the WI women over.' June looked down at her notes, pulled a yellow sheet from somewhere midway down through one of the many piles. 'I ran the times, just did a check with Traffic. He'd have made it down if he was fond of the throttle, wouldn't even have to pass a camera, apart from here.' She held up the sheet pointing to a stretch of road just north of Galway city. 'As it turns out, though, that particular camera has been off for a couple of days. Traffic are replacing it now we've let them know.' June threw her eyes up to heaven; *sometimes even when you have a dog you still have to sit out in the garden and do the barking, it seemed.*

'So he's a very real possibility.' Cullen began to brighten.

'Well, yes, but he'd have to have been travelling like the clappers all the way down and back up again – the chances of him making it without either killing himself or getting pulled in at some point are so slim – well, it'd be just freaky, right?' Grady looked around the room. The only one nodding agreement with him was Westmont and that wasn't a good sign, since he was the thickest guard in the building. Grady didn't like Boran, but he didn't figure him for this either. But then, the murder of Anna Crowe and her kids was so senseless could he figure anyone for it?

'Where's Slattery tonight?' Anita Cullen thrust her stubby finger towards Slattery's untidy desk.

'He's down the hospital with Maureen.' June had the words out before Grady had a chance to think. She was a true blue, no doubt about that, but she'd make Slattery pay for the fib in the long run.

'Well, that's something I suppose.' Cullen looked around the room again. Her eyes settled on McGonagle, and then out of the blue, 'What was Slattery working on today?'

'He was out at Crowe's, with me,' Iris said quickly.

'I see.' Cullen's words were soft and final and they managed to send a quiver of fear through Grady like he hadn't felt for many years, not since he'd managed to rise above the rank of sergeant and that seemed like a very long time ago.

*

Maureen's house was a lot cleaner than when Slattery lived there; gone was the smell of stale fags and the lingering odour of booze left behind after a few hours' kip. He suspected the frying pan was less often used too. Maureen was a martyr to her bowels, so there was more yoghurt than bacon in the fridge. Angela had rung after six; she'd never asked him for anything much out of life. Probably hadn't bothered on account of… well… he didn't want to think about those things too much. Anyway, once the sun had come up, he'd made his way as dutifully as he could to the ward, where Maureen sat waiting for him. Her coat was buttoned tightly, her bag perched on her lap and her lips pursed into a thin disapproving line, just in case he didn't know he could have collected her an hour earlier.

They travelled against the morning rush, gliding past drivers whose eyes saw nothing more than the bumper before them, the daily grind for most an obvious diurnal misery. *Perhaps*, Slattery thought, *they dreamed of golf, or fishing, or weekend trysts with mistresses young enough to be their daughters. What the hell was wrong with him?* When Slattery had hours to fill, he thought only of dead bodies, and murderers, of whiskey chasers and heavy dark Guinness, served in shady bars, surrounded by losers like himself. Maureen handed him the bag, walked a little before him, keeping up her pace so he'd never catch up. He wondered if she was embarrassed by him, or if she just wanted to be away from here, away from him, away from all they'd ever been. He couldn't blame her, felt the same himself. He knew he was wrong to feel it, for the damage that had been done could all be laid at his door.

'How are you feeling?' he asked when he'd finally taken his place behind the wheel of the car.

'How do you think I'm feeling?' she said and she turned her battered face towards him. It looked worse in the unforgiving daylight. There were dark purple bruises beneath both eyes, and a long gash that ran the length of her jawbone. He wondered fleetingly if people might think he'd done this to her. He'd seen worse inflicted on women over the years. She exhaled loudly. 'I just want to go home, Ben. Okay?'

'Sure,' he said.

She let him carry her bag and open the front door, but once they'd got into the hall she'd turned on him.

'I'll be fine from here now, you go on,' she said and her face was severe. She'd managed to get him out of the house only a few years ago; she didn't want him back in.

'Are you sure?' But they both knew he was glad of the excuse to get out the door as quickly as possible. He dropped her bag on the stairs and turned towards her. 'Maureen, I don't mind staying, make you a cuppa, and get you settled.' Her whole body had a look of weariness about it. It seemed to Slattery that she'd managed to shrink her normally rotund nature into the frail figure of an old maiden aunt that could crack in two given a light wind coming in the wrong direction.

'Sure you don't.' She looked at him, and he knew she didn't believe him, felt he wanted to be gone as much as she couldn't wait to see the back of him. 'Ben, we're too old not to be straight with each other – be off with you to find whoever it is you're looking for.' She shrank backwards towards her kitchen.

He followed her nervously; he hadn't stood in this room in almost three years. It was a room that had seen too many drunken arguments, too many miserable tears, too many let downs, too many excuses. But, when he hadn't been here, Slattery guessed it had been her cocoon. It was where she entertained the neighbours with cups of tea. It was where she'd stuck up every picture Angela had ever drawn and it was where she said her prayers at night before she climbed the stairs to her empty bed. He walked towards the kettle now, rinsed it out under the tap and filled enough for a pot of tea. When he looked around the kitchen he figured it hadn't changed much, it may have been painted a different colour, but not so much that Slattery couldn't remember what the colour had been before.

'What will you do when it's all over?' she asked and her voice was more measured than he'd ever heard it before.

'I suppose I'll do what I always do, wait until the next one...' He stood by the sink and looked into the barren back garden. Maureen had never been much for the garden.

'No, I mean, when it's *all* over. You must think about it... retirement? There's not all that long to go now.'

He took down two mugs and rinsed out the teapot with the warming kettle, tried to keep his voice as even as he could. 'I don't think about it.' The words had come out too low and he wondered when he said them if he'd actually voiced them at all.

'Oh yes you do, Ben, yes you do. I always thought you'd be dead long before,' she said softly. 'I prayed for that, for you.' She sat back in the only comfortable chair in the kitchen, a high-backed Queen Anne that sat next to the kitchen stove.

'I take it that was meant as an act of kindness?' He kept his voice light, hoping they could make some kind of a joke, move on, and talk about her health or the neighbours, people who meant nothing to him any more.

'We both know, I wish you no ill, Ben. Never have.' Of course, it would be a sin, but she didn't need to say this to maintain the higher ground. He made the tea, as quickly as he could, and checked that there was enough in the fridge to keep her going until Angela called later in the day. He hurried down the tea, taking hot gulps, whereas she seemed to sip hers with apprehension. 'You know, I thought I was going to die in there.' She didn't look at him as she spoke. 'And the one thing I worried about was you, Ben. You're a lost soul – and don't look at me like that, I'm not worried about you going to heaven or hell. I know I'm not about to convert you now. But I mean this constant searching, being surrounded your whole life by death and wickedness – you need a plan, so when you retire, well, so there'll be something to go on for. Something more than the pub.'

Slattery drained his mug of tea. He knew she was right, they both knew it. 'I've only ever been a detective, Maureen, you know that, there's nothing else for me.' He was telling the truth, he didn't know why he'd said it, wasn't even sure that she knew what that meant, he was damned if he knew.

'Oh.' She inspected her cup, as if from somewhere she might find some answers. After a few moments silence she nodded gently, that told more of how well she knew him than any words. 'Maybe, Ben, maybe you need those prayers more than I thought you did.'

He didn't say it then, but he had a feeling they'd both need them.

CHAPTER 21

Iris never thought it would be this hard. In all the time she'd wanted to get into Murder, she'd always assumed she'd know what she was doing when she got here. Now, here they were, with a list of suspects and the truth was, she knew, she couldn't tell her way out of the mountain of paperwork they'd built up since the beginning. Slattery had turned up like a bad house guest, there when you didn't want him and nowhere to be seen earlier when the whole team had an opportunity to throw in their opinions. He looked terrible and Iris assumed he'd been visiting his wife – she was afraid to enquire how things were since he'd barked at anyone who'd dared so far. He settled at his desk, staring blankly towards the deserted street below, a mug of tea cooling slowly under the weight of his contempt.

'We have nothing concrete, that's the problem.' Iris felt as if her eyes were ready to fall out of her head with weariness. Her ears felt even worse after the hours spent chasing up dead ends on the phone. At the back of the room, two fresh-faced uniforms had taken over from detectives who had finally given up chasing on the police computer system after Grady sent them home for a rest.

'It is,' Slattery grunted. 'If we can't crack Crowe now, after tearing up his house, well, then maybe there's nothing there to crack. Do any of us really think he's our man?'

'Well, there's definitely something off about him,' Iris said, but she knew, he didn't strike her as a murderer.

'Yeah, well we can't all be perfect,' he said under his breath but caught her eye and changed tack before she had a chance to snap back at him, 'perhaps he was having an affair, we know people don't break up for no reason – for all we know he might have been skiving off to his own house that night to meet up with his mistress, but that doesn't make him a murderer.'

'It's not about being *perfect*, no matter how alien that might be to you. There's the psychological report.' Slattery annoyed her, but no one wanted to let Crowe go without knowing for sure. It was just that he was the type that *could*. Of course, she wouldn't say this, because she knew Slattery would make some comment about watching too many cops on TV. Crowe's file had arrived from the Department for Defence. His record was clean. Almost too clean. He was a model soldier, just like he was a model employee and he wanted them to believe he was a model husband too. 'Something isn't right with him.'

'Maybe, but it's not enough to arrest him for murder, not what we currently have.' Slattery exhaled loudly. 'If we even had some kind of motive.' It was the one thing they truly lacked so far. 'That's it, isn't it?' Slattery didn't wait for an answer. 'Why would anyone want to kill Anna Crowe? There was nothing remarkable about her in any way.'

'No,' Iris said softly, 'apart from her past…' She caught Slattery's eye, for just a moment, that earlier case still lingered in both of their thoughts.

'Fine, maybe we should see if he can give us a motive for someone else,' Slattery said lumbering from his desk and heading off in search of Coleman Grady.

*

A couple of their burliest uniforms brought Crowe in. He'd come voluntarily. What Crowe didn't know was that, if they had to arrest him, then the clock started to tick and the pressure was on the team to pull everything together as quickly as possible. From the investigation's perspective, having Crowe 'help with enquiries' was a winning ticket. The psychological impact of helping with enquiries was almost as stressful as actually being arrested. Okay, so there may not have been as much panic on the part of the suspect, but there was a slowly building tension that escalated the longer the person was left to consider his situation. Iris knew this; she knew that the longer it took for Crowe's solicitor to arrive, the better for all of them.

Crowe looked as rattled as they had hoped. The presence of Slattery wouldn't do a lot to ease his nerves. If Ben Slattery was good at anything it was making others feel ill at ease. It was the small things he'd built up over a long career as a detective – his glares, his aggressive body language, it all added up to a big fat guilty feeling – nothing Crowe could do about it.

Slattery read out the caution, peering at it as he held it at arm's length, occasionally glancing up at Crowe, a disdainful expression on his face, as if he was holding down something sour between his wisdom teeth.

'Am I under arrest?' Crowe asked at the end of it.

Slattery shifted in his seat, eyeballed Crowe. 'Well, better safe than sorry, wouldn't you say?' He nodded to the recording device; the tape was already rolling. 'We're recording this voluntary interview under caution, present are myself – Sergeant Ben Slattery – Sergeant Iris Locke, Mr Adrian Crowe and his solicitor Mrs Barbara Morrissey.' He didn't add that just beyond the mirror, Coleman Grady and Anita Cullen were listening to every word.

Iris nodded across the desk, firmly establishing herself as the good cop. It was standard; everyone needed a friend to spill to when the going got tough. She wanted Adrian Crowe to feel she was there for him. Barbara Morrissey rolled her eyes; she was a big woman to Crowe's small neatness. Not much less than five feet ten, she was wide-set with burnt frizzy hair and lewdly mismatched clothes – a riot of orange, red, yellow and pink. She was good, though; maybe it was the fact that she worked alone, depended on her reputation for her week's wages – she was nobody's fool.

'So,' she spoke with a clarity that wasn't Limerick, maybe wasn't even Irish, 'what is it you think my client can help you with?'

'First,' Iris cleared her throat, 'we want to confirm Mr Crowe's whereabouts on the night his wife and children died.'

'And you have reason to believe my client has been less than forthcoming with you already on this matter?' she asked.

Slattery just smiled at her, a knowing, superior smile that left Morrissey in no doubt that hers was the weaker corner. She turned to Crowe. 'I must advise you that it is in your best interests to co-operate with the investigation as far as possible.'

Crowe looked belligerently at the floor. Iris watched him; his body remained completely still, his eyes fixed on some spot that had managed to grab their attention. Here in this meagre room, wearing a white shirt that seemed to drain all colour from him, he looked vulnerable, younger than his years and scared.

'Mr Crowe – Adrian – we know you left work that night. We know you were out of ABA for at least two hours.' Iris kept her voice low, gentle as if she was giving him a fighting chance.

Still Crowe kept his eyes down – there wasn't, Iris noted, so much as a flicker of recognition or an attempt to process the information so he could come up with a plausible explanation. The tape in the background provided the only noise in the room above Slattery's lumbering breath. Beyond the door, life was going on as normal. In the hallway, Iris could hear the usual comings and goings. Familiar voices rang out evening farewells, final instructions before the day was at an end; busy feet scurried along, a final report to be written, perhaps a child to be collected from crèche. They sat in silence for almost five minutes, until Slattery could take no more.

'Look, Crowe, it's like this – we know you were out of there. Better you tell us now – things are already bad enough for you.' He raised his hand towards the door. 'We've seen what was done to your wife, to your kiddies, better to come clean with the whole thing, better for you now.'

Adrian Crowe slowly raised his head and looked across at Slattery. He held Slattery's gaze for a long while, and then he began to laugh. Loud shrieks of mad laughter, hysterical sounds coming from a man who looked like he could hardly speak beforehand. Morrissey nodded towards the tape. 'I want to consult with my client.' She said the words flatly; they would hardly have been heard, but for the surrealism of Crowe. It seemed to Iris that everything in the room had intensified and she nodded towards Slattery who flicked the tape. As they got up to leave, the shrieking from Crowe stopped abruptly.

'How stupid can you people be?' The words were filled with disgust. 'I loved her, loved them all.'

'You don't have to speak now, we'll take a minute, clear your head, this has all been a terrible shock for you.' Morrissey laid a hand across his skinny arm.

'No,' the word was emphatic, 'no, I have nothing to hide. We may as well get this over with, and then they can do what they want with me. It makes no difference now. What have I got worth living for anyway?'

Once the tape was rolling again, Iris ordered tea to be sent in. No one wanted tea. They all just wanted to go home, or in Slattery's case to the nearest thing to his home. When Crowe spoke again, his words were measured. He rubbed his eyes; Iris saw tears. They were filled with regret. 'I loved her so much, but she thought I never really knew her. I never really understood. I don't see how I ever could have. You don't, do you? No one can, not really, not unless they've been through it.'

'Anna's sister? The missing baby?' Iris said, just loud enough for the tape, but apart from a slight nod of the head from Crowe, it was as if they'd never been uttered.

'She was taken before I even came to the village. I fell in love with Anna long before I ever heard about any of that. But then, once we got married… when you're living with someone,' he looked across to see if either of them understood, 'well, that's when you really get to know them. That baby was a huge part of Anna's life. Right up until the day she died.'

'Is it why she went back there?'

'Probably. I suppose it was why she did everything she did. It was always about the sister that had been stolen from her.' He sank his face into his hands at the uselessness of it all. 'I thought I was the one with a screw missing – you know, mild Asperger's – showed up as if I was almost psychopathic in some of the tests they ran in the army when I applied for cadetship. It's why I work nights, when I could just as easily work days – I like the seclusion, not having the stress of colleagues popping in and out, I'm supposed to be the odd one, I suppose. Then you see Anna, she seems so well adapted, so well able, and behind it all, she was haunted by what happened that day.'

'Do you think that her death might be linked to what happened all those years ago?'

'I don't know what to think. She was convinced the child was dead, buried somewhere in the copse between the cottage and Kerr's place. She was convinced that Ollie Kerr had something to do with the baby's disappearance. He still watched the cottage after that; she thought he was taunting her. That's why she took care of Pat Deaver; he looked out for her. Maybe she thought he'd look out for Martin and Sylvie too. Poor fucker couldn't look after a fly. Of course you couldn't tell Anna that.'

'Could Kerr have taken the child?' Slattery's voice was hard. He wanted a straight answer.

'He wasn't much older than Anna at the time. The way Anna told it, sure from the outside, either of them could have done it. The question is, more like, why would anyone do it?'

'Well, that's one we're not going to solve tonight, I think.' Barbara Morrissey moved uncomfortably in the chair that was too small for her.

'No,' Crowe agreed coldly and again Iris could see that vacant expression in him that made him look as if he was capable of unthinkable things. He reached up his sleeve, took out a perfectly pressed cotton hanky and blew his nose. He looked at Iris first, then across at Slattery. His words were emphatic, but Iris knew only too well it didn't mean they were honest. 'I went out to the cottage a lot of nights. It was one way of being close to them. I missed them so much when they left, but then, once Anna takes a notion… well, by the time she had her bags packed it was already too late.' He looked to the floor again, passing a small white hand through his fine hair. He sat back in his seat for a moment, as if allowing what he'd said to settle in for all of them.

'And that night? That last night, can you tell us what happened then?'

'I'd gone in to work as usual, forgotten to bring a sandwich – I usually have a cup of tea at about four in the morning. I told no one, but I decided I'd nip back to the house and pick it up. It took only a few minutes, so I thought I might as well take a spin out to Kilgee. I drove out, parked at the end of the driveway and sat on an upturned log outside the house for almost an hour. The place was in blackness, apart from a small light Anna had left on in the kitchen – she always had a light on, somewhere in the house. I sat there, I thought about our lives and where we'd ended up…' Regret, no wonder Iris had spotted it – she had seen enough of it in her parents' eyes.

'Did you see anyone else when you were leaving the cottage, any cars parked, anything unusual?' Slattery asked, his tone filled with sarcasm.

'No, I wouldn't have left there if I thought there was anyone hanging about the place, now, would I?' Crowe's face was open, his eyes steady – Iris had to admit she wanted to believe him.

*

It wasn't Crowe. Maybe that only confirmed what Iris and everyone else had felt all along, and maybe that wasn't smart policing, but sometimes you just know. She'd had enough for one day. She wasn't sure what made her indicate to turn right at Idle Corner. Perhaps it was the river, snaking black through Limerick's forgotten belly, perhaps it was the bells ringing across the city from St Mary's Cathedral on Bridge Street or St John the Baptist's calling from beyond the rooftops. Either way, she was headed down St Abbati's Terrace knowing that she would stop there for a while.

Boran was their only other official suspect now. His house, as before, looked as if it was home to a down-and-out squatter, not an artist whose work was probably hanging in the commissioner's living room. Iris pulled in just opposite, three to four houses back. She could have parked nearer, but why let Boran know she was keeping an eye on him, when it would probably come to nothing. Boran made her feel uneasy; something about him wasn't right. Maybe he hadn't killed Anna Crowe and her two kiddies, but he was a rotten egg and Iris knew it. She switched on the radio, looking for something, she wasn't sure what; restless and tired, a bad combination. She chose Radio 1, the old people's station; she was listening to it more and more these days. She sank back in her seat, rolled down the window slightly, taking in the smells of other people's dinners, other people's lives.

Then she spotted someone. It was Freddie the Mercury – not *Freddie Mercury*, obviously. No, this Freddie was born Frederick Murray. He'd started out as Freddie Varta, such was his liking for speed, but when he'd finally managed to kick the hard drugs, some wise arse had re-christened him and it had stuck. Most Limerick people knew Freddie the Mercury. Every other day he sang his lungs out down at the entrance to the Milk Market. 'Free range eggs; get your free range eggs here.' Of course what he really meant was: '*Da Players a hundred for forty, who's for da Players?*' Illegal fags, that was as far as it went with Freddie, so far as Iris knew, at least.

Perhaps there was more, but since their paths had never crossed, Iris assumed he'd never treaded the fine line into anything worse than anti-social behaviour with a constant sideline in illegally imported fags. The fact that he was left alone could only mean he was somebody's canary. But what was he doing outside Boran's house? Like it took a genius to figure that one out. Iris punched in a speed dial for an old colleague.

'Lorna?'

'Well, if it isn't Miss Celebrity – haven't heard from you in a while.' Lorna's voice was as Limerick as the mouth of the Shannon. They had trained together; Lorna had joined for a comfortable pensionable job. She'd never been in it for the action, so she was happy to park herself at a desk. In the meantime, she'd managed to get herself promoted and now she was married with twin boys and her once-size-six jeans probably wouldn't pass her ankle forever more.

'Hey.' Iris let her voice glide into their past acquaintance. They'd spent eighteen months sharing a dorm in Templemore, but it seemed like so long ago now. 'Are you on duty this evening?' She slipped back into sergeant mode – or at least informer of sorts. 'It's just, if you weren't doing anything interesting…'

'Go on…' Lorna had dropped her voice and she wondered now if they were both on the same track. 'I assume we're talking, but not talking?'

'You assume right.' Iris lowered her voice, conscious once more of her surroundings. St Abbati's Terrace wasn't exactly Soho. It was the kind of place, Iris figured, where the neighbours knew if you flushed twice within the hour and they would be counting. 'I've just been watching a guy called Boran and guess who's come to call?' Iris stopped for a moment and then continued drily, knowing that Lorna Williams would be watching a hundred and fifty Freddies every other day of the week, with not enough time or resources to really watch any of them. 'Freddie the Mercury,' she stalled for a moment, considered her position. If there was something there, it made no odds to her if the guy was shopped today or tomorrow, they could still cut a deal. Murder over smuggling; there was no comparison. 'I'd say that now is the time to get your guys down here, he's just after picking up his supplies, but you didn't get that from me...'

Bingo. Iris watched as Mercury left the house with a bulging bag full of what she presumed were excise-free fags.

'You're at Freddie's suppliers?' Lorna's voice was eager; she could almost hear her playing on the golf-ball pendant she wore around her neck, a gift from her father on the day he died.

'Well now, I'm not customs, am I?' Mentally, she shrugged, hoped the effect was heard over the phone. 'Anyway, this is just a friendly gesture, no need for thanks, like I say, if you're doing something more important...' She heard the phones going off in the background. Lorna was pulling a late, the only company were probably cranks, or lonely people like Iris who had nothing else to do and no one else to ring. The thought didn't exactly comfort.

Either way, Iris reckoned if she sat for an hour tops, she'd have a fair idea what Boran had going on. She turned the radio to Today FM, Friday night eighties' easy music. Sade, An Emotional Fish and the Eurythmics – not exactly favourites, but familiar, still hardly challenging.

Ten minutes later, she must have dozed off and she wasn't sure what woke her, perhaps the grace of God? But there was Slattery, bold as brass, walking up St Abbati's Terrace, walking right up, towards Boran's house. Iris rubbed her eyes, thought for a moment she must be dreaming, she'd wake up, back in her own nice familiar bed and all would be well. Except she wasn't, was she? She was sitting in her car, on St Abbati's Terrace, watching bloody Slattery walk towards a house that could be raided at any moment.

'You fuck, Slattery, you fuck.' Iris was suddenly propelled on a trajectory, as opposed to actually having taken any action.

Somehow, she'd bounded from the car, aware that at any moment, Lorna and her team could be careering into the street looking to pick up the smuggler who was supplying the Mercury and God knows how many more minor criminals around this city.

'You stupid...' Iris could barely keep the spittle from her voice. 'You stupid fucking fuck...' she finally managed as she dragged him into the car, hoping against all hope that no one had seen them, that no one would ever imagine they were police. At that moment, two cars blasted into the street. One was unmarked; the other was all sirens and warning lights.

'Jesus,' Slattery said under his breath.

'No, Customs and Excise, Slattery, but if they caught you in there, they might as well be the holy trinity, because Cullen would have had your arse for sure.'

Slattery smiled at her, a wrinkly, devil-may-care grin. 'I'll have to give these fags up someday soon, they'll be the death of me...'

Across the road, Boran was being led out by a plain-clothes officer; the two uniforms still probably sorting out the stock inside. When Lorna came out, she gave a small wave across to Iris. It was a good night's work for one division at least.

'I didn't know we were watching him...' Slattery looked a little stunned now that the initial bravery was wearing off. 'How come you're in on it?' He looked towards Iris now.

'Do you even know the guy's name?'

'Sure, he's Nixer Da Vinci, a fella down the pub told me I'd get a better price at St Abbati's Terrace. So I just thought I'd see for myself. Apparently, he's been flogging cheap fags for the last few weeks all round Limerick. You know the way it is, everything always tastes better without VAT.'

'It's Boran – our Boran, that's who's been supplying your cheap fags, Slattery.'

'Holy hell,' was all Slattery could manage and he threw his half smoked cigarette out onto the road in horror.

CHAPTER 22

It seemed like the only place to go; after the night's events Iris found herself sitting, disgruntled and irritably at the counter in the Ship Inn with Slattery. They'd hardly said two words to each other and it wasn't that there wasn't plenty to say, but they both knew that there wasn't much point. Instead, they'd sat at the bar, like an old married couple, wordlessly passing the time while she nursed her drink and he devoured his, listening to other people's conversations.

By midnight, Iris had had enough of pub talk. She'd parked her car a few hundred yards away from the Ship Inn, felt like she could do with a walk, but it wasn't the kind of place she'd go walking alone. She was almost on the old docks, an otherwise abandoned spot, the clinking of chains and see-saw of ropes buoyed by the tide the only sounds beyond the whispering wind and occasional lap of water from the Shannon. The developers hadn't managed to make it this far down river. Just as well. They'd taken enough of the country over, with faux stone and ruinous greed. She sat into the Audi. It wasn't a new car, six years on the clock and a guzzler on diesel, but it was flash enough for her and it gave her the balls nature had forgotten; a reminder to her colleagues that she could drive as fast as any of them and kick their backsides if she wanted to. She still needed to unwind and when she started up the engine, she knew exactly where she was headed. It was as if she hardly had a choice really, Anna Crowe was drawing her towards Kilgee from the first day she'd come on the case, now seemed as good a time as any to head out there.

The woods around the Crowe cottage were in complete darkness, her headlights a violent assault on the nocturnal activities of bats and badgers. She pulled the car in at the end of the drive, hadn't really planned on walking up to the cottage, but now she was here, well…

She pulled off her high heels, reached back for a pair of heavy boots she'd thrown into the rear seat. When she got out, she was struck immediately by the smell of autumn decay. It had rained heavily for the evening in Kilgee and now the mulch beneath her feet squelched noisily through the damp. In the distance, the waft of wet and rotting wood beckoned to her. The place didn't feel as if anything tragic had happened here in the last few days. She supposed that it must have felt a happy place to Anna too, even after the tragedy that had taken place in her youth. Otherwise, why would she have chosen to live here? No, the cottage felt like a safe place, a cocoon detached from the busy world beyond. It felt like home and maybe that's why Anna Crowe had come back here. Absurdly, Iris began to feel a well of emotion overtake her, as though something deep within her was ready to mourn. Not just Anna Crowe, the two children, that missing baby from years earlier, but maybe something closer to home, like the lost possibility of something that could never be – perhaps her place on the Murder Team.

What had she expected, coming here? She wasn't sure; possibly the feeling that the spirit of Anna Crowe somehow lingered on here. Iris knew that was just madness. Anna Crowe had died tragically and violently, but she had died and it was down to Iris to find out why.

She made her way along the narrow path, picking it out against the grassy verge to either side. It was rough and uneven beneath her feet, and the crunch of stones echoed far into the distance, making her feel as if she was somehow intruding on the stillness of graves. She had a torch in her pocket, that and her standard-issue firearm.

She hadn't come here to see anything, not really. Just to think, to get a sense of the place, of the person. The Ship Inn had made her feel as if she was stuck, as though somehow the information she had, the work she'd done, was stagnant. Maybe that was what had hit Coleman Grady. They were no further along than they had been two days ago.

She was at the cottage now. It stood in front of her, a looming black spot shading out the moonlight, hiding secrets she couldn't guess at in its darkness. She stood for... she couldn't say how long, found herself whispering a prayer for the Crowes – all of them, even the missing baby, whisked away too soon and never seen again. A chill wind creeping down her spine broke her reverie. She caught her breath; déjà vu suddenly, she'd been here, in this moment, before. But of course she hadn't, this was what murder did to you, too close and the lines got blurred. She backed a little way from the cottage, wondering at the unspoken link that had been forged on one afternoon in a coffee shop. She felt very close to Anna Crowe, maybe closer than it was good for either of them to be now. She wasn't sure if it was her imagination, or if in fact she'd been touched by a ghostly finger, but she turned to see if anything was behind her and in that moment hardly managed to stifle the scream that rose from somewhere deep in her gut. She was not alone.

*

He'd heard her car drive to the end of the road, opened his eyes as the lights died down, but not before they shone brightly into the trees, waking the sleeping birds, penetrating the darkness of night. He'd been up here for hours. He'd been coming here for years, since they were kids, just watching the house. Watching her. Occasionally a chink of light would struggle through the pulled curtains, but usually, it was just the knowledge that she was close that kept him here.

But this, tonight, this was more than he could have dreamed of. He moved slowly in the undergrowth towards her. Careful to keep his distance, but at the same time, drawn to her like a helpless pin to a magnet. Anna had had the same effect on him. Of course, he knew that this was not Anna. This woman was taller, more in command of herself and everything around her. Even here, in the dark of night, she walked with purpose, as though she had a right to be here; her shoulders straight, her back arched when she stood for a moment.

What had brought her out here at this hour of the night? There was nothing to see here. Nothing she couldn't see in daylight. And then it struck him. Did she know what had happened? Did she realise? Did she know what he knew? If she did, she'd have had a raft of big burly guards round his door, demanding that he come down to the local station, wouldn't she? Or would she? If he'd ever questioned the right or wrong of his actions, he knew now that this was meant to be. She'd come back for him, he was sure of that now, and when he revealed himself, she would come to him. Run into his arms and he would hold her, hold her so she could never leave him as Anna had done.

He moved forward in the brush, his foot finding a small twig on the damp ground. It snapped gently, but the sound seemed to echo through him. She tensed before him and when she turned around, the expression on her face was one of sheer terror. He knew then that their meeting may not go quite as he had planned.

*

She had her revolver: that was the only thought that whirred its way around her head now. It was heavy and cold in her pocket, loaded and ready.

'You came back to me, my lovely.' His words were hoarse, the accent was Limerick, but she hadn't come across the voice so far in the investigation. If this was their man, it was certainly not Adrian Crowe.

She stood in silence, cursing the clouds that played across the face of the cold moon, allowing it to pick out her frame malevolently, and maliciously, perhaps. She couldn't see his face, but the guy was big, even in the shadows, she'd give him six-two and a bruiser with it. Hard to tell if he was muscle or not, but he moved with the languor of a loafer. Still, if he got too close, he'd be hard to throw off. She reckoned the one thing she might have going for her is that she'd outrun him. That, and her hand gun.

'I wasn't sure if it was you or not – I came back after, but I was too late.' His voice was plaintive. *Perhaps he was just an innocent nut job*, she thought.

'Which way did you come?' she asked, still unsure how to play it.

'Through the woods, of course.' He laughed then, as though she'd forgotten. A rustle in the undergrowth told her he was moving closer, but she still could not make him out. When the moon tripped through the leaves again, he was gone and she felt panic rise through her; he could be anywhere, cutting off her escape route. She daren't turn round, hadn't heard him move behind her yet; surely he would hit a twig. Automatically she took a step backwards, her breath held tight, afraid to breathe. Could he see her now, could he make her out from his shadowy shelter? She had to get a location on him.

'Did you love her very much?' she asked, her voice soft but clear. There was no sound anywhere, not even a breath. 'Did she love you too… perhaps you had plans? Plans to be together, just the two of you…' She wondered, then, if maybe he was gone. But something, something small and cold told her he was very close, moving closer as she spoke.

She felt the cold draw in around her, a lonesome sensation. She pulled her coat around her, knowing it was futile; the kind of cold she felt out here was the cold Anna Crowe had felt before she died. She turned then, sensing the danger now far outweighed any lead she might hope to get. Whether this guy was smart or not didn't matter, he knew the terrain, he had the advantage. The path was uneven back to the car. She'd move as quietly as she could. The sky had clouded over; it would take at least two to three minutes to make it to the safety of the car in near blackness.

'Where are you going?' He was so close she could feel his breath on her neck, warm and sticky with a hint of booze, something pungent like lager or cider. 'You can't leave yet…' She felt him reach towards her, the sound of a jacket, moving in too close.

She didn't wait for any more; she ran faster than ever before, and cursed her heavy boots as though they were somehow going to slow her down. The road was more uneven than she thought. It heaved in troughs and bumps, small stones at angles with her shoes as she sprinted across them; she would have cursed aloud, but now she had to get away. Iris felt with certainty that the man a couple of feet behind would surely finish her off, right here, on the deathbed of Anna Crowe. The thought spurned her faster, but he was managing to keep close to her. She could hear his breaths, hard and heavy, too close.

And then he grabbed her. A long loose arm was on her back, pulling her down. She fought hard to stay upright, but he was on her now, pounding his weight down on top of her, and still she saw no more than his outline.

'I've loved her forever. What is it you want here now? Don't you see? It's too late.' She could hear tears behind his words. 'We're meant to be together, you must know that…' He was pushing heavily down on her, his weight immobile, fixed to her, no matter which way she turned. The various techniques she'd learned in training college at Templemore, all of them racing through her brain, but he'd caught one arm behind her, the heavy coat anchoring her further in his grip.

Then he started to cry, turned his face away from her. The movement was so slight, she hardly felt it, but it was enough to gain some kind of balance of her own. She stayed a moment, taking his full weight, tilting herself to one side, freeing up her left hand, gaining access to her pocket. Deep within it, she'd dropped the torch. He weighed heavily on the side of her gun; there was no chance of getting to it. In a single movement she had the torch out, blinded him before he had a chance to think. He screamed, more with fright she reckoned than the knowledge that she was going to be in her car before he had time to know what had happened.

High above, the moon was still hidden but the torch picked out her way. She pulled open the car door, threw her body into the driver's seat. Her fingers shook so much; it seemed to take an age to get the keys into the ignition. As the headlights came on, she searched out the drive before her. He was gone, and that only made her more uneasy. Was he behind the car already, waiting to crash something into the windscreen, yank her out like a rag doll and kill her too with his sick love? She threw the gear stick into first, was half a mile down the road before she managed to take the handbrake off. She stopped the car then, got out and threw up into the nearby ditch. She couldn't remember ever being so sick. She knew it was fear, a close shave with something darker than she'd ever come near before and worse, she felt that somehow, a connection had been made and he would not rest until he possessed her or killed her. She got back into the Audi, hardly able to think beyond the automatic movements of her body, bringing her home to some sense of refuge. His face lingered before her eyes, lit up bright and manic in the flashlight glare. It was no good – even if she had a million years to get over this night, she couldn't identify him no matter how much she tried. His face was a contorted nightmare. She'd probably see it every time she closed her eyes and never truly recognise him.

CHAPTER 23

Iris greeted the grey light tipping through her bedroom window with a sense of relief. Outside, far below on the street, she listened as Limerick slowly rumbled back to life. She had not slept, but then, she hadn't really expected to. At her bedside, a fat tumbler still two fingers full of brandy sat accusingly on top of some notes she'd made about the case. If it was anyone else, she'd tell them to talk to someone. She knew, as well as any, that bottling up that violent attack would do her no good, but she knew, too, that she hadn't any words to put on it yet.

She knew one thing, though, and this had occurred to her somewhere between the third and fourth bells of St Mary's Cathedral – whoever was out there in Kilgee last night, it wasn't anyone she'd interviewed so far as part of the investigation. Her attacker had been big, strong, athletic. It wasn't Boran, who was currently being questioned thanks to her tip-off to Lorna. Even if he'd managed to wiggle his way out, Boran was a string bean of a man – still wearing his adolescent rib cage as a badge of honour. He was a slippery reed of a man and her attacker was not. Well, it almost didn't matter anyway, he'd have enough on his plate when Lorna had finished with him.

Iris dragged herself from her bed and headed for her third shower in the last six hours. This one was long and hot and she hoped that combined with strong coffee it might cleanse her back to some kind of normalcy. The silence within her was echoing and when she turned on the news, it was as much to drown out the starkness as it was to keep up with what was happening in the world. She let the national headlines wash over her; it was the usual – politics, finance, murders and rapes. No mention of Anna Crowe and Iris wasn't sure if that was a good or a bad thing. No, she was pretty sure, it wasn't good.

'Short straw, I'm afraid,' June said to her when she arrived into the station. She was late, first time since she joined the Murder Team, but it had obviously been noticed and for today, it would cost her a full eight hours tied to a desk. 'You get the crazy detail…' June smiled as she shuffled into her coat.

'Where are you off to?' Iris felt a sting of panic ripple through her – she couldn't remember a day when June hadn't been fielding the phone calls. This was grunt work, she could do it in her sleep, but today she hadn't slept and today, she felt more vulnerable than she'd ever felt before.

'Cinderella is off to the ball with me,' Grady said, shaking his car keys to show they could take his car. 'We're heading off to see if we can't track down a bit more about the Fairleys from an aunt of Anna's who lives in a nursing home outside Galway.'

'Yes, and we might call in to check over the farmhouse once more,' June said. 'I haven't been out there and I just want to see for myself.' She spoke softly and Iris knew it was working this case, it had probably become personal for all of them, and June too, gathering information about someone she couldn't fully connect to… well, it was respect, wasn't it?

'Right, well, have fun,' Iris said, but they all knew, the cottage would be a desolate spot on a grey day like today.

By eleven, she was alone, the incident room empty, bar her own voice, checking out the crazies and they just kept coming. June had drawn up a database, listed each name, number and a brief synopsis of what they wanted to report. Mostly, they had come flooding in after the media appeal. Probably, they weren't worth the paper they'd been recorded on, but they each had to be double checked and then, if there was anything of merit within the threads of information, it would mean calling out and recording a formal statement. It was plod work, but it was important. Cold cases too often threw up instances where a crime might have been solved if the curtain twitchers had been sorted – because, occasionally, among the dross, there was gold.

'You're a busy beaver.' Anita Cullen parked herself on the side of Iris's desk just after lunch. 'How come you're here today…' It was funny, but when she asked a question, Iris always had the distinct impression she already knew the answer.

'Short straw and I got the crazies.'

'Ah, the loony brigade, don't knock them, they've made the difference in more than a couple of cases I've managed to crack over the years.' Anita smiled wryly.

'I'm hoping to strike lucky, but I've almost come to the end of the list and so far, everyone of them is a serial informer – they'd swear they saw Santa Claus surfing down the Shannon if they thought it would get them involved in a case.'

'They mean well, any of them I've ever come across, mostly they just have too much time on their hands and not enough company,' Anita said sadly. 'Anyway,' her features brightened up, 'I'm off for lunch, fancy coming along?'

'Aww, I've just eaten,' Iris held up the bacon roll she'd bought in the nearby deli only half an hour earlier.

'Not to worry, we can do it again sometime.' She made her way towards the door, her steps deliberate, her head high. 'Did you ever look into that old case, by the way?' she asked, turning then with a quizzical look in her expression.

'As much as I could, but there's nothing to look at. The files must have been destroyed or released before they were committed to the system, it seems that my father is probably the best source of information now and he's pretty certain that…'

'It was terribly sad.' Cullen's voice dropped, so that there was a trace of something that might almost have been maternal. 'That poor woman, she was hardly able to care for one child, there was never any doubt... she mightn't have even remembered what she'd done and even the daughter... well, you don't come through what that family went through without scars.'

'I suppose,' Iris managed, thinking of Anna Crowe that one time she'd met her. She wasn't stupid enough to believe she could tell from one conversation how emotionally damaged the woman was; after all, she'd worked DV and she knew, victims hid their wounds expertly.

'Some other time,' Cullen was saying now. 'Maybe later, dinner, I'll drop you a text.' She shook her head then and made her way out into the afternoon's drizzling rain.

*

It was only bread and milk.

'When I need groceries picked up, I'll get them myself,' Maureen fired at him and he knew she was reluctant to let him past the front door. All the same, she was still bandaged, moving about slowly and probably in more pain than even the Lord would expect from one of his most willing sufferers.

'I just thought... if you don't want them, I can bring them into the station and the boys'll make short work of them in tea and toast at the end of the day,' he grunted, laying the few provisions on the kitchen table. He knew better than to even suggest he might put anything into a cupboard or the fridge. 'Anyway, how have you been? Sleeping all right?'

'I'm sleeping as well as can be expected,' she said shortly and Slattery knew that if the pain didn't keep her awake, then the guilt of a young man's death on her hands would be enough to drive anyone from ever sleeping soundly again.

'You know, a lot of people, when they've been through… well, what you've been through, they go and talk to someone. There are groups who'll listen and people paid to help you get over the trauma of it.' He spoke quietly, and although the radio blared loudly from on top of the fridge, it felt as though he could hear her every heartbeat.

'I won't be needing any quack or touchy-feely group, thank you very much all the same. I've been through a lot worse than this and I'll manage just fine,' she said and turned her back to him, flicking on the kettle for a cup of tea neither of them wanted, but both of them hoped would be enough to move their conversation away from dangerous ground.

'Has Angela been over today?' he said looking up at the old plastic kitchen clock. She would finish work soon, but Angela was her mother's daughter and there was a good chance she'd have been over cleaning the front step before she even set off for work at seven in the morning.

'No, I told her not to bother.' She took down two cups, recognisable because it seemed they'd been here forever and yet unfamiliar in this surreal moment. There was a time when Slattery couldn't have imagined standing in this kitchen again drinking tea with Maureen. 'Of course, she's a good girl, you can't keep her away; she's worried sick about me, even if she doesn't say it.' Maureen sighed. 'And there's really no need, apart from a few cuts and bruises and they'll heal.' She scalded the cups, reached up for the biscuit tin, there were only sugar-free treats for her now, but still, she was of the generation that couldn't put a cup of tea before a visitor without something on the side. Suddenly, it struck Slattery that he had become a visitor in his own house. This was his house, his name on the deeds and his chair by the fire, even if he was glad to see the back of it all.

'She is a good girl,' Slattery agreed and stared into his tea, counting off the awkward seconds until he could leave again.

'You don't need to check up on me either, Ben. I'm fine, there's not a lot you can do for me anyway,' she said, but there was no accusation in her voice. She sipped her tea and examined her hands. They were old-woman hands now, much older than the rest of her. Of course, she'd spent a lifetime washing and cleaning: between here and the nearby church, Maureen Slattery had made sure that every surface she came across was as shiny as any soul in heaven. In the background Slattery heard the drone of the radio host and he wondered if Maureen listened to this every day and maybe, for the first time ever, he wondered what she did all day long. This house, well, when he looked about him now, there was no more cleaning left to do here.

'I always believed… or I convinced myself at least,' she said, her voice a fragile whisper, 'that He gave us the back to carry our cross.' She looked now at Slattery. 'You know, if I prayed hard enough, I could wipe the slate clean.' A small tear ran down her cheek and she rubbed it away with the viciousness of a nasty stain.

'I've seen too many terrible things to ever believe that, Maureen,' he said sadly.

'The thing is, I'm not sure my back is broad enough to carry *this* cross too.' Her words drifted from her softly. 'With Una…' She stopped.

It was the first time his sister's name had been uttered between them in years. Now, in the silence stretching between them in this claustrophobic kitchen that should have been theirs, it lingered unevenly, as though it might open up some long-forgotten box and unleash an ocean of memories that Slattery knew neither of them could handle. After a minute, he managed to graze his eyes away from examining the table to look at Maureen's face. He expected her to be crying, instead the expression was one of complete serenity, as if she had stepped into a completely different world and something about her sent a cold shiver rippling to Slattery's core.

*

Veronique shook her head, enjoying the sensation of clean, newly coloured hair. It had taken almost two hours to get roots and ends perfectly matching and now the aroma of ammonia and peroxide and sickly sweet apple pervaded every dank corner of the cottage. Better than the smell of wet dog – which was what had been the backdrop to Kilgee since she'd arrived here. Colouring her hair, picking up new lipstick, packing her bags – these were all steps in preparing for her new life. She didn't exactly have a plan, apart from getting out of Limerick, but she dreamed of making a fresh start, somewhere she wasn't known, somewhere warm and not so expensive to live. It wasn't a lot to start out with, but she would have enough in her pocket to get settled in a little flat somewhere cheap and maybe she could get a job, working in a bar or waiting tables. The first thing she had to do was get the cash in her hand and then she could make her way to the airport and out of this godforsaken country. She poured herself her second glass of vodka for the day.

She hated Limerick, the way everything about it made her feel like an outsider. From what she could see, it was a place built on secrets and lies. Even Ollie – he had his own secrets, him and Anna Crowe. She'd heard them together, their great big reunion. Fat lot of good that had done either of them, after twenty years apart. Of course, Veronique wasn't one for friendships much, but she figured whatever Ollie thought there was between him and Anna Crowe it had been all one-way traffic. Asking him to take care of her deepest secrets, indeed. Veronique had been itching to get a look at that box of treasure, knew instinctively that it was worth something more than just Ollie's sentimental gratitude for a friendship rekindled.

And she'd been right. Searching the house and every outbuilding had paid off handsomely. Five thousand euro and there would be more where that came from, she was certain of that. These people, they may not have been enormously wealthy, but a couple of thousand euro was nothing if it kept them out of jail.

The knock on the door when it came was exploratory, more than explanatory – as if someone was tentatively checking that anyone could live in this rundown cottage. Veronique checked her appearance before she answered, catching the backdrop of neglect and decay in the dark room behind her reflection.

'I am coming,' she yelled at the door and swung it open with a customary anger in her movements. 'Yes, what is it?' she asked automatically, but then stopped for a moment; she had no idea he was about to kill her.

CHAPTER 24

If this is what Cullen meant by taking it easy of an evening, Locke was glad they weren't house-sharing. The living room was like a mini incident room, all of the details played out on sticky notes against any surface that might hold them. She'd even managed to bring home pictures of Anna Crowe and her two kids. Unsettling pictures, photographs that let you see their personalities; photographs that made their deaths seem unimaginable. The photographs made them real and reminded Iris that once she'd met this woman, before these terrible things had happened. Once they'd been the same. Once this woman had held her hand for a long moment and looked into her face, as though they'd known each other a lifetime. Once there'd been a frail connection that Iris felt might grow into friendship. But then, the unimaginable had happened. Iris had seen their remains, smelled the odour of skin burnt, saw the three matching bullet holes where someone had callously stood over them and pulled a cold trigger, stopping the clock for them once and for all.

Seeing them now, Anna with her hair long and heavy, Sylvie snuggled safely against her smooth neck, Martin, his face a map of freckles and missing teeth, his eyes bright, filled with laughter and expectation, well, it was heartbreaking. None of it would mean anything, of course. Iris got that now, even if they managed to find their killer, it would mean nothing. Anna, Martin and Sylvie Crowe were gone, a whole family wiped away in one dark night, in one dark deed. They'd died, all the potential drained from them in a breath, and for what? Sure, maybe that was as much as they needed, to find out why they died, if they found out why, well, then they'd have a better idea who had done this terrible thing. And it was a terrible thing. Iris knew that she'd been so shit-scared of whatever had been lurking about that cottage, she'd lost sight of Anna Crowe and that was something she couldn't afford to do. She was reading transcripts now, carefully typed-up notes from the interviews with neighbours both in Kilgee and in Limerick city.

'So, maybe it's the Asperger's you were picking up on?' Cullen had the transcript from the interview she and Slattery had carried out earlier.

'Maybe.' She'd known a girl at school with Asperger's syndrome – Sandra. She was remote in the same way she'd found Adrian Crowe. Maybe her reaction would be similar if she heard her nearest and dearest had just died. She might have judged him differently if she'd had a different label for his apparent coldness. The thought didn't make her feel any better. At least the interview gave them something to follow up with the Department for Defence. Even ten years ago, there had to be some transparency around how people fared in competition for cadetships. 'So now we look at this Kerr guy?'

'Yeah, we look at him, sure. But the Baby Fairley case has been closed for over twenty years. If he had something stuck in his craw, I'd say he'd have choked on it well before now.'

Cullen hadn't wanted to consider a link between the two cases all along. Iris thought she could see why. It was old ground. Her father's case. Some cases are better left closed. That's what her father had said when she asked him about it. It was Anna Crowe's mother; they were all convinced of that. Jack Locke had looked at her and seen his own wife – the slow descent into a world away from reality. Maybe there was a tincture of vanity too. If he couldn't solve it, he sure as hell wouldn't want anyone else coming along and pulling his work apart, pulling his memories apart, pulling his reputation apart. Iris knew that no one would want to discredit her father; no one would want to upset the old man.

'But if she believed the baby was buried in the copse – it's not a huge area, shouldn't we at least...?'

'You're out of your mind, Iris.' Cullen's scorn-filled words threw her back to feeling like a newbie again. She felt the resentment bubble, and something build up inside her that made her want to run from this apartment, straight back to the station and pull every file on Baby Fairley and read right through till the morning. Except, of course, she couldn't, because at the moment there were no files. They had nothing. 'You know what the budgets are like now. You know how we're fixed. I can't open up an investigation based on a few words by a man who may just be trying – not very cleverly, mind – to get himself out of the eye of the storm.' Her face was white now, as if she'd just come face to face with too many buried ghosts; that's what missing kids did to you.

'Listen to me, just for a second. I know it was your first case of sorts. I know you were thrown it as part of your probation under my father. No one expected you to solve it then; he wouldn't have given it to you if he thought there was a hope he could solve it himself first time round.'

'So what makes you think we'll solve it now?' She was tapping her fingers against the side of her cold coffee mug. 'What makes you think it will actually improve anything for anybody by solving it now?'

'Jesus, you don't really mean that?'

'Of course I do. Think about it, the kid is dead – you said so yourself. What's to be gained from putting the likes of Kerr away for it now? He was only ten years old, if even that, when it happened. *If* he did it, if we could even prove that he did it – has he done anything since that makes you think he's a threat to any other kid? Has he done anything that makes you think that this was anything more than one stupid mistake by a kid who was jealous of a new baby? Think about that kid in Donegal. They created monsters by putting his killers away. Who won out there?' Cullen stopped; perhaps she knew she had said too much. One thing was certain, she had thought about this for a long, long time and maybe in her mind, she already knew what had happened to Baby Fairley. It was obvious; the one person they'd never pointed the finger at, Ollie Kerr was the person she held responsible.

Iris shivered, knowing it had to have been Ollie Kerr who she had fought off that night at the cottage also.

'There's never going to be any winners here, Anita. We know that, but wouldn't it be good to know that at least Anna could be buried with her sister – that even if they were separated in life that they might be…' Iris kept her voice even, not giving away anything, even if she was sick to the pit of her stomach beneath her calm voice.

'Don't give me that bullshit, Iris. It makes no odds to Anna Crowe now. The only one this is going to help is you and we both know it.'

'What do you mean by that?'

'I mean, you get to solve the one case your father couldn't. You get to walk about Corbally station thinking that you are better than him – you're not working in his shadow any more. You solve this and you're your own woman.'

'I can't believe you'd think that.'

'It'll take a lot more than a few words from a suspect and a sob story from you to make me fuck up my career just to put a couple of bones in a box beside Anna Crowe.' Cullen shook her head as though expunging some niggling notion that was being planted by a rival. 'We wouldn't find her anyway. The place was well searched at the time; if anything had been buried there, they'd have spotted it then.'

'Can't we just bring Kerr in and question him, ask him about what happened all those years ago?'

'Iris—' Even the way she said her name made her feel like she was back at school, humble, stupid, awkward. 'This is a murder inquiry; we don't just drag people in for questioning like it's a game of last one out.' She took up a chocolate biscuit and crunched it noisily. Iris knew that this conversation was over. *Well, over for now at least*, she thought.

Cullen picked up some of the notes that she'd left on the settee beside her. An arm full of crisp white sheets, reviewing most of what the team had put together. The 'book' was the bible of every case, essentially a log of every question asked and answered, not far off every coffee drunk. 'How are you finding the team?' Cullen raised her eyes over the smart glasses she wore for reading. 'They seem to be a grand bunch.'

'They're sound, well-knitted together, but very focussed on getting the case solved.' Locke smiled.

'Yes, Grady is a good man, you can see it in the unit. The only thing I'd worry about is that they're so well glued together at this point, it might be hard for an outside…' She let her words peter off.

'No problems there, I'm used to being out on a limb, but honestly, I haven't felt that here.'

'Slattery and Grady go back a long way, I do wonder if perhaps that's a good thing.'

'I don't know, they're very different, aren't they? Perhaps they balance each other out?'

'No danger of Slattery teaching Grady his naughty ways?' Cullen smiled indulgently.

'Old dog and new tricks? No, I think Grady is a straight down the line sort of fella, regardless of what he might see other people doing.' Locke picked up the photograph of Anna Crowe and Sylvie, aware that they were treading on thin ground; the last thing she wanted to be was the one who told tales to the boss. Not that there were any tales to tell were there? Well, apart from that empty bottle of whiskey in Slattery's desk, of course.

'Have you seen something?' Cullen's voice was low and even, just across the table as if she could read Iris's mind. Something in her manner had changed; now she sat like a large feline, waiting to pounce on her prey. 'Something of Slattery, something I should know about?'

'God, I don't know, you know Slattery probably as well as I do – I suspect most likely the same things you do, but what do I know? As any good detective will say, you can't base judgements on feelings, right?'

'Right.' But Cullen sounded unconvinced. 'Iris, you know that I would take it very badly if I learned at some point that you knew something that might compromise any of the officers on my team. I can't work with people I don't trust.' She didn't trust Slattery, it had been written all over her face since the day she'd arrived.

The threat was implicit, as invisible as it was tangible. If Iris wanted in, she had to spill, even if she had nothing to spill. What did she owe Slattery anyway; he was hardly likely to go out on a limb for her, right? Only problem was, and she knew this beyond any doubt, if she did spill, or if for any reason, Grady or June or even Westmont thought that it came from her, she could be on the team and forever remain an outsider. 'You're putting me in an awkward position here...'

'There's no need for awkwardness, believe me, I would never drop you in it. No one would know that it came from you.' And there it was. Cullen, for all her years, was honourable. Her rectitude was old school, so outdated that it was almost impossible to recognise it for what it was, but Locke knew enough to know she could trust her. And she knew, too, that she'd rather have Cullen as a friend than as an enemy.

'Okay, okay, I don't really know anything, but I suspect that there was a time when he might have been drinking in the station...' Locke exhaled, she knew from the way Cullen's eyes opened wide that this was exactly what she'd been hoping for. 'But that was once and I have no reason to think it's happening now.'

Then Cullen's phone rang with a singsong quality to it that reminded Locke of the circus, she had the showmanship of a practised ringmaster. Iris exhaled, saved for now by the interruption. By the time Cullen hung up on the call she was pulling herself off the sofa. 'Are you up for a spot of driving?' She threw the Mercedes keys at Locke, grabbing her coat and slipping on the shoes she'd discarded only a short while earlier. 'You should be happy; it looks like it's coming closer to home.'

'How's that?'

'We have another one – Ollie Kerr's partner.'

*

The place was cold and dark and bleak and Slattery knew before he went into the cottage that this was different. Maybe it was the fact that the place hadn't been torched, but he had a feeling it was something more, catching on the air before him, like a threat, drifting just beyond his reach. Cullen and Locke arrived before him, the Mercedes' taillights beaconing his way up the narrow road to the cottage. Typical, he harrumphed, but at the same time, it was odd, perhaps he expected more of Locke than to fall in with the likes of Cullen.

'The forensic boys are out in good time,' Slattery said, as two of the crime scene officers slipped into paper suits, at the side of a Gardaí van.

'Get someone on the end of the road,' Cullen hissed at Slattery. Iris eyed him disdainfully. She was still livid over the fags and Boran; it had been far too close for comfort. How could he be so stupid? Slattery knew the answer already, he was out of control, spinning fast towards royally screwing up and he had a feeling, when it happened, that there was little anyone could do to save his ass from Cullen.

The cottage was a 1960s' council build. Small and mean. Someone had painted it cream twenty years ago; it looked as if they still hadn't finished the job. The windowsills had never seen a lick of colour and Slattery figured the current owner had long lost interest in its upkeep. A high Mohican fringe of grass had brushed noisily against the underside of the Ford on the driveway and scattered around the house, an array of obsolete electrical goods and a long-dead Volkswagen beetle rested idly. It seemed they were going nowhere any time soon.

'Get down there yourself until a uniform arrives.' Cullen barked the order at Slattery; it was a long time since anyone had been so pissed off with him, but he was damned if it was going to lessen his swagger. He made his way back down past the parked cars to take up position, stout and obstinate. The last thing they needed was the press making their way up the narrow driveway. No doubt, they'd be here soon, all too often they were at the scene before the Murder Team, pushing their way as close to the crime as they could. That it bothered him, standing on sentry while the others were in the middle of the crime scene, could not be read on Slattery's face. All the same, the next uniform to arrive was left to take over and Slattery was relieved to make his way back towards the cottage.

The cottage inside was as dank as the outside led you to believe. Slattery remembered his visit here, only days ago. It had been a depressing place then, too, but tonight it was something else, a crime scene and that made it reek of something altogether more ominous. Veronique Majewski had not struggled with her killer. Her body lay hunched over the kitchen table. Beside her blood-matted hair, a glass that contained a large shot of vodka remained; her red-glossed lips had left their trace along its rim. She would have been beautiful, had it not been for the drink and drugs and general grimness of her personality that had wracked their own particular ugliness on her delicate features.

'Who found her?' he asked Grady.

'The boyfriend, partner, whatever you want to call him; he's outside now, we've left him with one of the uniforms, we'll get to him next.' Grady spoke with the firmness of the officer in charge, and it reassured Slattery; at least the DI would have his back.

'Well, what do you think?' Cullen ignored the forensic team who were moving slowly, quietly around them, widening their circle of investigation in movement waves away from the victim.

'No sign of Ahmed?' Grady asked, looking towards a guy called Fitzgerald. A nod told him he was on his way.

'Iris, you want to go first?'

'Sure. I'd say she knew her attacker; it doesn't look like a burglary, the place has been turned over, probably after she died. There's nothing in her posture to suggest a struggle. The place is untidy – but it looks like that's the way they lived, there's no obvious sign of a break-in.' She looked towards Cullen, checking that the other woman was in agreement with her so far. 'I'd say this was personal, just as personal as the Crowe murders.'

'So why didn't our guy set the place on fire?' Cullen asked Iris and Grady.

'Maybe he didn't have time. Maybe something spooked him.' Iris looked at Grady.

Slattery walked towards an old-fashioned dresser. Checked out its contents quickly with his gloved hands. Narrow shelves were crammed with the mismatched crockery of someone Slattery knew was long since dead. He picked up a photo of Veronique. She had a smiling full mouth below troubled eyes that watched the camera with an empty stare that was at once unsettling and entrancing. She had long fair hair, with the sallow skin of Eastern Europe and delicate features. The photo had obviously been taken at a local fair or festival, probably just a few months earlier; she was on the cusp of a new life, perhaps there was hope of something better then. Slattery handed the photo to Grady, who passed it along to Cullen.

'Jesus.' Cullen said the word almost under her breath, holding the picture before lowering it to look at what remained of Veronique. 'What kind of sicko does this?' She looked at Grady; his turn. Sometimes, the first impressions on a crime scene are tellingly accurate. Grady and Slattery had run through this routine thousands of times; it had been a long time, though, since either had found himself trying to impress his senior.

'The murderer knew what he was doing. There were two glasses here.' He pointed to a wet circle where a second glass matching the remaining one had stood wet and soaking into the week-old newspaper that covered half the table. 'My bet is our man took his glass with him. My bet is he wore gloves too. He's smart, there's no sign of any attack or fight back. It's not the boyfriend either.' He looked at Locke's puzzled expression. 'Why would he take away the glass; he could just wash it and put back in the cupboard. He does live here, after all.'

Cullen bent down to take a closer look at the victim's hands. Veronique's fingernails were long and synthetic; her rings were high and pointed. If she'd made any contact with her killer at all, there was lots of potential for picking up DNA.

'You don't think it's the same guy?' she asked Grady.

'I'm not sure what I think. It could be…'

'But?' Iris asked.

'Well, there's the obvious fact that the place hasn't been torched,' Grady began.

'But each of the victims has essentially been dispatched in the same way. One gunshot wound to the head, surely that has to be more than just coincidence, when you look at the proximity of the victims and the time frame?' Iris was chewing on her lower lip, suddenly looking much younger than her usual confident self.

Slattery, quietly on the periphery, had to remind himself once more that this was her first real murder investigation. 'Ballistics'll answer that sharpish,' he grunted.

'Well, yes, I certainly wouldn't rule out that it's the same person responsible for all these deaths, I just…' Grady looked around him. Slattery knew what he was thinking: *how did you say that there was something not quite right about it.*

'Something about the whole place just looks staged,' Slattery put in, even though his opinion had not been asked for. Grady looked at him now, the familiar sliver of a smile about his lips. 'Whereas, the Crowe house – being there, even now, would give you shivers down your spine.'

And that was it; it was as if the place had only recently been visited by a darkness that Slattery had not seen in a very long time. He wasn't exactly sure what it was, but perhaps it was the difference between murder, which is a terrible thing, and the murder of innocence, which is just unthinkable. Whatever it was, it wasn't something he was about to say out loud now. 'For what • it's worth, I'm just saying, I think at this stage, we should keep an open mind, that's all.' Slattery stopped, a commotion outside, the echo of shouting and general racing about drifted through the open door on the cold night air.

'Sir.' One of the junior officers appeared at the door, red-faced and out of breath, looking from Grady to Cullen, probably not sure which of them to report to. 'It's Ollie Kerr. He's just scarpered.'

'Well, isn't that just bloody perfect,' Cullen said and she stomped off out to give whoever had been keeping an eye on him the mother of all goings over.

CHAPTER 25

Iris shivered as she gulped down the last drop of wine. She'd searched the cupboards in vain for something stronger, something that would warm her and take the edge off her fear. It was almost four in the morning. She knew it was being out there, near where Anna Crowe had lived, near where they had all died, near where she could have died herself. It had triggered this unstoppable shaking that was sending tremors through her, so even her bones seemed to rattle in her body. Delayed shock. That's what they'd call it. She knew the best thing for it was a warm drink. Keep warm. Stay calm. They hadn't left Kilgee until three and when she'd arrived back at the apartment it had suddenly hit her. She'd gone through the motions, she knew them well enough, had dealt with enough victims over the years. She was no victim, was she? She could have been, though. So easily, that night out in Kilgee, she should have said something, to someone – she knew then what she had to do.

She'd rung Grady first, wouldn't have known where to find him otherwise. His home wasn't what she'd have expected. A two-up, two-down in a nice old brick terrace that would once have been working class, but now its location made it a bit yuppie, a bit bohemian – this was Limerick, not enough ground to be one or the other. But then what did she expect, some kind of lad's pad – he was too old for that. He'd led her into the kitchen, a tasteful stainless steel and ash combination, unused, cold. His eyes were as tired as her own. She could see this was the last thing he'd expected.

'I didn't know where else to go,' she said simply.

The house was quiet, but it seemed to absorb her as if somehow making her feel safe. In the hall a Swiss clock rang out the half hour; it was a familiar sound. They had had a similar clock in their own hall when she was a child.

'Can I get you something?' He was taking down two tumblers from a shelf. It looked like it was the most used shelf in the house with all the daily provisions stored there. He poured a generous measure of Bushmills for each of them. 'I was going to have one anyway.'

He smiled at her and she realised it was the first time she'd seen him smile, a real smile that went all the way up to his eyes, crinkling the skin so he looked softer, older, gentler. He'd been morose since she'd first met him, if not scowling, then certainly sullen, but it suited him, she decided. He was dark and big and old enough to know himself. Maybe that's what marked him out as much as his looks; he was what he was and he was at peace with that. If he was haunted by anything it was ghosts from the past, there was nothing in the present or the future that would faze him.

They sat for a while, in his small 'front room', just sipping their whiskies. She began to feel the warmth envelop her and soon she felt as if she just might fall asleep. It was safe here, and beyond expectation, she actually felt comfortable, as though the place insulated her from the fear she'd felt earlier on. But the terror would come back; she knew that even as she felt it float away.

'I went out there… a couple of nights ago, to Kilgee.' She said the words softly. 'I'm not sure why, I'd left the Ship Inn, everyone seemed to be… going somewhere… I suppose I had nowhere else to go.' She smiled at him; she'd never imagined herself being so honest with anyone. 'I drove up to the Crowe cottage, had a look about. It was very dark, darker than it was out there tonight.' She gulped down some of her drink and shivered slightly. Grady looked around the room. Had it been a woman's house there might have been a throw, but the sitting room was bare of cushions or blankets. A grey suite of furniture, a bookcase, a couple of table lamps and a cast iron fireplace managed to fill it up.

'You're freezing.' He got up and walked to a switch beneath the stairs. He flicked it on, the heating she assumed, but she wasn't really cold, she didn't bother to say so, though.

'There was someone there.' She didn't want to go into all the details, but she had to tell someone. Perhaps, and this was one of the worst things that had struck her tonight – perhaps if she'd told him sooner, Veronique Majewski would still be alive.

'Did you see him?' Grady asked, leaning forward now in his chair.

'No, but I felt him, he was big, tall and sturdy, maybe slightly overweight. But he was strong and fairly fit.' She didn't have to say another word, the description fitted perfectly with Ollie Kerr.

'What happened?' Grady closed his eyes and she figured part of him didn't want to hear this any more than she wanted to tell it. 'What happened to you?'

'It was fine.' She did her best to make light of it – she'd never planned on being the quarry. 'He grabbed me, came up from behind, we struggled, and then I managed to give him a dig. I was on my way back to the car before he managed to get upright again.'

'Would he have seen you, your face, could he identify you?' Grady's voice was even, but behind his eyes she could see he knew it had been close.

'No, I doubt it, he was probably watching me for a while, but it was so dark, hard to tell what was what. He'd have seen the car, though, the number plate.'

'You had a station car?'

'No, my own.'

He sipped his drink thoughtfully. 'It would have happened anyway.' He looked across at her, maybe sensing that she was beginning to drift away from the conversation. 'Tonight, Veronique, you can't think anything else now.' His words were firm, his eyes steady.

'You don't know that, maybe if I'd said something.'

'You didn't because you were in shock; sometimes, fear can do that to you, you just went away and buried it. You're smart enough to know that you couldn't help that, it's just a coping mechanism.'

'It had to be Ollie Kerr, hadn't it?' She felt a raw shiver curl along her spine. 'Out there that night, the more I think about it now, it almost felt as if… he was waiting for…' She didn't finish it off, but they both knew it felt as if he was waiting for her.

'Maybe,' Grady murmured then sipped his drink thoughtfully. 'We discounted him earlier because it looked as if the place had been ransacked; the evidence of a second drink removed as if to wipe any trace of a stranger, but maybe he's smarter than we gave him credit for.' He was thinking out loud. She suspected that her visit here, her revelation, had somehow permitted her, for a short moment, to see into how his mind worked a case.

'So, Ollie Kerr is our killer?' Could it have been that simple all along, really? she wondered. 'What now?' She drained her glass.

'What now, indeed.' He sat back in his chair and exhaled deeply.

When she woke, she wasn't sure where she was, or what had happened. He'd thrown a blanket across her while she'd slept. The sound of her keys landing close to her ears woke her none too gently.

'Come on,' Grady said. 'Time to get moving.' He was already showered and dressed for work; she could smell fresh aftershave. Her watch showed her it was after seven. Her brain told her she was stupid to have let herself fall asleep here, stupid to show her vulnerability. 'I'm heading in now. I presume you'd like to get back and have a shower before you go to work?' He was standing over her, waiting for her to leave. She got herself up from the chair, mortified; he'd never see her like this again.

CHAPTER 26

Cullen was at the station before him; Grady wasn't really surprised. He closed the door to her office; you never knew who'd be knocking around between now and eight o'clock.

'We have something,' he said, before sitting opposite her.

'Is it a problem?' She eyed him over her glasses.

'Only if we make it into one.' He could see that she was waiting for him to tell her Slattery had managed to fuck something up. 'Iris called round to my house last night.'

'I'd guessed as much…'

'No, not like that.' Under different circumstances he'd have been tempted. 'She was upset, she told me that she'd been out in Kilgee some evening last week; she was attacked, but she said nothing.'

'How badly?' Cullen's face was serious now.

'Hard to say, I assume it was just a scuffle – at least I hope so.'

'Maybe she thought if she said anything we'd have taken her off the case,' Cullen said quietly.

Grady raised an eyebrow at her. 'Maybe she'd have been right.' They both knew it would have been the only ethical thing to do. 'Anyway, at this stage, what difference does it make?' He'd already decided he was going to fight to keep her on the team. There was no special reason, other than he knew how much she wanted to be there and she was a worker, he could see that. 'If he was still hanging around there last night, he'd have surely taken a stroll over to the Kerr place; more than likely he'll have spotted her again, though she reckons he can no more identify her than she can him.'

'Did she have anything at all?' Cullen asked. Already she looked tired and their day hadn't even started yet.

'She didn't see his face; it was dark, and he jumped her from behind. She said he was big, tall and heavy, maybe overweight – sounds like Ollie Kerr even just from that.'

'So he was on her?' Cullen lowered her eyes, Grady wasn't sure if she closed them tight, maybe trying to rid herself of what Iris might have been through. 'Christ.'

'Look, it gives us something to go on, right?' He looked at her now, squaring his jaw up, knowing he didn't really need to say what he was going to say. 'Obviously, we don't say where we got our description, such as it is, from…'

'Obviously.' The word was dry and cynical, but Grady felt she wouldn't let Iris down either.

'So we bring him in for questioning today?'

'Soon as.' Cullen's eyes lit up. Finally, they both knew, the trail was warm.

Grady's only worry as he headed back to his own office was of Slattery doing something wildly inappropriate. Perhaps Iris would make sure that didn't happen. He'd seen another side to her now, a side he'd never have imagined. He recognised something of his own remoteness in her, as though she would keep people at arm's length for as long as she could. Most of his colleagues knew nothing of his past. Apart from June and Slattery, they had no idea that he was alone in the world apart from this place. He didn't need a counsellor to tell him it was this emptiness that made him push away anyone who got too close. Shrinks would say it was a fear of loss. Slattery said, *Death fucked you good and proper, no point fighting it.* Still that was his story and he didn't have time to think of it today.

He decided now he'd talk to Iris about working Murder. She wanted Dublin, but that was a closed shop, where as Limerick… He knew that she wouldn't be talked out of it – he'd been the very same, and maybe Iris Locke was even more determined. She was, after all, her father's daughter. If she was going to work Murder anywhere, he was going to do his damnedest to make sure it was here, where at least he could keep an eye on her, keep her safe.

*

He'd arrived before any of them. Picked his spot good and early. He was going to find her today, find her, follow her and then… He had watched her the previous evening. Did she know it was him? He'd wondered if perhaps she'd just been playing with him.

'Sorry, mate.' One of the press guys who had arrived after him was hogging his space.

'Watch yourself, fucker. I was here first.' He growled at the camera operator. A small, butty bloke, no match for him and they both knew it. He wrapped his coat close around him. It was cold this morning, cold and damp and he was planning on staying here for a while. He'd like to take her home with him, keep her there forever; she belonged in Kilgee, belonged with him.

The morning was beginning to brighten around him. Overhead, the sun was making a valiant attempt at breaking through the ocean of clouds that knotted and bolted across the sky. It would be overcast again today; too much cloud cover to expect any clearance. About him, he felt a swell of excitement in the reporters who'd managed unwittingly to give him cover, a sort of human form of camouflage. They'd descended from across the country to salivate over the latest Limerick murder. The connection with the Baby Fairley case fuelled their curiosity. They all looked the same, leather jackets, jeans, gloves on the camera men, scarves on the reporters – an unofficial uniform – their noses red from the early morning and maybe a late night beforehand. He'd had a late night, but he'd slept soundly, maybe that was because he had a plan now.

The rustle around him had almost grown to fever pitch. He craned his neck to catch a glimpse of what the reporters were becoming animated about.

Across the road, just outside the station, he saw her. Walking along, like she hadn't a care in the world. She was wearing the same clothes as last night, but her hair was done and she looked well made-up. He fancied, that even from here, he could smell her perfume, but he wasn't stupid enough to actually believe that. He walked along, behind some of the reporters, to get a better look before she ran up the steps into the station. He was by far the tallest man on the pavement, but still, he found himself reaching onto the tips of his toes to garner a better view. One of the men in front of him shouted something across the road at her, whistled too, trying to get her attention. He swiped a large palm across the back of the bloke's head. The blow knocked him sideways into his colleague, who was filming Iris making her way into the station. Both men ended up on the road, their clothes wet and dirty, their expressions shocked. *Teach you a fecking lesson.* By the time the guy got to his feet, he'd be well gone. Last thing he wanted was to be in the middle of any scuffle, last thing he wanted was notice. He moved cautiously along the pack, no one was going to pick a fight with him anyway. He looked mean and he looked dangerous.

CHAPTER 27

The case conference had not lasted long. It seemed to Iris that all the work had been done before they'd sat down to review Veronique Majewski's murder. The big brass sat stony-faced and silent at the top of the incident room. It shouldn't have gone this far and Iris felt a wrench of guilt once more for not telling someone what had happened that night at the cottage.

'We're bringing in Ollie Kerr today, that's Veronique's partner. Westmont, take a couple of uniforms out to the barracks in Kilgee. He's meant to call in today for an interview,' Grady said. He walked the length of the case board, a new murder added more pressure than they needed.

'How come we're so sure of ourselves all of a sudden?' Slattery asked, a sneer from the back of the room. He looked as if he hadn't gone home for the night, instead found a bar stool and slept where he sat, maybe didn't sleep at all. As far as Iris knew, he'd had five minutes at the murder scene; perhaps it was enough to put his nose out of joint. She wondered as she looked now from him to Grady exactly how much history they shared. How far would one go to look out for the other?

'We've had a description of someone hanging out around the Crowe house in the nights since Anna Crowe and her family were murdered. The description best fits Ollie Kerr.'

'That was kept quiet,' Slattery frowned.

'It was an anonymous phone call this morning. I just happened to pick it up, early.'

Slattery had to know he was lying. He'd seen too many good liars to be fooled by someone he'd known for so long. Iris wondered if they were acting on her information alone. Had what she'd said to Grady really been that important to the case? He'd been so cool with her when she'd woken in the morning, left the house so quickly she began to wonder if she'd dreamed the night before. He'd seemed so sincere, so genuine. Then, this morning, it was as if she was dealing with a completely different person, a blank wall of a man with not a shred of warmth.

'What about Boran?' June asked.

'Ah, I'm afraid Darach Boran is helping us with our enquiries in another area at the moment.' Cullen smiled at Byrne. 'Customs and Excise made a swoop on his home; seems Mr Boran was running a lucrative sideline in importing illegal cigarettes. Storing them in the house on St Abatti's Terrace, too, so no wonder he was jumpy when two detectives called to visit.'

'Jesus.' It was obviously news to Westmont. 'That scumbag, we just knew he was hiding something.'

'Anyway, it seems his last big shipment came in off the coast of Donegal the night Anna Crowe was murdered. While his WI ladies danced the night away to a local crooner, Boran was out unloading his cargo.' Cullen smiled across at Grady. Normally, Iris would want to take the credit for this nugget, but this morning, with another victim in the morgue, her contribution had lost its sheen for her – still, it had been down to her, so that was something.

'Aye, he's a cool customer all right,' Slattery said from the back of the room, as if this was all news to him.

'And Deaver?' Westmont asked.

'We felt at the time he wasn't in the frame. Of course we'll check out to see if he has an alibi for last night, but if he's been in the cottage we'll have his DNA picked up soon enough,' Grady said. They'd thought about getting him onto a sheltered housing list, but Deaver needed more than that, so Grady had managed to pull some strings. For now, he was staying in an addiction treatment centre – he was lucky even if he couldn't see that yet. He was drying out, it would be up to him which way he turned after that.

'So that just leaves Adrian Crowe…' someone at the back of the room barked.

'We've found nothing to put Crowe out at the scene once the fire was started when his wife and family died,' Grady began. 'I had a feeling when I watched our last interview with him that he'd told us everything he knew. What about you, Slattery?'

'Felt the same, but so long as we have victims and no accused, I'll not be happy to let Crowe rest on his laurels.' Slattery puffed.

'The man is grieving, Slattery, give him a break,' Cullen said drily.

Grady called Iris aside as soon as he'd delegated the work around the room and motioned her to follow him back to his office. When he switched on the light, she had a feeling he hadn't been here since yesterday; if he left early this morning it wasn't to come in here.

'About last night,' he began.

'I'm sorry.' She kept her eyes straight ahead, couldn't meet his. Last thing she'd ever wanted was for any of them to see her as weak. She tossed her hair away from her face and when she sat opposite him, she sat tall and straight, smoothing out her skirt to cover as far down her legs as possible. 'It was silly of me to react like that, probably just being out there again last night. I shouldn't have bothered you with it.'

'It wasn't any bother, you needed to tell someone. I only wish you'd said it sooner.' He sat back in his chair, looked at her now.

She smiled, glossing over the fear, the embarrassment. 'It was just one of those things, stupid, stupid.'

'It was dangerous, he could have killed you…' Grady stopped speaking and she felt his presence, strong and resilient, reminding her of why she had gone to him last night, this sense that he might protect her in some way.

'Well, he didn't. So, it's all right.'

'I'm not taking you off the case, if that's what you're worried about.'

'What's that supposed to mean?'

'Oh, come on, you know, if you'd told me this a week ago, I'd have had to take you off the case immediately…'

'Bloody hell.' She had blurted the words before she had time to think; he raised a palm to stop her going any further.

'But,' his tone was unrelenting, 'I'm going to have to insist you speak to someone. Not here, outside. I'll get some names for you.'

'You're not serious? I'm fine, I don't need counselling or debriefing or whatever it is you want to call it.' She watched as a dark cloud channelled across his expression.

'Locke, you had debriefing last night. You came to my door, God knows why, but you needed to talk to someone and maybe I was the only one you could think of. Either way, we're dealing with a dangerous killer now. He has murdered four people, and if it wasn't for the fact that he didn't have time to plan with you, we might be looking at five bodies.'

She felt as if he'd just thrown a bucket of water over her. She couldn't speak, couldn't think.

'I need you to work with Slattery today. Keep an eye on things.'

She was tempted to ask, *Don't you trust Slattery?* but knew she was already treading on very thin ice.

*

'It seems to me that the easiest way for us to find out anything about that missing kid now is to ask your old man,' Slattery said, but he didn't look at her.

'I suppose.' Iris exhaled deeply; perhaps that was half the problem.

'So, ask him?'

'Ask him what?'

'Ask him what we need to know.' It seemed reasonable enough when Slattery said it like that. Her father had always been happy to talk about old cases, well, the ones that he solved anyway. 'Look, he's probably the only one left around now who actually remembers everything there is to do with it.'

'Cullen spent a bit of time on it too…'

'Did she?'

'Yeah, when she got made up to detective sergeant, kind of like an exercise while she was still on probation, I think my father asked her to look at it.'

'Wouldn't have been unusual way back then, especially for a woman gaining rank, but she doesn't seem to like talking about it much.'

'No, who does want to talk about the ones they never closed, though?'

'True.' He seemed to mull over something for a few minutes, gazed out at the passing wet streets of Limerick.

'And anyway, she's certain there's no link,' Iris said, but her words weren't convincing and they sure as hell didn't take in Slattery.

'Do you think maybe she doesn't want you to look at it for some other reason?' She could sense a smile forming about the words; they were softly spoken; but his eyes never left the road.

'No.' She answered too quickly. 'No, I don't think she's trying to cover anything up, I…' *Did she really not think there was more to the missing baby case than met the eye?* She thought back to the transcripts from Adrian Crowe's interview, and to her last conversation with Anita Cullen about the case. She hadn't wanted to examine her own motives too closely since and so she'd buried any misgivings she had. 'How do you mean?'

'Well, I don't know, maybe one of them messed up. Maybe, if there was anything left worth looking at, it just might show that someone had fucked up big time along the way – and that wouldn't look good for either her or your father, now would it?'

'My father was not the kind of man to cover something like that up.' As she said the words she knew what she sounded like. 'I'm sure of it. Anyway, even if they did,' she corrected herself, 'even if *she* did we have no way of finding out now.'

'Oh, dear girl,' Slattery said wearily, 'there are always ways to find out things.' He held out a hand. 'Left here.'

'Cullen doesn't want us anywhere near the Baby Fairley case, does she?'

It was the first time she'd actually admitted it. Cullen did not want the earlier Fairley case looked at; that was just wrong, and no matter how badly she wanted into Murder, she had to ask herself on what terms she wanted to be there. If she didn't look at the Fairley case now, what would she be asked to ignore or maybe do in a future investigation? And sitting here with the smell of stale fags off Slattery and the unending drizzle of Limerick rain petering down the windscreen, she knew. This was not about one-upmanship on her father. It was not about making her name in the Murder Team in Limerick. This was about a baby who went missing, a baby who meant enough to Anna Crowe to send her back to a killer. It was about a baby that somehow had connected with Iris. This was about a missing baby that was never found; probably a dead baby. Perhaps it would make no difference to Anna Crowe now, no difference to Baby Fairley, but Iris knew with certainty it would make the world of a difference to her.

'I might know someone… if you're interested.' He motioned her to turn the car around and they were headed back towards the city centre before she had time to think. 'This guy was a councillor back in the day, spent his time on various committees. I think he knows more of what goes on in this country than the *Irish Times*. He knows more about the police than the Minister for Justice.'

They pulled the car up outside a small jewellery shop on Grundel Street. It was a shop that had seen better days, probably made as much now on second-hand jewellery as it did on anything shiny or new. Jackie Tiernan looked like a man in his eighties, crooked and squat at the back of his little shop, but behind his thick glasses, his eyes were quick, his handshake was strong, and his welcome for Slattery was warm.

'So, you're still in the land of the living, hah?' He looked over Slattery, and Locke wondered if he was gauging who would be first to die.

'When I'm planning on heading off towards the watering hole in the sky, you'll be the first to know. You might even be there to welcome me!'

'Who's to say, but I'm not planning on going anywhere for a while, too many grandkids to keep an eye out for, you know the score.'

'Ah, sure, has to be done,' Slattery said and Locke wondered if Slattery could have grandchildren. She couldn't imagine him ever having had kids, but she knew now, he had a daughter – Angela. Before that phone call, she'd have laid money they'd be born detectives, probably come out with a cigarette in one hand and a warrant in the other.

'You keeping busy these days?' Slattery looked around the shop; it was empty save for themselves.

'Ara, sure you have to keep active, don't you,' he tapped the side of his head, 'good for the brain… keeping all sorts of busy up.' He smiled at Slattery, at some unsaid joke that Iris wasn't privy to.

'Good that you're still in tune. Can you check something for me, but it has to be as silent as that grave we're both running away from.' Slattery lowered his voice; Iris reckoned there was no need. Apart from the odd neighbour calling in here, it wasn't the busiest spot on benefits day. Jackie Tierney probably bought as much as he sold when it came to gold these days.

'Do you remember the Baby Fairley case, years back?'

'Jesus, Slattery, everyone remembers that case. I had small kids of me own then, put the fear of God in me, that one did. Ye ever get anyone for it?'

'No.' Slattery sniffed. His lower lip curled into a sneer that said whoever did it wouldn't come out too good if Slattery got him first.

'What kind of things are you thinking – paedo rings? 'Cos anything I ever heard along those lines I've passed straight on to you, you know that.' Paedophiles were scum as far as any decent criminal was concerned, hardly counted as human beings at all.

'Sure, and I understand how you feel, but I'm kind of thinking, maybe someone fucked up on the Fairley case. I want to see if there are any connections that aren't... obvious to us in the force, if you know what I mean.' He smiled at Tierney; they evidently had their own secrets and Iris was happy not to know too much about them. He lowered his voice further, looked about furtively and she could see that Tierney was enjoying being part of something of enough importance to bring two detectives to his door. 'If there was a connection between her and a senior officer in the police, maybe, or someone who could make things disappear.'

'Can you give me a name?'

'I can, but it mightn't mean anything to you. You know the way these things work, one to do the nasty...'

'Aye, another to fire the balls?'

'Exactly. Either way, check out an old bird called Anita Cullen, she was in Templemore until a couple of days ago...'

'She rattle your cage?' Tierney smiled with a wisdom that was disarming.

'She's a pencil pusher, Tierney.' He reserved for the words as much disdain as any voice could carry. It was as if she was worse than a child molester, or maybe in Slattery's case, a pioneer. 'Anyway, you have my number, right?'

'I'm sure I have it somewhere.' Tierney looked around the shop and Iris figured she wouldn't want to be going looking for a name card among the decades of slips of paper and bits of notes that were scattered along the shelf behind him. 'Might as well give it to me again, just in case,' he said, taking the card Slattery had managed to have ready to hand over to him. If they heard anything back from this old codger it'd be second-hand information. That didn't bother her too much; she had no desire to get caught up in any kind of contention with Cullen. Slattery, on the other hand grinned, delighted to be digging for a bit of dirt on her.

When they got out of the shop, Slattery lit up a fag. 'That won't take long,' he said as he admired the sliver of smoke that peppered the light breeze settling in around the city. 'And the thing about Tierney is I've never found him to be wrong about anything.'

'So how...?' Locke knew she didn't need to finish the sentence.

'He knows everyone. If he doesn't, he knew their fathers, or their grandfathers and that doesn't just go for Limerick. He was involved in everything from the Jewellers' Association of Ireland to the Irish Farmers' Association back in the day. I think he even had a foot in the door of the NUJ.' Slattery smiled to himself. 'He's a little-known treasure here in the centre of Limerick, and I'll nearly guarantee you he'll be back to us with something before the day is out.'

'If there's anything to get.' Locke didn't want to rain on Slattery's parade, but she wasn't sure she wanted anything on Cullen.

'Yeah, sure, that's if there's anything.' Slattery's voice was flat, but Locke could sense a bristling excitement from him.

CHAPTER 28

The post-mortem results were pretty much what they had expected. Grady sent Slattery and Locke along. Of course, Slattery bitched about having to attend, it was only afterwards he admitted to Grady that he'd known the victim. PMs were never easy, even less so when the victim was known to you beforehand. Burn victims were the worst. Slattery reckoned it was the smell. Grady thought it was the fact that the face and body screwed up so it looked like they'd be forever in agony, their spirits only drifting away long after the damage had been done.

'Veronique Majewski died from one bullet to the head. Probably taken at a range of about eight feet,' Grady told Cullen who had raised her attention away from what appeared to be CCTV footage on her computer screen.

'So her killer hadn't been close, probably the other side of the kitchen?'

'Exactly. If it was Kerr, why not come up as close as he had with Anna, Sylvie and Martin?'

'More personal?'

'That would make sense if it was the other way round, surely?' They were taking random shots, hoping to hit a target. 'It's a different gun.'

'Well, Kerr has plenty of those.'

'Not like the ones we saw at the cottage.' Grady had never seen a private collection of guns so vast. Most were legal, licences were hung on the wall above each firearm, but there were a couple that shouldn't have been there. Westmont had reckoned there was one from Iraq, one that had probably come from Lebanon, maybe thirty years ago. No doubt, Kerr had a taste for guns, but had he a taste for murder?

'He shoots things, doesn't he?' Cullen said, as if somehow that was enough. But, Grady knew, his own father had a shotgun. Double barrel, his mother had hated it, his father had gone out twice a year, with a local club. He was no murderer though.

'Bit of a difference between going out and shooting ducks and killing the neighbours off.' Grady raised an eyebrow. 'I'd say the DPP might agree with me too.'

'Still, he has opportunity; he certainly has the means...' She tapped a button on the screen before her, smiling slightly to herself, paused the footage she'd been searching.

'And the motive?' Grady looked at her. 'Give me the motive and we'll arrest him now, shall we?'

'He's a bloody weirdo, Grady, that's as pointed as the top of Croagh Patrick.' She looked at him now, softened her expression. 'Any word from Westmont?'

'Nothing. Kerr hasn't turned up to collect his dole anyway.' Grady didn't expect him until the afternoon at least.

'Maybe give the boyos out at the cottage a heads-up too. If he turns up there, nab him.' She looked thoughtful now. 'How come we have no interview recorded with him, have you thought of that? Every neighbour in the village was questioned, most of them twice over, but we never actually managed to talk to him.'

'Yeah, I know, I've gone through the interviews with Dennis Blake. Nothing.' It was as if he'd slipped through the cracks of each visit. They'd only known about him because Veronique had mentioned him in an interview with one of the uniforms.

Grady looked out the window. Still on the path opposite a crowd of reporters waited for news about the case. Grady scanned the crowd again, searching for something; he wasn't sure what, something or somebody who shouldn't be there. 'I thought I saw someone there earlier,' he jerked his thumb towards the window.

'Oh?' Cullen craned her neck to see past him.

'Probably nothing, overactive imagination.' He shrugged, but he still hadn't shaken off the feeling that chewed at him today. Someone was watching them, not just camping out waiting for a story, but stalking them, waiting for them to make a mistake, or maybe waiting for something else. 'Do you fancy the same murderer for both?'

Cullen looked at him. 'Yes.' He didn't need anything more than that. 'You?'

His eyes drifted once more towards the street outside. 'What are the connections, apart from geographical? They were two women, within a decade of each other in age, living within a couple of hundred metres of each other. There it ends. It might be enough if Anna Crowe and her kids hadn't seemed so personal, but it was just business with Veronique. A bullet to the head.' He thought for a minute. 'But then what does that make it – a big coincidence? We don't get many of those in Murder, do we?

'So it's Ollie Kerr?' Cullen looked uneasy. 'See, that's where it gets awkward, isn't it?'

'Not if it's two different murderers.'

'So then we're back to why…' Cullen sat back, considered her cup for a moment and then left it on the desk.

'For Anna Crowe, I'm betting passion.' Grady looked at her with such conviction, it was easy to go along with the theory. He held up a hand. 'I'm just putting it out there. From what we know of her, she was everything some loopy loo would focus on – beautiful, talented, removed, mysterious and – to her own downfall – kind.'

'So, either the husband or Deaver? Kerr or Boran?'

'You see that's where we've run aground…'

'Even still, you don't sound very convinced.' Cullen smiled.

'That's because I'm not. We've looked at those two and there's nothing, nothing that truly persuades me either of them is guilty. Let's face it, neither of them are blokes you'd especially warm to; it wouldn't be a scourge exactly to see them put away for a while.'

'But?'

'Kerr is a bit of a loner, isn't he? I'm betting if we had a profiler in here, he's the first one they'd pick out.'

'Doesn't mean the profiler would be right, though, does it?'

He looked thoughtful, checked the window again. 'How did we miss him before?'

'He wasn't there, I suppose. As you said, it was only because Veronique mentioned him that we even knew he existed.'

'Yeah, but he was never interviewed, there's not one word from him. He was never there.' Grady tapped the side of his head, leaned forward just a fraction, then his eyes darted towards the window once more, his voice Arctic. 'Perhaps, he's been here all the time.'

'Did Slattery know about him?' She nodded towards the screen before her and Grady bent across to see what she was watching. 'Did Slattery know about him?' Her voice was sterner now, but Grady hardly registered it.

Instead, he felt a cold trickle of sweat trace down his spine, his head spun, just a fraction, enough to make him want to vomit. The screen was a jittery white before him; a shadowy figure had paused midway, like a fat marionette, the puppeteer just beyond the camera lenses. The shot was taken in a corridor that ran to an exit at the back of the station – no one ever used those rear entrances. Or at least, that's what Grady and obviously Slattery had believed. A cartoon version of Slattery standing in the Ship Inn shot like a steam train across his brain. The familiar thick body, with a short fat arm, extended towards the bar counter, taking up his pint, or his half one. Bending his left arm and throwing his head back slightly as he swilled like he'd never manage to get quite enough into him. The shot before Grady now had paused

Slattery midway and there, though slightly blurred thanks to the freeze frame, was a quarter bottle of Jameson, three swallows flying towards Slattery's open mouth. Might as well have been holding his own hand gun, cocked with a finger on the trigger, because Grady knew with certainty, that before the day was out, Cullen fully intended to blow Slattery away.

There was nothing more to say. Grady left the office, headed for his own quiet corner and slumped at his desk. It felt like he'd walked in on Slattery's wake, only no one had told Slattery he was a dead man walking.

Grady sat in his cramped office, looking about him. It was the end of the road for Slattery, this much he knew. If they went back over his HR file, and they would, he'd been warned before, suspended at one stage for drinking on the job. He'd already had a fair reputation when Grady had struck up with him. But there was no denying he was still a good detective, and, Grady knew, that if he wasn't a guard, well then, he might as well be dead. He'd given it everything he was worth over the years, given it so much it had cost him his marriage and his daughter – they'd never forgive him. And none of them, not Byrne or any of the rest of them, had ever tried to stop him. None of them had said, 'Go home, Slattery, enjoy your kid, mow the lawn for Maureen, take a break – be normal.'

Was he any better? Grady turned his chair to look out the window. Beyond the station, on the footpath opposite, a pack of journalists and cameras, waiting for news on the investigation. He scanned the crowd. Some of the faces he recognised, most not. They were a raggle-taggle of news reporters, probably a few freelance, hoping for something to flog that might pay the rent for the week. Grady didn't like them, but he could hardly blame them for doing their job.

He began to turn away, when – from the side of his eye – something caught his attention. Something familiar, a mouth or a jaw bone. He'd just caught a flash of something moving through the crowd, watching him, but when Grady looked back again it was nowhere to be seen. He scanned the gathering once more, moving methodically along the lines, taking in the faces, the clothes, the draggle of equipment, but there was nothing and after a couple of minutes he wondered if perhaps he'd imagined it. Not that he could say exactly who it was, but just that it didn't belong on his doorstep on a miserable afternoon.

He was tempted to run from the office, take the wide stone steps two at a time and rush to the other side of the street. Taking each face in turn and studying it, just to be sure, but he knew he wouldn't. Whoever he'd seen there or whoever he thought he'd seen there were well gone by now, weren't they? It was probably some innocent passer-by, who'd got caught up in the throng for a moment while making his way home. Still, Grady felt uneasy. He pulled the blind down slightly, feeling he was under surveillance now, the prey and not the hunter. When his phone rang, it startled him. He found it beneath open files he hadn't read yet. It was Westmont, breathless and excited.

'We're out at Kerr's place,' he said, shouting above the din of the gathering wind.

'Is he there?' Again an uneasy feeling swept across Grady, but he brushed it off.

'No, but we've found something else…' Westmont's voice moved away from the phone as if his attention was shared with something far more interesting.

'I can hardly hear you,' Grady said.

'Sorry, sir, I'm moving outside now. It's just I had to ring to tell you. We've found a box of photographs, newspaper cuttings, like someone was building up a file on…' His voice cut off, the line breaking up again. Grady could just imagine him, jumping about, trying hard to keep out of any cow pats, trying hard to sound as professional as he could, maybe fooling most of the techies there that he actually knew what he was doing. 'It's like a whole file on the Crowes: from what I've seen it's going right back to when the baby was taken.'

'Have the forensic boys got it now?' Grady wiped from his mind the vision of Westmont hugging it to him, delighted with his prize, destroying whatever bit of DNA evidence they might be able to take from it. Grady shuddered despite himself.

'Yeah, it's gone for analysis – they say it won't take long, they're going to make copies and send them across.'

'Finally, something is going our way, thanks for that, Westmont.' He'd needed some good news. He moved towards the window once more, lifted the blinds and tried hard to ignore the uneasy feeling that was making its way through his bones. Grady lifted the blind slightly, looked out the window. Still on the path opposite a crowd of reporters waited for news about the case. Grady scanned the crowd again, searching for something; he wasn't sure what, something or somebody who shouldn't be there. And then it dawned on him, perhaps it was why they hadn't interviewed Kerr – how could they when he'd been here all along?

*

By four o'clock Iris was wrecked, feeling the tiredness of the previous night's lack of sleep. There was a briefing in an hour, a quick wrap-up of everything they'd been doing for the day. It had been sixteen-hour days since Anna Crowe and her family had been murdered, most of the squad was exhausted. Either way, Iris decided that if there were going to be any detectives waiting on late, she was going to be one of them. She had no commitments; no one would really care if she never got home to bed, and most of all she wanted to show she was keen. She wanted in to Murder in Limerick and she was going to do her damnedest to show that she was the woman for the job. She decided to nip back to the apartment, just for an hour, grab a shower, and change her clothes.

That should make all the difference in the world to how she felt. She was still wearing the same suit she'd had on the previous day. It may not have smelled exactly, but it had looked better all the same.

The evening was drawing in, damp and dark, but it was only a fifteen-minute walk to her apartment so she pulled her coat collar close to her throat and set off. The fresh air would do her good. She soon left Corbally station behind, the rally of press photographers lying in wait, hoping that there would be something to report today, good or bad. It was all news, and she wondered if it mattered much to them either way.

Iris walked on, past the Georgian buildings that marked Limerick as a city worth fighting for. It had been a city of sieges and rebellions over the years, and even today, the blemishes of battle remained on city walls. Ahead of her she saw Thomond Bridge, the traffic bumper to bumper, everyone in a rush to leave the city behind. The wind was whipping up nicely, and if Iris thought she heard a footfall behind her, it could as easily have been carried from some distance off on the breeze. The mist started to thicken and she picked up her pace. It felt as if she'd been indoors forever when it massaged her cheek, a gentle, cool cleansing that she hoped would wash away some of her fatigue before she got back to the apartment.

She pulled her phone from her bag. This, all of this, Limerick, Baby Fairley, Anna, her kids and now Veronique – they deserved more. She punched in her father's number, bit down the last of her pride. She left a message, wasn't sure what to say, something about the old Fairley case, if there truly was a connection, well, it didn't bear thinking about. He'd call her as soon as he got a chance, the mention of a child would be enough to make him want to help. She knew him like no one else; he'd do anything to keep a child safe.

As she turned in towards the apartment, she felt a shiver run through her. She shook it off as a flashback to the night out in

Kilgee. Occasionally, it struck her that this case and in particular that night in Kilgee had left a handprint on her. Perhaps it would fade with time, or at least that's what she was telling herself. She'd come across evil before, the terrible things people do to each other, so often there could be no explanation. The thing was, though, and perhaps this was what had driven her to Coleman Grady's house in the early hours of the morning – she'd never known what it was to be the victim. If she was honest, it wasn't a label she could carry easily. But now, in the cold misty streets of Limerick, she wondered if maybe she wasn't over reacting. *It's late afternoon, with lots of people and traffic about, and here I am, still spooked.* A small voice worked its way from her brain, calming down her nervous system, so that the tingling feeling that had begun to riddle along her spine quelled somewhat. She couldn't let that kind of fear take her over, not now, not when she was so close to getting onto a murder team. Had she really been that afraid? She struck in the number combination to open the front door of the apartment block, stalking her way across the empty foyer. She did not notice the hand that held the door ajar behind her. Did not see the eyes that travelled to the fourth floor where the lift stopped to let her out. Did not guess for one moment that she was in the sights of a pursuer, did not realise that an invisible clock ticked in his brain and as he circled closer his excitement grew at the thought of her.

CHAPTER 29

It was clearly a summons, not a request; Slattery was to head for Cullen's office immediately on return to the station. Do not pass go, do not have a cup of tea, do not waste any time in getting there. Slattery knocked, not too lightly, on her office door. He was looking forward to a fatty rasher sandwich when he'd finished with her. He'd guessed it was the fags, what else could it be? He hadn't, so far as he knew, stepped on too many toes recently, certainly nothing that might warrant an official complaint, and as for the fags, well, these things happen, don't they? Just an unfortunate incident of being in the wrong place at the wrong time, and thanks to Iris, no harm done.

Cullen was on the phone, peered over glasses that had more frame than lenses – *Too small for her fat face*, he thought. They were too stylish to sit on her plain features; they jarred with her jowls and with her thinning hair. Mostly, they highlighted her small eyes that seemed to fall further into the folds of skin that drooped from her lids and bulged from the bags beneath them. She'd never been a beauty and age had not helped her. She motioned towards an uncomfortable chair and he took it. *Won't be long here*, he thought. When she put the phone down it was with a thoughtful click, as if she was moving onto the next unpleasant part of her day.

'Slattery.' Spoken with a sigh, as if even the thought of him pained her. 'I'm not going to beat about the bush here.' She looked towards him. 'You're a big boy and regardless of whatever else you are, you're nobody's fool.'

It was more than he'd bargained for, he supposed. If he'd worried about what she'd thought of him, apart from intense dislike, then she'd have said, 'thick as an ass,' all brawn and attitude, no brains worth talking about. And maybe, she'd have been right. For all he knew, and for most of what he believed, at this stage well over two thirds of his once working brains were now stewed in the alcohol in which he continued to steep them. He had lost hours of his life. Vanished. Couldn't say where he'd been for them, who he'd spoken to – or probably insulted – and he knew with certainty those times would never return. He figured, too, that these absences would occur more frequently as time went on, and he was okay with that. Really, there was damn all he could do about it anyway.

'It's come to my attention that you've been boozing…'

'That's hardly news.'

'On the job.' She looked at him now across the top of her unfortunate glasses. 'Here, in the station, Slattery, and we both know what that means, don't we?' She managed a thin smile. He figured it had been wide as a mile when she'd picked up this nugget.

'Can't say as I remember having anything more than a whiskey with Grady at the end of the last case, but if that's a problem, well, then…'

'No one's ever had their knuckles wrapped for an end of day drink, when you're off duty, when it's shared at the end of a case, when it's…' she looked at him meaningfully, '*not a problem.*'

'My drinking is not a problem.' He spoke with conviction. The booze didn't slow him down, he was as quick any of the new bright sparks that had come through the door.

'You have an unpleasant manner, Slattery, and a bad attitude. We could overlook one, if the other was just a little less noxious, but the two together? Well, you're lucky to have lasted this length.' She looked down at the papers before her. 'I'm putting you on suspension, pending disciplinary.' Her words began to fuzz into a stream of meaningless sounds. 'You'll get full pay when you're off, but… and I'm not saying this lightly, once the disciplinary is over, you're going to be out on your butt.' Her eyes glided to her diary. Moving on.

'Hang on a minute.' Slattery felt himself, as though waking from a coma, coming back from a nasty shock. 'You can't do that; you can't just throw me out on a couple of words. You…' The words would not come. He was fighting a losing battle, this wasn't about the drink, and it wasn't about the job. This was about Anita Cullen and the fact that he'd screwed up her chance of promotion and now she was going to watch him pay for it. Slowly and satisfyingly. Anyone else would get a warning, counselling and plenty of leave – this wasn't about supporting him. This was all about her and what had happened so far back in time it was barely a blur to him any more. But for all that, she couldn't throw him out on his butt just on her word, could she?

'Oh, Slattery,' her voice was soft, knowing, irritating, 'do you really think that I'd risk my reputation on you?' She swivelled her computer screen towards him, a freeze frame of him in an empty corridor lifting a bottle of whiskey towards his mouth.

'Have you told Byrne?'

'He will be fully briefed.' She smiled sweetly, evasively.

He had too much on Byrne over the years for the old man to screw him like this. 'We'll see about this.' His voice was even, he couldn't remember a time when he'd been more sober in his life. He took out his identity card, and his hand gun, placed them on the table between them, stood silently and headed for the door. 'It's not the last you'll be hearing from me, you auld bitch.' He could hear her laugh as he banged the door behind him. It was, he knew, a fair cop.

To say that Slattery was shell-shocked only half covered his mental state as he managed to make his way through the incident room. No sign of Grady either. No sign of anyone. What could he say to them even if they were there? He was practical enough to know, there was nothing Grady could do for him now, the only one who could help was Byrne.

'Feck off,' he'd told June as she had hovered about his desk while Slattery, through eyes burning with temper, had searched for he knew not what.

'You all right?' June had just asked once she'd taken in Slattery's general air of *don't mess with me* bullishness.

'Oh yeah, I'm just brilliant, how do I look to you, kiddo? Like a fucking survivor, do I?' If he shouldn't take it out on June it wasn't something that was going to keep him awake.

'I'm only asking. You look like shit, Slattery; if you don't begin to wise up…'

'Too late.' Slattery put up a hand, not in defence, so much as in peace.

'How do you mean, too late… I'm just saying, a good night's sleep, lay off the gargle for a bit…' She wasn't even looking at Slattery now, wouldn't maintain the eye contact and so Slattery knew, she didn't want a row.

'Answer me this, *friend*.' He leaned so hard on the word, June could only wonder if it was ironic or not. 'You came looking for me a few days ago, found me in the corridor.' He jerked a thumb towards an almost unused emergency exit sign. 'Am I right so far?'

June had the good grace to avoid his eyes; looking out for him had been her full-time occupation since her husband had died – was this what she thought was best for him? He was too blind with rage to think clearly now.

'So, you slunk off, saw what you saw and kept it to yourself.'

Slattery could feel his fury rise through the centre of his body. Was he having a heart attack? But he suspected, no, this was just disappointment, regret and something else he didn't want to put a label on. A great big, volcanic eruption of emotion. Was this what it felt like to kill someone? Was this what it felt like to die? Part of him, the cynic, thought in those few moments, when his heartbeat had doubled and his blood pressure was probably at its highest ever, *Bring it fucking on, baby, bring it fucking on.* He managed to stop himself from lunging at the woman, from taking aim, grabbing her by the throat and throttling her until all life had left her sorry form. Whatever trouble Slattery was in now, however blind was his rage, he knew for certain that an assault on a colleague would be the final nail in his coffin. And Cullen would be like the cat that got the cream.

'So,' Slattery managed, with some effort, to keep his voice even. 'So, you held onto it for a few days, slept on it, chewed on it and probably offered up a couple of prayers for me, thinking you'd manage to sort me out. Didn't you?'

Slattery didn't wait for a reply. Instead he just grabbed his jacket, turned the key in his locker. There was nothing there, not even an empty at the moment if they looked, just foul socks and reports he'd never finished, never filed.

'And then what?' June was following him now, defiant, but she shrank when Slattery turned on her, maybe knowing how thin the ground was beneath them suddenly.

'Like you need to ask. Then you hightailed it into Cullen's office—' He raised his voice, a whimpering whine, an ugly bitter smirk tying his mouth up at the corners. He hated June now, hated everyone in this shitty place. '*Please miss, Slattery's drinking in the corridors, I saw him with my own eyes, I did.*' He moved closer to her, into her space, into her face. When he spoke next his voice was a whisper, a threatening murmur filled with spit and hate. 'It's like this, June; you'll get yours for this. I might not be around here any more, but these things tend to come back and bite you in the arse when you least expect it. No one's going to work with a squealer. Word will get out.' Slattery was almost nose to nose with June now. 'I'll make sure of that, don't you worry.'

When he turned on his heel, Slattery was only vaguely aware that June was speaking, hardly heard her words.

'That wasn't me. I never said a word to Cullen.' But Slattery was already volleying along the corridors towards the evening cool air. He was going to get as pissed as he'd ever got. Now, he had an excuse.

*

The man could feel his hands sweat. The nerviness tingling through him sent beads of perspiration from his forehead, down the back of his neck, even his toes seemed to crackle with an electric current that streamed his body. He was so close now. He'd managed to steal through the open front door, he'd stood then for a while in the darkest corner of the foyer, watched as the lift counted out the floors. She was at the top; there was no mistake, no stops in between. In the silence, it felt like there was only the two of them in the whole universe; and maybe in some ways there was, they were the only ones who mattered any more. Anna was gone – this was down to him now.

The foyer was dimly lit; the walls and doors ran seamlessly into each other, a muted grey. The lift doors were a dull metallic. At his back, mottled brick silently recorded a century of change. He stood as close as he could to the bricks, his breath shallow, his heart racing. Damn, the light switches were on the far side of the hall. He'd prefer to have darkness when he crossed to the elevator. That was the hunter in him, he'd already spotted one camera and it looked top of the range. Still, good and all as it was, if he kept his head down, moved fast, kept his back as much as possible to it, he knew that it would be hard to identify him from it. The problem was there could be more than one. Hanging around at the lift doors, waiting for it to come down four floors that was a lot of footage to be checked through.

He sloped back deeper into the corner, biding his time. He was here for Anna, here for all the time they wouldn't have, all the time they'd lost. She was dead, her soul, that thing that made her what he'd loved for all these years had slipped from her. An invisible, intangible thing – he knew that the greatest minds in the world argued about the existence of the soul.

Across the hall he heard the rumble of the lift begin. It stopped once on the third floor, and then descended – was he ready? Part of him wanted to slink back into the brickwork, stay there until she emerged, and watch her from a distance, just as he'd done with Anna. All had been well while he'd stayed back. He could admit to himself that once they'd spoken, once she'd told him what she knew, his whole world had turned on its axis, and maybe too so had hers. It was meant to make things better, should have made things perfect. The world would probably have been a much better place for all of them if he'd left well enough alone and just kept watching her.

The lift was down now; he could hear the slight clang of metal, the whoosh of hydraulics as it seemed to dip below the floor level and mini bungee back up the few millimetres to let its passenger exit. He felt his heart dip with it, the anxious anticipation of earlier had risen to a pitch now where he feared that he might vomit. Here. All over the fancy carpet. Wouldn't the guards just love that? Enough DNA to put him away for a lifetime. It was something he could honestly say hadn't occurred to him before – not really – that those patronising detectives might actually cop onto him. They might realise that he knew more than they did and put him away. The thought chilled him, a searing second of panic shot through him. He couldn't survive being locked up. He'd spent his life outside, working, hunting, free. He could still turn back; he didn't have to go near her.

The elevator doors began to open slowly. He started to count to ten. If he made it to ten, then he'd turn on his heels, not get into that lift, not confront her, not do what he knew he'd come here to do. He'd walk away. Silently he'd counted them out – two, three and four. The lift doors opened. Five, six. A tall, fair-haired youngster, maybe a student, stood inside carrying a huge folder, flat and black and the size of a half door. Seven, eight. He struggled for a second, and then turned sideways slightly. The lift began to close on him again. Nine. He reached out, a slim hand pressed flat against the door button, and they swung back obediently. It took only one more twist of the case to manoeuvre it out through the lift doors. They were still wide open as the student made his way past his unseen voyeur. Ten.

It was a sign. Anna was calling to him, asking him to do one final thing for her, and if he didn't run now, it might be too late. Somehow he had to put things right for her.

Something propelled him from the wall into the lift. He jammed a fat thumb on the button to bring him to the fourth floor. He hummed, softly if none too tunefully, just low enough to calm himself, 'Scarlett Ribbons (For Her Hair)'.

CHAPTER 30

She stood beneath the hot jets of water for a long time, her eyes closed, the case rushing through her brain, until some of the tension washed from her body and her mind felt clearer than it had in days. It hadn't just been the case, either. She thought about Anita Cullen, about Ben Slattery and Coleman Grady. By the time she'd finished, she knew there was nothing to be gained from worrying about what might be; all she could do now was get on with it, work like a beaver and if a post came up, apply like everyone else. After the shower, she felt better, as if some invisible pressure had been washed away. As for Slattery and Cullen, she was sure that nothing would happen there. After all, they needed all hands on deck now. Cullen wouldn't go pulling the team apart in the middle of a murder inquiry, would she? The buzz of her phone pulled her from her thoughts.

She picked it up on the third ring.

'Iris?' It was June Quinn. 'Where are you?'

'I just popped back to the apartment, figured it might be a long night ahead.'

'Grady's just asked me to ring around a few people to check in. We have the briefing in under an hour.'

'Yeah, I knew that. Anything else turn up in the last while?'

'Funny you might mention that.' She could hear June smile as she spoke on the other end of the call. 'Grady is pretty sure that Kerr is our man for the Crowe murders.'

'Oh?' Iris grabbed a towel, clenching the phone under her ear she began to dry off her arms and legs.

'He thinks Kerr's been watching the station for the last few days. He wants to know if you've noticed him.'

Iris wracked her brains for a second. 'I've never met him.' A small shiver ran through her, but she wasn't cold. She walked towards the bedroom, pulled out fresh clothes for work and began to wriggle one-handed into them.

'Oh, he seemed to think that you might have run into him at some point?'

'I… might have.' Iris dropped to the bed. *That night… in Kilgee…* she shivered at the memory of him. Her voice when she spoke next sounded scared even to herself, but she tried to keep it as even as possible. 'Did he say where I might have bumped into him?'

'Um…' June sounded distracted now, as if she had calls to make, things to do that were more important than this empty conversation. 'No, but if you'd met this character, I'm sure you'd remember him, he has a face even a mother couldn't forgive.' She laughed a little to herself, and then she said, 'Big, ugly and dirty, from what I can gather, not a lot of personality either.'

Locke didn't need to hear any more. She mumbled something into the phone before dropping it. She didn't hear June telling her that Grady said to be careful, to keep an eye out, and to take no chances. She flopped onto the bed, lay there for a few seconds and then with a determination to her movements set about putting on the rest of her clothes. She'd have a coffee before she left, gather her thoughts together, by the time she was leaving, she'd feel much more confident, less scared. She was still spooked enough to strap on her gun belt, leaving the Sig Sauer on the table, until she'd finished her coffee.

She was searching for a hairdryer when she heard the noise at the door, more a careful tap than an actual knock. The tap was so light Iris might have missed it had she not been padding past. She walked to the door distractedly, a million other thoughts streaming through her brain. Opened it without checking. Swung back the door, expecting to see Cullen or her father or at least someone she recognised.

When she'd tried to bang it shut again he jammed his foot beneath it, his hand reaching out. She backed away from him, terror racing through her body. She'd never seen his face before, but there was no mistaking who he was. He towered over her, dominated the doorway, his presence taking over the room. For a moment she felt herself reel backwards, thought maybe she was about to faint. Somehow, against a sturdy pine table she managed to steady herself. She watched as he turned, casually, slowly, and locked the door; as if he was a jailer, locking her in, keeping her from the world beyond. When he turned around, he slipped the key into a large pocket at the front of his shabby jacket. She knew then she had no chance of making it through that door, no chance of getting out of there, not unless she killed him first.

When he began to smile at her, she found it hard to keep fear-fuelled bile from rising in her throat. He handed her a photograph that sent shivers down her spine and his first words did little to comfort her.

'Hello, *Janey*. You and I have a lot of catching up to do, haven't we?'

*

Slattery surprised himself by not going to the pub. Not immediately anyway, he told himself, as the car he'd *borrowed* from the lot moved at a steady pace away from Corbally station. He wasn't quite sure where he was off to, one of two destinations. At Idle Corner, he made his decision, turned right and figured he could always backtrack later on.

The house, when he pulled up outside it, was in darkness save one light in the sitting room. Maureen would be watching the news, the weather and then taking down her rosary beads. He leaned back further into the seat, breathed deeply and closed his eyes for what seemed like just a moment, but probably lasted nearer half an hour. In the silence, it was not the case, not the drink, not even Cullen that crowded out his brain, but rather it was Maureen. By the time the concerned doctor – '*call me Maedhbh*' (she put her finger to her lips as if to silence their fears) – had come along, he'd already known. She brought with her too much sympathy to blanket out the bad news. Slattery felt suffocated; his brain woollen with inadequacy.

Alzheimer's, she'd said, as though it was a complete sentence. A life sentence, more like, for both of them – another responsibility to run away from, perhaps. For now it was their secret. Just like when she'd been expecting, something they shared for a while before the world needed to know, before they guessed and descended upon them with wise words they didn't need and Slattery resented. The good doctor was sorry, she couldn't tell them any more yet. They'd have to wait and see what the progression was like; there were pills, there were pills for everything now. But there would be no pills when the time came. Nothing could stop the descent for Maureen away from the people she loved, away from the places she knew, into a terror-filled world that would rob them of all dignity. Dementia would take from Slattery whatever he might have had left in this shambles of a life he'd created. He thumped the steering wheel, he wasn't sure if it was in anger or anguish.

He'd put his phone on silent when Grady had tried to ring him, twice already. He needed more time, not sympathy for the mess he'd let happen with Cullen. He needed a game plan. He needed ammunition. He tossed about the notion of walking up the short drive and knocking on the front door. What would he say? He'd already mulled over the many possibilities. Best he could come up with was that he'd been passing by the door, got caught short, could he use the loo?

It was over an hour since he'd met with Cullen, but he was setting things straight – in his mind, at least. Come what may over the next few days, he had a feeling this time would be important. When he started up the car again, somehow he felt like he'd made a difference just being here, even if Maureen didn't know. Perhaps if he came here often enough, one day he'd go inside and say what needed to be said. Only time would tell.

Slattery drove his car back towards Idle Corner, full intentions of heading towards the Ship Inn. Now he could sink into his misery. He had a feeling it'd take a lot of alcohol to convince himself that this fuck-up hadn't been his own doing entirely. He pulled the car up at the lights before turning onto O'Connell Street. He failed to ignore the eclectic mix of Georgian buildings with a couple of nasty-looking moderns thrown in. *Typical Limerick*, he thought to himself, *it was always the one or two bad apples that brought the place down*. With that he felt his phone vibrate in his pocket. He thrust a clumsy hand about his jacket, seizing it just before the caller rang off. Jackie Tierney. He almost didn't bother answering it.

'Just getting back to you on that little matter earlier in the day.' There was a lightness to Tierney's voice and if Slattery hadn't been so tied up in knots over everything else that was going on, he might have twigged that it was early days to be coming back with a big fat nothing.

'Go on.' He pulled in. It was hard to smoke, drive and talk all at once. Last thing he needed was some eager uniform pulling him over; he figured that Cullen would just love that, especially since technically, he was now driving a stolen Gardai vehicle. 'Amaze me with your intel.' Tierney was well used to Slattery's cynicism.

'Hey, if you're not interested, this stuff could get in the papers. It's the kind of thing some would pay for.' If he was trying to whet Slattery's appetite, he'd managed.

'Okay, let me have it and then we'll see if it's worth you passing it on.'

'Hey, I might just pass it on for the fun of it, Ben. You'll find out soon enough, it doesn't take a lot to amuse you when you're out of the game for a while.'

'Tierney, we'll never be out of the game, we both know it.' Although he said the words with some confidence, Slattery didn't quite feel the bravado.

'Okay, your woman Cullen, one with an arse the size of a family shithouse?'

'Yeah, sounds like her, what did you get?'

'She's some big wig, yeah?'

'Yup, as she likes to remind us all daily.'

'Bet she doesn't remind ye that she shouldn't be there at all.' Tierney's voice was sing-song, at least he believed he'd hit the jackpot.

'How d'ya mean?'

'She never made it through the entrance exam, didn't make the Irish and she's too short. From what I heard, she's never been five-six in her life, not unless she was standing on top of a friendly superintendent, that is.'

'Any particular super?' Slattery could feel a terrible thirst rising from the back of his throat. There was nothing new in guards managing to squeeze around these things back in the day, though it was never admitted. But Slattery had to agree, it had been plain to all that the closest Cullen had ever got to five-six was if she played bingo.

'Someone we both know quite well.' Tierney paused, savouring the moment. 'The sterling Superintendent Locke – with his perfect record and his medal for service.' Tierney hadn't liked Locke since the old guy took him down for misappropriation of funds with a charity Tierney had set up to do with Chernobyl. It was a long time ago now, but Tierney was a man who never forgot.

'So what, she was banging Locke and he got her onto the force as a farewell gift.'

'Who said anything about farewell? Locke turns up again and again over the course of her career, generally around interview committees, he's given her a boost every step of the way.'

'Wonder what she's done to deserve that kind of mentoring,' Slattery guffawed.

'Well, I suppose, that's for her to know and you to find out, my friend.' Tierney rang off, satisfied that he'd passed on all that he knew. But, of course, what he knew was little more than anyone who went looking could have found. The thing was, until now, no one had gone looking.

Slattery sat for a while, thinking about what Cullen might have done to deserve such special care and then it dawned on him. It wasn't so much what she had done, as what she hadn't done. *Jesus*, Slattery thought, and a thin film of sweat covered his forehead. She had something on Locke, something far bigger than an affair. For feck's sake, every one of those big boys wearing the shiny brasses has been bonking left, right and centre for years. *Probably give out medals for it in their secret clubs*, Slattery thought. No, Cullen had something on Locke and it had to do with the Baby Fairley case. Now, Slattery felt his thirst rise, the sweat seeping from his every pore. He had to talk to Iris, because whether she realised it or not, she was probably their best chance at solving this case. He started up the car, a smile trembling on his lips.

'Fuck.' Slattery felt a wave of something that might have been considered joy in anyone else; he'd settle for giddy excitement. Wouldn't it be sweet, if this once the mouse might trap the cat? He flicked his indicator, drove up O'Connell Street, passed by a parked traffic patrol, headed for that swanky pad Iris lived in. It was his best bet for answers, he'd wait until she finished at the station, wait a week, if he had to. They were going to solve this case after all, and he had a feeling that it would be a lot sooner than any of them had expected.

CHAPTER 31

He'd pushed past Iris with a violence that seemed to characterise his every movement now. His voice was low and something in it gave away the urgency of the deeds she figured he planned to commit.

'I'm not Janey, I'm Iris,' she said as evenly as she could manage. She'd stayed standing, her feet planted firmly to keep her balance, trying not to shake, trying with every fibre not to tremble. She knew if he was a little less excited he might have noticed. As it was, she could sense his edgy instability in the way his mouth twitched, a nerve pulling somewhere taut along his bearded cheeks.

'Don't say that, for God's sake, don't say that…' He shook his head. 'I know it was all a long time ago, but you're still that girl to me, still…' He looked at her now, his expression softening. 'This could be a second chance, don't you see?'

'I don't see, tell me.' For some stupid reason his name had fallen out of her head. She couldn't for the life of her think of anything beyond the seconds in which he spoke. All that came back to her from basic training was to keep him talking. While he talked, maybe she'd figure out a way of getting out of here. 'Tell me what happened a long time ago.'

'Don't you know, haven't you worked it out yet? It was all over the papers, changed everything for everyone. *The Fairley Baby* – no one else had a look-in after that.'

'That was what?' Iris took a shot in the dark. 'Almost thirty years ago?'

'Yeah, it was that and more.'

'And you waited until Anna came back to Kilgee?'

'I wasn't waiting for her, I thought I'd lost her, don't you see? She'd blamed me, blamed me for years until she met you.' He smiled at her now, handed her a faded photograph and somewhere behind the weather-beaten skin and the unkempt hair and ragged beard, she thought she could see a drop of sincerity. Maybe this man meant her no harm.

She examined the photo he'd handed to her. It was creased and worn and yellow with age. The colour had faded, a pink blanket and a little lemon hat. It was a newborn baby; snuggled into a pram that probably dated the picture somewhere in the eighties. From the hood hung a brown scapula and a miraculous medal. She could almost feel him hold his breath, as though he was waiting for some great wisdom to shine upon her. She stared at it for some time, turned it over; the caption just said, '*my baby sister Janey*'. She rubbed her fingers across the faded ink.

A sensation of familiarity flooded through her body, as if some part of her had seen this before. Then she turned it back, looked at it more closely; there seemed to be something in the baby's right hand. She drew the photo nearer, strained her eyes and then she knew – knew with the certainty of one who is baptised in light. Baby Janey and she shared the same birthmark on their right hands. Many times over the years, her mother had brought her along to various specialists to try and have the mark faded. It hadn't bothered Iris, caused no pain and she rather liked it, felt it marked her out as special. Like small rosary beads running about her thumb and over the back of her hand.

'That's how she knew you. The little marking on her sister's hand had never vanished. She knew then for certain, when she met you, that her sister was still alive. And thank God, she knew that I had not taken you and done the terrible things she thought.'

'Was she killed for this?' Iris heard the words, hollow in her own throat. Suddenly her head felt like it might implode, her brain only processing what was before her in a standby mode. There had to be some mistake, some terrible coincidence at play here, she couldn't believe that her whole world was being turned on its axis by a man she didn't even know. 'Was she killed for this?' She whispered the words again. If the answer was yes, there were only two people who might have murdered Anna Crowe and now she had a feeling that Ollie Kerr wasn't one of them.

'I don't know, but…'

'And Veronique?'

'Yes. She was killed for this.' It was said without sentiment.

'I'm so sorry,' she whispered automatically. There was too much confused emotion swirling through her to extend any real sympathy towards the woman whose corpse she'd stood over in that little cottage.

'I'm sorry, too. I didn't love her, I think I was gone beyond loving her, by the time I met her, but well, you… you and Anna, you set me free. I've lived with so much guilt for years. I'd almost convinced myself I had taken you. Taken you far away and killed you. Of course, now we know what happened, don't we?'

'Do we?'

'Oh Janey, of course we know, your *father* was in charge of the case. You're the detective around here… surely you don't need me to figure it out.'

'Why didn't Anna tell me?' Iris tried to take in the world that was being thrown at her from a lifetime ago. 'Why didn't she tell me I was her sister?'

Even saying the word, *sister*; it was what she'd always wanted, but here, now, in the quiet of the apartment, the word sounded hollow and unreal.

'She had to come to terms with it too. I think she had to get her head straight. She left Crowe the week after she met you, never told him why, never said a word, so far as I know, the only one she told was me.'

'And Veronique?'

He smiled at her, an evil grin that pulled up the corners of his mouth into something that was more mocking than happy. 'I met her on the streets. She was a drunk; I knew it from the first day she moved into the cottage. Thanked the Lord me mother couldn't see what I'd been driven to.'

'And then you told her?'

'No, she was bad news, I'd never have done that…'

'You didn't kill her?'

'No, I never thought I'd have to bother. She was doing that all by herself. I expected to come home one of these days to a stiff anyway. We had a fair deal going. I got what I wanted, when I wanted, paid for everything and she drank from when she got out of bed until she was getting into it again at night.'

'So what happened to her?'

'I think greed. She was getting all she could out of me, but she knew I was keeping an eye on Anna. Maybe everything I knew, she knew.' His voice seemed to dip to a depth further than Iris had ever heard, as if his words might be coming from hell. No doubt, he was a tortured man. 'Anna asked me to take care of a box of files, little things she'd built up over the years: newspaper cuttings, that photo, lots of different stuff. I pulled a photo of you from that big case you worked in Dublin, couple of weeks ago, it clearly showed your thumb, the back of your hand. Something clicked with Veronique; something must have made sense to her. I think she contacted your father…'

'Oh God.' Iris couldn't believe she was hearing this. She wanted him to stop talking. She wanted to protest, but these were the answers they'd all been so hell bent on finding and now, well, they just weren't sinking in properly. The words seemed to stand on the air between them, resounding for much longer than possible after they were spoken.

'Yeah, well, you can't tell a drunk, can you?' His voice was empty; the emotion had long since been drained from it. 'Remember, when Anna confronted him she ended up dead. Veronique's death wasn't exactly going to keep him at up at night by comparison to murdering your sister, was it?'

Somehow, above all of the things she'd learned in the last half an hour, the idea that Jack Locke was capable of killing two sleeping kids and their mother was probably not really going to penetrate her consciousness at any real level for a long time. Maybe she'd always known he was capable of doing anything to keep her safe. Tonight, there was so much to take in, suddenly it felt as if they were talking about a total stranger, not her father. This was not the man she'd known all her life, not the man who meant the world to her.

'That night, last week, out at the cottage, I thought you were going to kill me.' She spoke gently, the memory still scared her. She knew now, looking at him, that if he wanted to kill her with his bare hands she wouldn't stand a chance.

'You *are* the reason she's dead.' His eyes bore through her now. The words were simple and she wondered if that had been his intention all along.

'Why did Anna think you'd taken me all those years ago?' She felt a quiver of fear rise through her as she asked the question not entirely sure that she wanted the answer.

'I resented you. I told her that I wished you'd never been born. As soon as you arrived, she had no time for me. I was glad when I heard you'd been stolen. I laughed and jumped and thumped the air. It was like all my birthdays had come round together. I thought everything would go back to normal again.'

'But they never did?'

'No, they never did. And now,' he said, taking a hunting knife from inside his coat, 'now they never will.'

They were four floors up, with two exits, both locked. Bar a battering ram, there was no getting out the front door without wrestling the keys from Kerr, and she knew that in a brawl she stood no chance. The other exit, a narrow window that led onto the fire escape, would be locked also; she wasn't even sure where the keys were and even if she could lay her hands on them now, she knew she'd never make it out the door before he'd catch her. Basic fire safety – lesson learnt for next time, if there was a next time to learn for. He was beginning to cry now, tears streaming from his eyes, falling into his thick beard. She knew better than to speak to him, knew she had to wait and let him take the lead. One wrong word and it could all go pear-shaped.

*

Everyone was in, a full house, save for Slattery and Locke. She'd be along later, no doubt. 'Okay, okay. I know you're all tired, but here's the deal. We're seriously considering Ollie Kerr for the Crowe murders now.'

'It's like musical feckin' chairs, first the husband, then the artist, now this Kerr guy.' A uniform from the back of the room had obviously decided to take up where Slattery had so recently left off. He had the good grace to half apologise into a throat-clearing cough. More than Slattery might have done.

'Not for Veronique Majewski's?' A youngster in his freshly minted uniform had slipped quietly into Slattery's chair and for some reason the move irritated Grady more than he'd have thought possible.

'Not at the moment. No.' Grady sounded far surer than he knew he had any right to feel. 'Anyway, we've talked to Alan Gains tonight – he says that Kerr was always hanging around after Anna when they were younger. They assumed he was a bit slow, didn't pay too much heed.'

'How come he didn't show up before?' Cullen said from behind Grady's back.

'Maybe not as slow as Alan Gains thinks?' Grady said. 'He was meant to drop into Kilgee station today; there's been no sign. I have reason to believe that he may have been watching the station here over the last few days.'

'And now?' Cullen arched a neglected bushy brow.

'Now, I have Westmont keeping an eye out.' Grady turned to look at Cullen. He hadn't spoken to her since she'd told him about Slattery; now all he felt for her was contempt. 'We'll put whoever we have out in Kilgee tonight; see if we can't catch up with him before morning.'

'Whatever you think.' She lowered her head, checking an incoming message on her phone. 'We should put someone out at the cottage.' He knew she was thinking of Locke, and the night she'd come across him hanging around Anna Crowe's cottage. Somehow, he felt that Kerr had moved from there, was sure he was much closer to home now.

'Sure, I'll see if I can't get two of the night-duty boys to hang out there.' He looked around again; still no sign of Locke.

'We've had Adrian Crowe on the phone wondering if Veronique's death is connected to his family's murders.' June looked up at Grady.

'And?'

'I said we were treating that as a possibility.'

'Did you ask him where he was at the time of the murder?' Cullen lifted her head from the phone.

'Yes, this time it seems he has a watertight alibi.'

'Oh?'

'He spent most of the day making funeral arrangements; he was with the local parish priest, picking out hymns and whatnot.'

'That's okay then.' Cullen levelled a look at June that said conversation over. Grady felt the room was beginning to become stifling; he wasn't sure if it was the number of people or the presence of just one too many.

'So, bright and early tomorrow morning, yes?' he said to the tired-looking team before him. He knew they'd put in far more hours than they'd ever get paid for, and there was little more they could do tonight, apart from picking up Kerr. He really didn't think that Kerr was going to strike again, or at least if he did, he had a feeling that he'd leave things as they were for a while. Any witnesses he thought might have given him up were gone.

The place emptied out noisily but quickly. They'd all had enough of this whole investigation. Grady walked to one of the tall windows that overlooked the street outside, opened the bottom sash just a fraction before turning off the lights. Just as he leaned towards the wall he spotted something on the floor, a bag left behind by one of the female officers. He kicked it beneath the nearest desk, noticing as he did that it was Locke's. *It was odd*, he thought, and stood for a moment considering the bag. Then he fished out his mobile and rang her number, a cooling sense of panic rising up his spine. It rang out, went to messaging. Not like her. She usually picked up by the third ring. He scrolled down through the numbers. Got June.

'Did you manage to get Locke for the briefing this evening?' he asked, keeping his voice as even as he could.

'Yeah.' It sounded like June was driving, the phone attached to her ear rather than the hands free device her sons had purchased for her. 'She was back at her flat, cleaning up beforehand – beautifying herself, more like.' She cursed, obviously missed a light. 'I didn't see her at the briefing, though, was she there?'

'No.' The one word and in that second, Grady had a feeling that he'd been wrong. Ollie Kerr had one more piece of unfinished business. It was why he'd been watching the station, why he'd moved off so quickly out in Kilgee rather than face Locke and gamble on her recognising him. 'Where's the flat?' He listened while June rhymed off the address. He knew the place well enough; it was a recent redevelopment, high-end living in what had been, until Ireland became so obsessed with property, low-end storage.

Grady didn't wait to pick up his coat; he just grabbed his keys and headed for the car. He had to get there before it was too late.

CHAPTER 32

Iris felt as if they both spotted the gun at the same time. Then: that wasn't possible, since Kerr's back was turned on it – but something made him bolt, perhaps he'd noticed her eyes, slip towards the small table, calculate how likely it was that she'd make it there before him. He was a step away from her, directly in her path to her hand gun. If he realised what she was thinking in that moment, she knew he'd have reached out and finished things there and then. When he turned towards her, she still had a chance. He hadn't seen it. He hadn't figured what had flashed, for one brief, mad moment through her mind. If she killed him with it, would it be premeditated? Would anyone have to know what had been said here tonight? Would anyone have to know what had happened all those years ago? *But you'd know,* a small voice whispered deep inside her head, *you'd know.*

'I thought, once she'd found you, all would be well. I thought everything would be exactly as it should be. I've spent a lifetime in a half world, trying to convince myself that I'm not some kind of monster.' He looked at her, his eyes holding out a flicker of hope. He was consumed almost completely by wretchedness, apart from that one small glimmer. He scratched his beard, perhaps drying the last tears that had fallen, part anguish, part anger, maybe some guilt, too. Impossible to tell how much of each; she knew she couldn't take any chances with him. 'Now it feels as if I'm sitting on the edge…'

'The edge – I don't understand,' she said carefully, keeping her voice low and even, careful not to change her body language too much. She needed him to sit. If he just sat on the low couch, even the movement of having to hoist himself out of it would be enough to slow him down; she'd have the upper hand before he knew what was happening. He'd have his back to her then – could she shoot him in the back?

'I think,' she paused. 'I think we should sit down for a while. Please, tell me everything.'

'I…' He eyed her warily, and then looked at the arrangement of the sofa and chairs. To her frustration, he dropped down into a single chair. To the side of his head, only slightly beyond his line of vision, the Sig Sauer sat cold and ready on the table. 'I've watched the cottage for years, even when there was no one near the place. I think I was watching it for you, hoping against hope that somehow you'd come back, that fate or maybe accident might send you back. Then she found you and I still watched the place, looked out for her.' He quivered slightly. 'Maybe I knew then that he couldn't let her live, not once he knew.'

Iris sat back in the chair, mirroring his movements as much as possible, still hoping he'd sit back and relax a little. The words were hanging in the air between them, too awful to fully take in.

'The day Veronique was killed I'd taken a shot gun out across the bogs. I came back to see a big hulk of a car parked before my front door. Habit, I suppose, but I slipped back into the trees. I watched him come out. I could see it on him then, something in the set of him. He will kill again to keep this secret.' He cleared his throat; his voice was becoming thick with emotion. 'I thought I heard her move.' He bowed his head.

'Inside the house?'

He nodded. 'So I let off one bullet into the air. It was enough to spook him, I guess. He got into his swanky car and drove off.'

Kerr started to unsettle himself in the chair, but she couldn't stir. It was as if time had stood still, complete silence about them, as though the world beyond this room had stopped. Iris felt her chest constrict. Felt as if she'd never breathe again, as if all of the oxygen in the room had finally given up and been gobbled by the blackness. Then he shifted, just a little nearer to her, held out his hand to her and she knew that regardless of whatever else happened, regardless of who was what or whether her world would ever be the same again – she wanted to live.

Maybe he was no threat, but by now adrenalin, and training and too many close calls in undercover were all kicking in together. She dived towards the small table; half ran, half jumped, so she felt as if she'd almost taken flight. She grabbed the gun and fell to the ground, turned as quickly as she could to face Kerr. It was the last thing she wanted now, but she'd shoot him on the spot if she had to; let him bleed to death slowly while she rang Grady or Cullen or whoever decided to answer first. She levelled the gun, felt as if everything was moving in slow motion, pulled back the release, her hands shaking, tears and snot now streaming down her face. He'd brought her as low as it was possible to go. This was Limerick, it was Murder, and it was what she'd wanted for so long. What was wrong with her? *Pull the bloody trigger.* She knew, in that instant, she couldn't shoot him from behind and so she walked slowly, her back to the wall, sidestepping so she kept her eyes on his hunched figure. One more step and she would be facing him. She dropped her eyes on his face first, a knowing, sly look pulled his mouth upwards; his eyes were hard, the glassy stare of a hunter who has no empathy for his prey. And then, she looked downwards and she began to tremble, for there, through his great overcoat she could see where he'd plunged the hunting knife as close to his heart as he could manage. *'Away with us she's going, solemn-eyed; hear no more the lowing…'* She heard the words drift across the room a soft song emanating from a dying man.

'I've told you all I know, it's time to go back to her now.'

*

Grady didn't get bad feelings so much any more. Sure, when he arrived at a crime scene, there was always the odour of something foul. He could still be shocked by what man could do to his fellow man, but he'd managed, somehow over the years, to quell the revulsion, the sick shaky feeling that things were not right. He figured it was the only way to survive. Early in his career, he'd finished work and cried for the dead, cried for the living and drank himself into a stupor with lads of his own age. They'd called it craic; it was survival. At some point, he'd looked around him, knew that if he didn't harden up – well, the role models for that path weren't too inspiring. Maybe the feeling in his gut now was as much about the fact that he was praying he would be in time to save her. He took the steps two at a time, his adrenalin pumping because until he knew otherwise, there was hope.

He rang the first bell. The apartment belonged to a *G. Birmingham*. He answered almost immediately and buzzed Grady through as soon as he'd explained who he was and that he was concerned about a neighbour who wasn't answering the door or the phone. Just as he was about to go through he spotted Slattery, bounding like a madman along the path towards him.

'What the…' Slattery said as he rounded the steps to him.

'I think our man could have Iris up there.' Grady kept his voice low, knew that there was no chance Kerr would hear him, but he needed Slattery to calm down. He watched as the older man took in his words.

'Come on, what are we waiting here for?'

'You can't come… you've been suspended, remember.' He felt like shit, knew that he could do with Slattery covering his back, but at the same time, knew that Cullen would have him for breaking and entering if it all turned out to be Grady's imagination working overtime.

'Has the paperwork actually been submitted?' Slattery said with a smile, a familiar devil dancing in his eyes.

'I wouldn't think so.'

'Well then, maybe she shouldn't be counting her chickens just yet.' He took a look at the list of names on the door frame. 'Fourth floor. Lift for me, I think.'

Grady ran the four flights of stairs, conscious that he should be conserving his energy. Kerr was a big man, it'd take both of them to arrest him if he gave trouble. The corridor on the fourth floor was silent as the Burren in January snow. The door when he touched it was solid oak, with a Chubb lock and a spy hole.

'No battering down that baby,' Slattery said and reached for the bell. 'This will be a nice surprise for her anyway, if she doesn't already have company.'

Grady hoped that whatever Slattery had up his sleeve for Cullen and perhaps Iris would just be enough to get him reinstated. He reached out and pulled Slattery's hand away from the bell for a second. 'You're sure you know what you're doing here?'

'You know I'm a sly enough old dog not to make a move unless I'm certain.' He depressed the button with the smile of a madman about to hurl himself off the Cliffs of Moher. No answer.

Grady moved closer to the door, there was a whimpering noise coming from within. Someone was crying and when he motioned to Slattery to listen, the sound quickly wiped him clear of anything but complete disengaged panic. Grady felt like one of those poor sods who comes home after a bad day at the office to a house full of people shouting 'Surprise!' from the darkened corners of his living room. Except this surprise couldn't be seen at any level as being pleasant. Automatically, both men fell away from the door, down to the ground, Grady pulled out his hand gun. Slattery was unarmed – Grady knew, that somehow, that was actually a good thing.

The place was silent again. Not one neighbour stuck a head round a door to see if everything was okay. This was Limerick – people knew better than to get involved. Grady shuffled awkwardly, moved his head so he could shout through the door. 'Stand back from the doorway; I'm going to shoot off the lock.' Still no sound from inside. He held up the Sig Sauer, aimed it from above at the Chubb lock and fired, just the once. This was the real world. Every single bullet had to be accounted for. He flung the door inward, still shielding himself to the right of it. Waited for a moment or two, until the silence from the room beyond had settled heavy enough on his shoulders so he could wait no longer. The smell of sulphur in his nostrils was gritty and strong – Slattery opposite signalled to him, *What's the hold up?*

Kerr was sitting slumped in a chair before him. He walked towards him, taking no chances but he knew immediately the man was dead. A large knife protruded through layers of unwashed clothes. The chair he sat on was already crimson with his blood and his face had taken on the blank stare of someone who'd died long ago.

'Kerr is dead,' he called to Slattery who had been only footsteps behind him. They both stood over him for a second; aware that somewhere in the apartment Iris could be dead too. Grady took in the room, a tasteful, expensive mixture of exposed stone and brick, an open-ended U of deep white couches and chairs faced a large wall-mounted TV. Grady made his way along the wall, walking slowly. He found her, a whimpering, shaking heap, crouched behind a single chair, her Sig Sauer held tight against her chest. When he took it from her, her eyes were blank, unseeing beyond the bloody mess before them. There were no injuries, no physical injuries at least, that he could make out.

'It's okay, now. I have you, you're safe.' He said the words over and over into her hair, felt her body relax into his, an occasional quiver reminding him that she was badly shocked. *Was he comforting her or himself?*

'We need to find him.' She spoke so softly he thought for a moment he'd dreamed it. Then she moved away from him for a second and looked into his eyes. There was no escaping the terror behind them. 'We have to go. He's not going to leave any loose ends.'

Slattery listened while everything tumbled out of Iris, the past and the present jumbled up – a lifetime destroyed in a moment. Five lives lost to repay the debt of Baby Fairley and all the time the answers were right here in front of them. Ollie Kerr had carried a heavy secret and tonight he'd passed that burden on to Iris. No doubt, she was in shock, but her version of events made sense. She clutched the photograph in her hands, held it like it was the Book of Kells. The most precious thing in the country, the most precious thing in the world. Slattery, more than anyone, knew that truth was a costly commodity; he knew it because from what he could see, it was rarer than hens' teeth.

Cullen arrived just as the ambulance was leaving. Grady had no time to talk to her; there'd be plenty of time for explanations later. He half carried Locke out the door with him, leaving Cullen to clean up the mess. She eyed Slattery with the disdain people would normally keep in reserve for pond scum.

'You've been busy,' Cullen said, stepping before him and block-ing his path, as she surveyed the bloodied living room.

'Aye, all in a day's work, ma'am.' He knew the term would annoy her, make her feel that she was far older than him.

'Yes, except it's not, is it?' She looked at him, a cruel smile playing about her lips. 'In a day's work, that is, because you're not working any more, are you?'

'Amn't I now?' He smiled evenly back at her, so she moved a step away from him; gauging him as much as the room around them. He wanted to be gone with Grady and Locke, but this had to be done, too, and without it, maybe he had no place going anywhere near Woodburn. 'You really wanted out of Templemore, didn't you?'

'I missed the real world, if that's what you mean, yes, who wouldn't?'

'Believe me, Cullen, I more than anyone can understand that.'

'I'm sure you can.' She wasn't softening, despite her words.

'Would you have sold your soul for it, though? Or just lied through your teeth? Or maybe the reason you wanted to come so badly was why you had to lie.' He watched her now; she hardly blinked, cool as an Irish summer. 'You know one of the things I learned very early on, Cullen?' He didn't wait for an answer. 'It's a small world, and a smaller country. That's the thing about Ireland. People try to have secrets, they can try as hard as they like, but everyone is connected, it's like we've all buggered each other, somewhere along the way. What is it they call it? Six degrees of separation. Only with us Paddies, it's more like three degrees, at most, wouldn't you say?'

'I'm sure you've had lots of time over the years in the boozer to mull over these philosophical issues with your beer buddies.' Her voice was bored but her eyes were wary. She hadn't moved an inch. Her posture remained exactly as it had been before he began talking. He hoped he could see a little rigidity creeping in, but if he was honest, it was probably just wishful thinking. Anita Cullen had done every training course going to spot a liar: duplicity should come easily to her. She knew how to cover all the bases.

'Funny you should mention that,' he said, smiling at her now. He too had long since learned a few tricks and he knew how to smile a threat better than most. 'What you'd call my boozing buddies, I'd call contacts – they're informers and they've been more than helpful over the years.'

'So we've been paying for your loser pals to tell us what the dog in the street probably knows.'

'The dogs in the street don't know everything now, do they?' He ignored her snort of derision. 'But it's amazing what they'd *like* to know.' He moved closer to her. 'Like, I'm sure the dogs in the street would be very interested to know that a senior officer who was leading out the investigation into one of Ireland's most publicised crimes was actually covering her own tracks.' He watched her expression – hardly a quiver, but there was one small movement, just beneath her left eye. It was like bait to Slattery. 'I'm sure they'd be very interested to know that one of Ireland's most respected female officers actually got where she was by covering up for a more senior officer and of course keeping quiet.'

'I don't know what you're talking about.'

'Oh, I think you do. I think we both know that you got your start thanks to that missing baby all those years ago. I think we both know that you knew a lot more about things than you ever committed to any files, official or otherwise.'

'How do you mean?' Her words were even, there wasn't so much as a flicker and if Slattery hadn't caught it earlier, he knew he'd think this was all bullshit now. But he could bullshit too, bullshit better than any of them.

'I mean that you should never have been a guard at all, you never made the height, never passed an exam and then Locke put you onto a case, *the* case, to cover up his...'

'You have no proof.'

'What proof do I need exactly, just a phone call to a local reporter would do the trick from where I'm sitting.' He smiled at her now, a smile that he loaded with as much threat as he could. 'If I'm going down, dolly, you're coming with me.'

'You need to be careful who you're pointing fingers at, Slattery.' She was brusque, not even denying it. He knew then that there was more than a ladle of truth to it. She turned on him, ready to walk out the door. 'The forensic boys will be here soon, we'd better leave them to it.'

'You have two hours. I have every intention of continuing on this case, of heading back to the office in a few hours' time, of sitting behind my desk, having a cup of tea and being my normal obnoxious self.' He leaned closer to her now, so he could smell expensive sweet perfume – deceiver perfume – but it didn't quite cover the fear. 'When I look into my desk drawer, I want to see my warrant card and my Sig Sauer. If there's so much as a whisper of suspension or any other kind of shit, you'll be front-page news before you know what's happened to you.'

Cullen looked at him, calculating just how much she could push him perhaps. But his eyes were hard, he had no intention of losing this battle and in that moment, perhaps she realised that to fight on would be futile.

'Does Byrne know?' he asked as she stepped aside to let him pass through the front door, trying to avoid the pieces of metal and wood that had been strewn confetti-like about the floor.

'No.'

'Good, that saves me having to have a word with him too.' He smiled to himself, Byrne wouldn't have been all that easy, but he had enough on him to keep him in his place at the same time.

Slattery walked out of the apartment with lightness in his step. He handed the keys of the Ford to one of the uniforms – Joyner. He was new, but already he had a bit of a reputation about the station – he liked fast cars and speed. 'You can drive, lad, guarantee you more excitement than you're going to see around here tonight.' No point getting done for dangerous driving, at least not until he was sure his suspension was lifted. He was headed out to Jack Locke's place, with a little luck they'd make it in time.

*

Iris was blind with hurt and rage. The streets of Limerick passed by in a blur. The car radio played low, The Cranberries, thumping out their heavy drum heartbeat, a slow unending pulse, throbbing and enduring, like the Shannon, pounding its way through the centre of Limerick. They crossed the river at Thomond Bridge. The oldest bridge in the city, its seven arches held steadfast, strong and noble, tonight its sturdy permanence was reassuring. It connected the city up to and over the longest river in the country. As they crossed it, Iris felt some small encouragement that she could be resilient enough to see through the next few hours, at least until the morning light shone again. She had to remind herself now that it would.

Grady took a series of narrow roads away from the horror left in her apartment. These were back roads she wouldn't have known, winding down long narrow working-class streets. They travelled in broad silence through the underbelly of the sleeping city until they came to the fringes of suburbia. It didn't take long; he knew the streets well and once they hit the open country he put his foot to the floor. She hardly noticed that he clipped corners at twice the legal speed limit.

The house, when they arrived, was in darkness, bar one light shining at the rear – hard to tell if it was inside, or a tripped security light at the back. They'd hardly opened the gate when Slattery arrived in a Ford, barrelling its way too fast down the quiet drive. Joyner, a big bruiser of a bloke, still in uniform, jumped from the car with the enthusiasm of a beagle on a scent. For a moment, Iris almost forgot that if they caught this guy – well, he wasn't just anyone, he was the man she'd called 'Dad' for almost thirty years now. Could she really put her own father in prison? Jack Locke, a great teddy bear of a man, a doting father, a loyal husband, a good man. Where had all that gone to in the last hour? Iris knew that there were no answers now, none that would really make any sense to her tangled mind.

Grady looked at Slattery. 'Front door?' It was unlikely he'd make it round the back without collapsing; the short gallop from the car had almost finished him.

'I think so.' He made his way up the short path. They left Joyner standing guard to the side of the house, patrolling front and back, back-up at either side. Iris could hear the bell sounding as Slattery stood in the faded light at the front door. It seemed then, looking at him standing there, as if everything had suddenly gone into slow motion and Iris wasn't sure if she heard the doorbell ring out through the darkened house or if she just imagined it. Then Grady jolted her and they were moving quickly around the side and towards the kitchen garden her father had been cultivating since his retirement.

To the rear of the house only two things struck Iris: the first was how quickly her senses adjusted to the garden; the second, and it took a moment for this to settle in, was the smell of petrol. As if the whole place was bathed in it. Grady before her, stood for a second, taking in all that lay before them.

'Are we too late?' The words escaped from somewhere at the back of her throat. Were they dead already and they were just arriving in time for the bonfire?

'Maybe not.' Grady pointed towards an open drum of petrol. It had obviously been tipped over. Some of it now lay, fresh and pungent, a small pool of filmy fuel, trapped in the worn grooves of stonework leading towards the back door. 'It's hard to know how much he's taken inside.'

Grady moved closer to the door, put a hand against it and pushed it easily in. The oil trailed along before them, a ribbon of translucent terror.

In the darkness beyond the warren of rooms to their left, a clock struck out the hour. It echoed throughout the slumbering house. Grady slipped a small torch from inside his jacket and switched it on with a soft click. They were in a small anteroom, just off the kitchen. The door before them led towards the main body of the house. She pushed it forward gently. Everything had been left unlocked, the price of innocence, perhaps – if only. More like he had nothing to lose now. The rooms beyond lay in silent darkness, the day's activities discarding their own scent about the place. In the kitchen, her mother had cooked an omelette. Its odour still hung on the air, a lingering reminder above the petrol fumes that everything had been normal not so very long ago. The corridor from there opened out into the stairs and the living room, closed up for the night. Jack Locke would not be there. The trail of fuel beckoned them upstairs. Iris opened the front door gently as she passed it, nodding at Slattery as he slipped his bulk into the hallway. On the stairs, each step creaked its own groaning protest. They did not belong here, none of them, not at this time of night, not in darkness. Each of the doors at the top of the stairs lay slightly ajar. There was no light from them. Iris felt with certainty that they were too late.

And then, one, ominous grunt. It seemed to echo throughout the whole universe, loud and prophesying all that Iris did not want to think about. She could hardly move. She knew that once she looked around, her life as she'd known it would be over for good. She felt Grady, at her side, stiffen, only slightly. He moved the flashlight slowly towards the sound. The movement when it hit the spot was quick and light. Her father surely couldn't move like that? It had taken refuge behind a slightly ajar door and part of Iris knew then, it might have been better for all of them if they'd just been too late.

CHAPTER 34

Maybe Jack Locke had always been a nasty fucker, and maybe Slattery had always known it, who could say at this stage? But the expression Slattery spotted for just a moment when the moon caught his eyes told him Locke was a dangerous man now. It had been just a movement, little more than a shadow, but somehow Slattery had managed to pick him out.

'Mrs Locke – Theodora?' he shouted, loud as he could, hoping it would be enough to halt Nessie before he did something they would all regret. He took the steps two at a time, feeling Joyner behind him. He was at the top of the stairs now. Grady and Iris stood, flashlight in hand, ready to pounce. There was no waiting for Slattery. Ben Slattery bounded through the door, switching on the light as he went, one blustering movement, and he was at Mrs Locke's bedside. She was sleeping, soundly. He could see some small lift in the bedclothes, her shallow breaths working away rhythmically, and then he smelled it. Petrol. The place had been doused in it. Jack Locke was standing on the far side of the bed, the bed he'd shared with his wife for over forty years. Tonight he stood watching her, maybe for the last time for all of them knew now; lighter in one hand, his eyes full of sadness, his posture ready for murder.

'Dad?' Iris said the word gently from the doorway and Slattery watched as Locke's face crumbled into desperation.

'Iris, my love, you shouldn't be here.' He looked at Slattery as if somehow he should have kept her away, but they both knew that this was about her. Iris was the reason he doused his home in petrol, her voicemail telling him that she was on her way armed with the truth was the only ignition Jack Locke had needed to know the lies had to finally end.

'Dad, it doesn't have to be like this, nothing has to change, come on with me,' she pleaded.

'Iris, you go, I'll be right with you.' His eyes were pinned to Slattery. Slattery looked down at Theodora again.

'Oh God. Something's wrong.' Slattery moved closer to the gently sleeping form. The smell of petrol almost knocked him backwards, but she hadn't woken. 'He's given her something.' He said the words almost to himself and thought, *Where the hell was Grady?* 'What did you give her?' He'd almost flung himself across the bed. 'What have you done to her?'

'Never mind, you're too late for her now.' Locke held the lighter up, raised his lips in something that was meant to be a smile. 'Go on, Iris, get out of here, let us sort this out.'

'I can't go, you know that.' Slattery heard her voice, steady as a pioneer at closing time and he marvelled for a second at her nerve – not even undercover gives you that kind of strength. 'What did you give her, Dad?' She moved closer to the woman she'd known all her life as her mother, raised her head and shoulder from the pillow in one arm, hoisting her higher in the bed. 'I can't let her die, Dad, don't you see?'

'No. We can't let her live. She will have nothing to live for when this comes out. Believe me, Iris, this is kinder. She doesn't know you know the truth, let her have that much at least.' His eyes were hard now and Slattery knew that if Iris tried to take the woman out, he could turn on her just as easily as he did on Anna Crowe.

'It's too late, Dad, they already know, they know everything. Best now if we get to the hospital and…'

'They don't know, they haven't the first iota. How could they?' He looked across at Slattery. 'Look at him, hardly married five minutes and he was a father. Twelve years – Iris, we were twelve years and then your mother said that she was pregnant. We had a baby boy, baby Idras. Your mother chose the name, it was meant to mean feisty.' He laughed now; a cruel wounded laugh that wrenched even old Slattery's worn-out gut. 'Ye were born side by side, you arrived just a few minutes after him. Theodora and the Fairley woman had exchanged addresses before they'd both been discharged, they planned to meet up. Perhaps, if things had been different, ye'd have been friends.'

When he spoke again, his words were flat, all emotion had gone. 'Our boy died after fourteen hours. I never realised, it was all done so quickly. Your mother never let us see him; I never got to hold him when he was alive. Then she went out and came back with you. She wasn't gone an hour. By the time I got home from work, they'd buried Idras. I don't know, if you hadn't been a girl, maybe I'd have been none the wiser. But then, your hand. There was no mistaking the markings on your hand. The Fairley woman was so shocked, she never mentioned it, but the girl, Anna, she remembered, right up until the end, she remembered that damned birth mark.'

In the hall a radio cackled into life. Slattery heard movement, wondered briefly and then Coleman Grady stood in the doorway. 'Jack, let me take her. You make up your own mind, but don't make up hers.' He looked down at the pathetic form of Theodora Locke. No bigger than a child, curled up, her hair halo-like across the pillow, seemed to take up more space than her whole body. 'You've had to visit too many crime scenes not to know the score. This is pointless, do for yourself if you have to, but not for her, let her choose.'

Locke said nothing, but he bent over Theodora, kissed her softly on her lips, lingered for a moment. Slattery watched as one slow tear slid from his cheek to hers. Then he stepped away, a lifetime of regret etched on his face.

'I'm sorry, Dad, we have to take her now.' Iris said the words slowly, but her voice was strong, there was no mistaking the intention in her eyes. Slattery knew that once Grady had the woman in his arms, they would both go up like a Halloween fire candle if Locke flicked the lighter. Iris held on to the woman's head, supporting her with gentle hands, while Grady lifted her from harm's way. Surely he would not harm Iris? Slattery wasn't sure; he was far from sure about anything.

'What about the boy?' Iris stood now with the sleeping woman draping into her arms.

'They buried him in the garden. You can see the spot from my study, just beneath the yew tree…' His eyes were sad. 'I didn't realise what they'd done at first, even when I got the call out to Kilgee, but either way, you were ours by then. I'd seen the Fairley woman going downhill. She could hardly look after the daughter she had, never mind let you back there.'

'And Mum was so fucking stable?' Iris almost spat the words at him.

'You were always going to be fine. I looked after everything.'

'You and Anita Cullen?' Iris fired back at him.

'It wasn't like that. She was in the house when Idras died.'

'She helped to bury him?'

'She buried him; your mother wouldn't have been able. Anita was very young. Maybe she didn't know what else to do. But your mother arrived back with you and… well, maybe she knew… maybe not.' He took a long deep breath. 'I think it was only as the publicity about the missing Fairley baby really took off that she realised what had been done – the enormity of the thing. I had to do something for her, and she made a good guard. I knew she would.'

'I'm going now, Dad, I hope you'll come with me.' Iris turned away, and Slattery could see her eyes were closed, as if with each word she was counting out the seconds before she could get away from this place. Slattery watched as Jack raised the lighter in his hand, his eyes manic, but she was gone, couldn't see him. *Just as well*, Slattery thought, *she's seen enough.*

He could hear them as they made their way downstairs. It was only Slattery and Locke now. Their lives didn't mean as much as anyone else's. There would not be the same sadness if they both perished in flames, that there might be if they were better men.

'So, what's it to be?'

Slattery knew now he wasn't afraid to die here. In fact he'd be tempted to take out his fags, go with a smile on his face at least, sit back smoking, two old fuckers burning. He knew that, low and all a value as he'd usually place upon his own existence, the news about Maureen had thrown his currency completely out of sync. There were, on the one hand, so many fewer reasons to live. He didn't want to watch her disintegrate into a frightened, confused mess. He didn't want to have to make the choice of walking away, or staying to see that. But she'd stood by him; maybe but for her, and her nagging and her constant checking, he'd have been dead a long time ago. He held out his hand for the lighter. Maybe that was reason enough not to die here tonight.

'Ah, Ben, you know that I can't go inside.' Spoken as if he regretted the life he saw passing by his eyes, moving away from him.

'She still loves you, you're her father no matter, it could be…' He wasn't sure what else to say. Tell him that the court would see he was just trying to protect his beautiful, vulnerable, unstable wife? That was Jack Locke all over; he'd been loyal to the things he'd held dear all his life.

'Ah, no, we both know that everything has changed now.' His eyes were sad, but that steely determination that had set him apart as a detective settled now so Slattery knew that there would be no talking him out of what he planned to do. 'Go on with you now. I won't be going, but you have another few years to try and get kicked off the force.' He smiled a small quiver of a smile at Slattery and they both knew that it was the only way.

'Good luck,' Slattery said as he closed the door behind him. He took the stairs maybe more slowly than he should have, called out to anyone who still might be inside. 'Out, out, everyone out.' There was no sound. Just as he reached the front door, he thought he heard the spring of a lighter and then that small quaking flame. Before he reached the gate the place was ablaze. Jack Locke didn't make a sound. It finally ended here.

*

Iris barely made it to the gate. Grady had carried Theodora and half dragged Iris down the wide stairs. Whatever strength she'd summoned to confront Jack Locke was well gone now and Grady kept a firm arm about her back to ensure she remained upright. Outside, some way from the house, an ambulance had drawn up to administer whatever medical aid would be needed. Theodora had been well doped, so she still had no idea that her world was crashing down around her. Her husband had slipped something into her night-time routine that knocked her sideways.

'He was not a bad man,' Grady said softly to Iris. She was shivering and silent, violent rattles overtaking her body every now and then. She was suffering from shock; it had drained the speech from her lips. Grady wrapped his coat about her, hovered as if there was more he wanted to do, but some invisible force stopped him. Soon, they were speeding through Limerick; headed for the nearest A&E department in St Dominic's; Theodora was travelling in the ambulance before them. They'd left Slattery, left Jack Locke and in the distance, they could hear the scream of sirens, rushing towards the hades they were leaving behind. Of course, what they'd learned had changed everything. Iris had watched as Slattery made his way towards the gate. She knew then that she'd never see her father again. Knew it was the only way out for him. She vaguely wondered at what would happen next. The fire brigade had rushed past them. It would be too late for Jack Locke.

'No?'

'No, he was a good man, caught up in a terrible situation. You could just say, he loved too much.'

'Yes.' She'd known that all her life. Iris watched while he'd made excuses for her mother, papered a fine veneer of happiness over their lives. Still, she'd never guessed at the true reason for the hollow hub that had been at the centre of their world. For years, she'd assumed it had been her mother's frail personality.

'Maybe this was the only way for him?'

She couldn't answer him, but she caught his eyes as they turned towards her. They were filled, not with pity, nor with empty sadness, rather, she thought she saw that he cared. Maybe, it was just what he felt for every victim he came across?

'You and I...' Her words were hardly audible to herself, but he shifted slightly in his seat.

'Yes.' He reached across and held her hand for what seemed like an eternity. It seemed there was nothing more to say, not now.

CHAPTER 35

Byrne's house was snuggled in an upmarket cul de sac, just off the North Circular road. A detached eighties-build, upgraded with all that money and current fads could throw at it. At either side of the front door two bay trees struggled against the winter cold; Slattery knew they would not be the only thing that wouldn't survive the season. He could have phoned. In fact, if right was right, it should be Anita Cullen making this call. Of course she never would. Not as he intended to, at least. It was going to be the truth, the whole truth and nothing but the truth. He'd waited until the very end. Waited until the flames had been doused into submission, waited until the crackle and hiss of the dying house had become a subdued undercurrent in the night. He'd waited until Jack Locke's body had been examined, photographed, loaded into a black body bag and taken away from that terrible place. There had been no sign of Cullen. All right, so she was at the scene of Ollie Kerr's murder, but knowing Cullen, that wouldn't have stopped her getting across the city to stomp through a second murder scene.

'Busy night?' Byrne said drily when they were sitting at his kitchen table. He flicked the switch on the kettle and set about making two strong cups of tea. Slattery held his words and didn't say it was more than tea he'd need. It took about forty minutes to get Byrne up to date, he'd made him backtrack once or twice, but Slattery managed to keep his voice low and steady. There was no good news here, but then neither was it his job to break it to Byrne gently. 'What evidence do we have?' Byrne asked, deflated by the end.

'We have enough to arrest her, enough to make sure that she's put away for the foreseeable,' Slattery said soundly.

'I see.' Byrne got up from the table, took down a bottle of Glenmorangie. The seal cracked as he opened it, but that didn't account for the heaviness of his movements. He poured them two large measures, sat back for a while considering. Eventually he moved forward in his seat. 'She's still one of us, Ben.' The words were so quiet, Slattery wasn't sure if he heard them at all.

'Jesus, Byrne, have you not listened to a word I've said?'

'I've heard every word.' He pursed his lips, drew up his knotted hands to them. 'The least we can do is give her twelve hours.'

'She'll be fucking well gone by then.'

'She won't; she rang earlier on, she's probably only just left the Kerr death in the last hour or so.'

'I don't bloody believe this.'

Byrne cleared his throat. 'We leave it till morning, give her time to get her thoughts together, get a brief in place and...'

'It's a feckin' wipe over...' Slattery could feel the bile of resentment and injustice rising in his throat; he couldn't be part of this.

'And I'll forget the tape she emailed me earlier on today; forget that she almost had you out the door.' Byrne took their two glasses, rinsed them in his spotless Belfast sink and stood with his back to the draining board. There was nothing more to say. Slattery gathered his anorak around him and headed out into the night.

*

Anita Cullen had lived frugally her whole life. She'd bought a place in South Africa many years before it became anyway fashionable to holiday there. Truth was, she'd only been there a handful of times. Nevertheless, it had the right climate, or at least the right legal climate, it was bought and paid for ten times over, and now she had quite a nest egg wrapped up on the sunny continent. Even with the property crash, Cullen had managed to keep her investments safe. She'd spent her whole career waiting for this day to come, resigned to its inevitability, dreading it, planning it and now that it was here she thanked God she'd planned so meticulously. She'd almost made it to the final fence, obviously she'd rather they'd never found out, have the last laugh without them realising it. Damn it.

There were no direct flights from Shannon to Port Elizabeth; she had to fly to Heathrow and onwards from there. It hadn't taken long to arrange as much as she needed arranging, most things she could do online. There was only one thing she wanted to do before she left. From deep in her bag, she took a small envelope. She'd kept it with her for twenty-nine years. The only thing she could keep to remind her of the baby she'd buried in scratchy blankets on that windy day. She'd taken them when Theodora wasn't watching. It had been easy; once Iris had arrived, she'd had no interest in the little boy she'd given birth to. Anita had gently snipped one dark curl from the baby's head, slipped it and his identity bracelet from the hospital into her purse. Later she'd transferred them into an envelope, carried them like a talisman all these years. But they weren't hers. Maybe they weren't Iris Locke's either, but that was the name Cullen wrote on the outside of the envelope, then she left it in Locke's cubby hole. It was something, wasn't it?

By the time Slattery was having his miserable breakfast in the grotty canteen; Anita Cullen was sitting in a taxi headed for her little apartment in the sunny suburbs of Kabega. Despite her bulk she almost skipped up the small path to her complex. She knew she'd never set foot on wet Irish soil again – it had all worked out as she planned in the end.

CHAPTER 36

'It's a right shaggin' mess.' Slattery said the words low before taking a long sip of the whiskey Grady had poured for him.

'It is that,' Grady agreed, but at least the mess was no longer theirs. He'd packaged up everything they had on the Crowe murders, the Baby Fairley disappearance, Veronique Majewski and Idras Locke. Everything had been sent by courier to the Director of Public Prosecutions. It was up to him after that. Grady thanked God it wasn't his job to decide what happened next. He sipped his whiskey thoughtfully.

'I think the saddest thing is that tiny baby.' June looked into her barely touched glass. 'I've never seen anything so pathetic as when he was taken from the ground.' Grady had been there, they all three had been there – as much for each other as for Iris. She was one of them now – whether she came back or not, she was one of them from here on in. 'Any word from Iris?' she asked now, maybe thinking what they were all thinking.

'No,' Grady lied, but he kept his voice steady. He'd been talking to her earlier, of course; somehow, she'd stirred something deep inside him, something he thought he'd lost forever. Family? He still wanted to protect her even if he couldn't quite figure out why. So, he rang her, every day. Same conversation. Same replies. She wasn't ready yet. She wasn't ready for anything yet. Grady wasn't sure she'd ever come back to Corbally station; maybe she'd never be a detective again. Every reason she'd had for the job had been snatched away from her, as surely as her family had, as surely as her whole identity had. She was on extended leave of absence – Grady figured it would be some extension to get past everything she'd learned over the last few weeks.

'Damn this; I say we go for a right good drink.' Slattery drained what remained of his Bushmills, pulled his anorak on so it sat at an angle and he looked more like a belligerent schoolboy than a hard man detective sergeant.

'Slattery,' June said softly. She looked across at Grady but the slight shake of his head was enough to tell her that it was not a good time. He'd spoken to Angela earlier in the day, told June already. There was nothing they needed from anyone now, just time, as much of it as the Alzheimer's would give them, and maybe then, when they needed help, they'd know who to ask. June took a sip of the whiskey, grimaced as though she'd been poisoned. 'I think I'll pass on the pub, lads, I just want to go home and have a bath – wash this case from my skin.' She stood beside Slattery; put a hand on his arm.

'Thanks, June.' His tone was low and gruff, but Grady and June knew what he meant.

'You're welcome,' June said as she made for the door. Neither of them was built for too much sentimentality, especially not towards each other.

'Come on.' Slattery nodded at Grady, and, as he closed the incident room door behind him with a rattle and a click, Grady knew the Crowe case was finally closed.

EPILOGUE

Woodburn was gone. Razed almost to the ground and with it everything that Iris had taken for granted as her past. She pulled her woollen scarf closer to her neck, feeling a shiver run through her that had little to do with the windy autumn afternoon.

Darkness settled about the trees around the property now, even here, in the garden, she felt the chill of secrets and lies encircle her.

Idras Locke had laid buried here for almost thirty years. It was inconceivable that they had lived their lives walking past his unmarked grave and there had never been a word. Not so much as a mark put on their son's resting place.

Iris bent down to touch the ground that had so recently been pulled back. The damp of the earth clawed out whatever warmth was in her, so her heart clenched just a little more in her chest.

There were so many things she probably should be doing, but Iris felt as if someone had stopped winding the hands to her heart that terrible night. It didn't seem to matter where she was, here or at the hospital with the woman who had been her mother for almost thirty years – she was numb. She couldn't stay in her apartment any more and so she'd taken a place in a nearby guesthouse where the other lodgers were mostly foreign students. Her room was basic, dated, wearing the stamp of someone else's taste, a strangers' history permeating its every fibre. It was a study in beige, so neutral that it didn't even register with Iris.

Early days. That was what Coleman Grady said when he called her. Even Slattery had been in touch. He caught up with her, spent an awkward half hour sharing a pot of weak tea neither of them wanted, but he left her with the feeling that somehow she was not alone.

She thought about Theodora again. Lying pathetic and afraid in a hospital bed. *What will happen to me?* she had asked with huge tear-filled eyes.

Indeed, Iris had thought, *what will happen to all of us?* Her phone buzzed in her pocket, she took it out, annoyed that it interrupted the thoughts that she knew would continue to swirl about her brain regardless.

'Come in to Corbally, just for a few hours, we need you, Iris,' Grady said again. Of course, she knew, they didn't need her at all.

'I'll see,' she lied. She wondered which was worse, to feel she wasn't wanted, because they thought she wasn't there on merit or to be wanted because they feared that left alone there was no telling what might become of her.

'Don't *see*. Just come back, it's not going to do you any good, thinking about it over and over…' His voice petered off and then, as though a whisper, 'I know what I'm talking about from experience.'

'Oh.' The word escaped her before she had a chance to pull it back. 'Anyway, I'm not sure that I can…' There again, that feeling that she hadn't earned her place.

'There's a vacancy, on the Murder Team…'

'Who's gone?' That's how it worked, she wasn't stupid, there were only so many desks, so much in the pay budget, new posts weren't just created out of thin air or pity.

'Me,' he said, but there was a lilt to his voice.

'No.' She couldn't imagine working Murder in Corbally without Coleman Grady.

'Well, Anita Cullen's not going to come back, so I'm working something out with Byrne… for now, at least,' he said. 'Come back, Iris, we really do need you here.' His voice was thick and hoarse and she wondered if he might be about to cry.

'I'll… call in tomorrow.' It was the best she could do. Night was falling in around Woodburn and she thought she could feel the years of laughter lap mockingly against her skin on the breeze. This wasn't her home any more. She wasn't even sure if she was entitled to those memories when she thought of that poor innocent baby forgotten in the ground beneath their feet for all those years. 'Yes, I'll call in tomorrow,' she said softly in the breeze, perhaps like Slattery, Grady and June, the Murder Team was welcoming her home when she needed family about her. Yes, perhaps Corbally was where she belonged now.

A LETTER FROM GERALDINE

Dear Reader,

I just wanted to say a huge thank you for choosing to read *Her Sister's Bones*, the first book in the new Corbally Crime series. If you did enjoy it, and want to keep up to date with all my latest releases, just sign up at the following link. Your email address will never be shared, and you can unsubscribe at any time.

www.bookouture.com/geraldine-hogan

I've been so looking forward to introducing you to Iris and Slattery and as you might imagine, there are many more stories waiting to unfold around this pair. Already, as I write this note to you, book two is about to wing its way to my editor and I promise, it's as full of twists and turns as this one, but also filled with familiar faces from Corbally who are continuing to fight the good fight – even if some of them seem to be a bit misguided at times!

The next book follows Iris as she tries to patch together what remains of her life after the explosive end of this story; Slattery is finding his way too, except he's back-pedalling around a wife who may need him, but certainly doesn't want to admit it. And overlaying all of this, a murder that looks as if it might be solved already, except no one wants a missing vulnerable girl to be their killer.

I count myself very lucky each day I sit at my computer and call myself an author. It really is living the dream as far as I'm concerned. I've always adored books, reading stories and making them up.

And there's nothing nicer than hearing back from readers. I'd love to hear your thoughts on this story, so if you have time, please do post a short review or share it on social media. I'm always up for a bookish chat on Twitter: or find me on Instagram or Facebook. There's something very moving about reading a review that really 'gets' a book!

If you enjoyed this book and you want to keep an eye on what I'm up to next, you can follow me on Amazon or check out my website *www.geraldine-hogan.com* where I'll let you in on what's going on in my world of books!

Thanks so much again, until next time,

Happy Reading,
Geraldine Hogan

 @GerHogan

faithhoganauthor

GeraldineHoganAuthor

www.geraldine-hogan.com

ACKNOWLEDGEMENTS

Every author, when they start out, dreams of writing their acknowledgements at the back of their precious story – it is like reaching a special milestone somehow, as if finally, all the words are written and the work is complete.

Of course, as you read this, my place in this story is now nearing an end and I'm handing it over to you, to make of it what you will – but hopefully enjoy it and maybe recommend it to someone else!

The funny thing about writing a book is that even when you think it's finished, there's always something else and this is very true with *Her Sister's Bones*.

In becoming the story in your hands today, I want to thank most sincerely the following people.

First, Abigail Fenton who saw within my manuscript the story it could become. It is thanks to Abi that this book has taken shape and landed in a very happy home at Bookouture. I am so grateful for your guidance and keen eye and for championing my book when you came across it!

It was my very good fortune to be placed in the hands of Lydia Vassar-Smith with this book. Lydia, you are a legend and you'll never know how much that first email with the cover really touched me, thank you for putting in so much thought, energy and genius on my behalf!

Speaking of Bookouture – there are so many people who have not only made me feel very welcome, but also who have helped enormously in bringing this story to life. My thanks to

Jon Appleton, Leodora Darlington, Lauren Finger and Alexandra Holmes for their editing skills and to publicists, Kim Nash and Noelle Holten for shouting about it from the rooftops!

I count myself as very lucky to be a J girl – thanks to Judith Murdoch, my agent who is kind, witty, savvy and very, very wise!

I would also like to give a mention here to Russell D McLean, Lesley McDowell and Jane Jakeman – all of whom gave me encouragement and expert advice on the journey to publication of this book; it is very much appreciated.

A writer's life can sometimes seem a little cut off from other people – as you might imagine, there is a lot of sitting alone making up stories involved! So, I would like to thank all of my author friends across the Lounge, the Savvies and on Twitter – you make coffee break even better!

Since I began to write, I've been lucky to fall into a community of book bloggers – too many to mention and much too generous to forget. They share a love of books, generously and enthusiastically – you're a rare gift!

To you my reader – thank you for picking up my book – I do hope you enjoyed it and you'll come back for more…

And finally, to my wonderful family, Seán, Roisín, Tomás and Cristín, you make every day special. To James for his unwavering support and enthusiasm, I still can't believe my luck to have you at my side. To Christine Cafferkey for so much more than I can write here.

Finally, thank you to Bernadine Cafferkey, for walking every plot step with me, reading every word and finding something in them to praise always – I count my blessings every day!

Made in United States
Orlando, FL
22 November 2025

72942611R00164